SUDDENLY . . .

He barely knew Miss Gregory. And yet, he felt as though he knew her as well as some of his most trusted soldiers. He knew she was smart, fearless, loyal, and proud.

What would it be like to be her *beau* in reality? He had suddenly become aware of things about her he had barely noticed since he first encountered her on the street in front of the pub several months ago.

Such as the curve of her hip beneath her utterly proper muslin gown.

And the few tendrils of reddish hair that had escaped from her eminently practical bun and were curling along the base of her long, white neck.

And the way that her eyes sparkled with admiration . . . Who would have suspected that a rural schoolmistress could be as enticing as the most skilled courtesan in London?

BOOK YOUR PLACE ON OUR WEBSITE AND MAKE THE READING CONNECTION!

We've created a customized website just for our very special readers, where you can get the inside scoop on everything that's going on with Zebra, Pinnacle and Kensington books.

When you come online, you'll have the exciting opportunity to:

- View covers of upcoming books
- Read sample chapters
- Learn about our future publishing schedule (listed by publication month *and author*)
- Find out when your favorite authors will be visiting a city near you
- Search for and order backlist books from our online catalog
- Check out author bios and background information
- Send e-mail to your favorite authors
- Meet the Kensington staff online
- Join us in weekly chats with authors, readers and other guests
- Get writing guidelines
- AND MUCH MORE!

**Visit our website at
http://www.kensingtonbooks.com**

A RAKISH SPY

LAURA PAQUET

ZEBRA BOOKS
Kensington Publishing Corp.

http://www.zebrabooks.com

ONE

"Demme, Finchwood, but you are having a devilish string of good luck," Sir Basil Winston said with wry regret as he tossed his remaining cards and last counter onto the table. "This play is too deep for my meager pockets. I believe it is time for me to repair to my lodgings."

"I couldn't agree more," said Henry Seabrook, pushing his chair back. "A man can only lose so much in one evening before having second thoughts. And I've had a few third thoughts in the last hour or so." The blond man braced his hands on the edge of the green baize table as he rose, rather shakily, to his feet. He adjusted the peacock-blue silk patch that covered his left eye, permanently injured at Talavera. The patch exactly matched the elegant waistcoat he wore. "Congratulations, Finch. Good play."

Francis Burnham, Viscount Finchwood, scanned his distant cousin's face for signs of sarcasm, but there was nothing but bleary resignation on Seabrook's florid features. Winston looked equally neutral. Good. Finch was no cheater, and the last thing he needed was to have his fellow club members accuse him of foul play. Although a good duel might liven things up a bit.

He bade his fellow players good night and swept the pile of coins on the table into his purse. As he stood, he realized that he was almost as wobbly on his feet as

Seabrook. When had he lost his talent for holding his drink? Or was it just that he was trying to hold more than usual?

He dismissed the question from his mind and focused on walking steadily as he made his way across the card room at White's. *Never show weakness.* He heard his old commanding officer's voice in his head as clearly as if Lord Holt were standing next to him.

But of course that was impossible, since Lord Holt was back on the Peninsula with the rest of the battalion, schooling other men in the art of army intelligence. And Finch was living the life of a gentleman of leisure in London.

He didn't have much choice about his life of ease, Finch thought as he left the club. He pushed the too-familiar rancor to the back of his mind. Demme, he wasn't going to think about that tonight.

He signaled to the doorman to have his horse brought round. Really, he should have taken the carriage, but there were nights he longed to be back on horseback and this had been one of them.

As he waited for his mount, Finch reviewed the evening's events. Five hours of vingt-et-un, faro and, finally, commerce had netted him a total of about two hundred pounds. Not bad for a night of idling. He should be careful, though—he had come by the money honestly, but that sort of luck was bound to bring accusations of cheating.

The money was nice, but truth to tell, he didn't need it. He would have enjoyed the evening exactly as much—which is to say, not much at all—if he had lost every penny in his purse. But wagering large sums on cards and dice was about the only thing guaranteed to amuse him these days—that, and the attentions of his latest paramour. If he hadn't just given Sue Brightman her *congé* the night before last, he might be tempted to pay her a visit.

Then again, he might not. Relations between them had become somewhat stale, which was why he had told her it was time to find a new protector.

"Can't say as I'm surprised," she'd said with a cheeky grin. "You ain't noted for your longevity."

He'd raised an eyebrow.

"With relationships, I mean." Her grin, if anything, grew wider. "I looked ahead."

"You—"

"—have another gentleman in the wings. In my line of work, it always pays to plan for a rainy day."

His grin matched hers. "I'm relieved to hear it. I would hate to see you stranded."

She kissed him on the cheek. "No fear of that, Finch. Hasn't happened yet."

He'd miss Sue's sense of humor and cheerful outlook, most certainly. But trekking over to her snug little house in Chelsea had begun to seem like more of a duty than a pleasure of late.

Until then, however, it had served well to distract him, and distraction had been his main priority since his return from Spain. After an evening with Sue, he could sometimes fall asleep without the echoes of groaning men and frightened horses reverberating in his brain.

Besides, having a prominent paramour—Sue was an actress of some standing—added to his rakish reputation. And that reputation was useful in keeping all but the most avaricious mamas and their daughters at bay. It had been amusing, before he had gone to the Peninsula, to be the object of hot pursuit in the Marriage Mart. But in those days, he could fool himself into thinking that the young women were at least as interested in his charms as his purse. These days, his charms were somewhat diminished, and the ugly truth was that the size of his inheritance was his main attraction.

He shook his head. When, exactly, had he become so

self-pitying? It was not appealing, and it was high time he put such thoughts behind him. He simply must try harder to find more elevating means of distraction than gaming hells and courtesans.

Not that he hadn't been trying for the better part of a year.

A groom led his horse to the edge of the curb. "Here you are, m'lord."

Finch tossed him a coin. Gripping the reins in his left hand as he buried it in the horse's mane, he awkwardly wrapped the crooked index finger of his right hand around the pommel and prayed it would hold as he swung up into the saddle. He wondered if it would ever feel natural to mount a horse this way. He doubted it.

With a slap of the reins, he was off at a gentle trot. Fortunately, Sophie was an old mare, and a gentle pace was all she was equipped to provide. There were days when Finch would have killed for a good gallop, but *killed* was the operative word. He needed both hands to manage a mount going full tilt, and it was suicidal to think otherwise.

He had to stop focusing on the things he couldn't do, and he knew it. After almost a year of attempting to rebuild his life in London, he seemed further from establishing a purposeful existence than he had been when he stepped off the troop ship in Portsmouth. He still missed the mornings in Spain, when he would awaken in his tent with a clear idea of the things he needed to accomplish that day and a clear sense of the reasons for doing them.

Perhaps the coming London season would bring some entertaining diversions, he thought as he turned Sophie toward Mayfair and home. One never knew.

St. James's was still lively with activity, even though it was well after two in the morning. Squads of swells stumbled down the pavement in merry abandon. On the corner of St. James's and Jermyn Street, two young dandies were tossing the pieman.

"Heads," called the vendor as a silver coin glittered in the moonlight, twisted and fell to the pavement.

"Tails!" cried the taller dandy, holding out his hand. With a sigh, the hapless pieman handed over a meat pie, which released a cloud of steam into the crisp April air. Finch hoped it wasn't as hot as it looked, for he knew what was coming next. The vendor barely had time to turn his back before the pie ricocheted off his bald pate, leaving a streak of ground meat and grease before it fell to the ground.

Without a backward glance, the two dandies rejoined the throng on St. James's Street, having completed what was a nightly ritual for many young men with too much money and too much time on their hands.

Finch cast the pieman a sympathetic look, leaned down and handed him a handkerchief.

"Thank you kindly, sir, but I've my own," the vendor replied with a rueful grin, extracting a large checked cloth from his pocket. "It's not the first time I've needed it, and it won't be the last."

His words recalled Sue's cheerful acknowledgment that she would always need to keep one eye open for a new protector. How could people whose circumstances were so much worse than his own be so much sunnier about life?

Perhaps it was because they were used to adversity. Finch, on the other hand, had always had everything in life presented to him like a gift-wrapped box: toys and pets as a child, a splendid horse when he was thirteen, a superior education at Eton and Oxford. The only thing he had ever been denied was permission to enter the army, and he'd managed to overcome that obstacle with barely any effort at all. And look where that course of action had brought him.

Stop it! He was tired of the whining voice in his head.

It was as though he were trapped in a ceaseless eddy. The more he tried to escape, the more strongly his dark thoughts pulled him back into the whirlpool of disgust.

Finch knew that the source of his distress was greater than simple boredom, but boredom was a part of it. It was too bad he didn't suffer from the lack of imagination evidenced by the two dandies, who could amuse themselves quite handily by tossing pies at street vendors.

It wasn't as though he hadn't tried to find useful things to do with his time since he had come back from the Peninsula last summer. But his efforts to take up his duties at Gilhurst Hall had met with cold condescension.

"The estate has bumbled along quite well in your absence," the Marquis of Gilhurst had written. "Don't trouble yourself to take an interest in it now."

It was the first letter Finch had received from his father in more than five years, despite the dozens he had written from Salamanca and Corunna, Oporto and Talavera, Busaco and Albuera and Sabugal. Only the letter he had dictated from his camp bed in Badajoz, telling the Marquis that he was to be invalided home, had received a response.

Finch would be demmed if he would contact his father again.

With that resolution in his tired mind, he guided Sophie into Brook Street and drew up before a small, redbrick townhouse on the corner. Light gleamed palely through the fanlight above the green front door. As usual, he gave thanks that he had had the foresight to invest part of his inheritance from his uncle in this property before leaving for Spain, and to let the property to tenants during his absence. The rents had accumulated to a tidy sum while he had been away, and he had become quite fond of the little house during his year in residence.

A lantern blinked on the walkway leading to the stable at the rear of the house, and a sleepy-eyed young groom came into view. "Evening, m'lord," he said, touching his cap. "Fine night, i'n't it?"

"Fine, indeed," Finch said as he leaped to the ground. Dismounting, he found, was far more graceful a procedure than mounting.

As the groom led Sophie away, Finch climbed the short flight of stairs to his front door. Weariness engulfed him like cold, damp mist.

"Good evening, Lord Finchwood." His butler, Watkins, stood as Finch entered the small, black-and-white tiled foyer. "I trust you had an enjoyable night?"

"As enjoyable as always," Finch replied, biting back the cynical reply that had been on his lips. Watkins was simply being polite. Finch unbuttoned his greatcoat and leaned back so that the shorter man could remove it easily from his shoulders, then handed his beaver hat to the butler as well.

"A letter came for you this afternoon," Watkins remarked, nodding toward the hall table. "The messenger who delivered it said it was quite important, but that it could wait until your return this evening."

"Thank you," Finch replied, trying to mask his surprise. Invitations to routs and balls rarely came with such instructions, and he received precious little else in the post these days. He lifted the missive from the table and broke the seal. Unfolding the single sheet, he took in the simple, heavy letterhead and felt a pulse jump in his throat that he hadn't felt in many months. It was as though a beam of sunlight had scorched and scattered the fog of exhaustion.

Francis Burnham, Viscount Finchwood
Brook Street, London

Dear Sir:

It has come to my attention, through our mutual acquaintance Lord Holt, that you boast some abilities of which we could make great use. If it is convenient, I should like to meet with you tomorrow at three o'clock in the afternoon, at my offices in Whitehall. I shall explain the reasons for this message in more detail then.

Cordially,
William Sands, Lord Barton

The letterhead bore the seal of the Foreign Office.

Finch barely restrained himself from throwing the letter in the air and leaping about like a delighted child. After almost a year of studiously casual inquiries, he had finally caught the attention of someone in the Foreign Office. He knew of Barton, although he had never met the man reputed to hold great sway with the Foreign Secretary himself.

Perhaps, finally, he would have something more than cards and brandy to occupy his days.

The clock in Barton's office seemed insufferably loud.

It was quarter past three. Finch had arrived on the dot of three. Well, to be more precise, he had arrived at two-thirty, and spent the ensuing half hour pacing the streets of Westminster awaiting his meeting.

At three, he had been ushered into Barton's office, with assurances from a private secretary that Barton would join him momentarily.

For probably the tenth time, Finch surveyed the framed engravings on Barton's walls. They were unremarkable.

He drummed his fingers on the arm of the leather club chair.

Tock. Tock. Tock.

Perhaps Barton had forgotten.

He ran a finger beneath his neckcloth, which suddenly seemed uncommonly tight.

The door flew open and a rotund man in a dark jacket and breeches hurried in. Bushy side curls stood out like flags from his somewhat disheveled gray hair, and a set of spectacles dangled from his neck on a silver chain. He looked more like someone's eccentric great-uncle than a key member of the Secret Service. Finch stood.

"My apologies, Lord Finchwood," the older man said, proffering a hand. "Barton."

They shook, and Barton motioned Finch back to his seat.

"I was meeting with the Foreign Secretary to discuss some matters pertinent to my meeting with you, and it took longer than I expected to resolve all the issues." He tossed a pile of papers onto the cluttered desk. "I assume you suspect why we have summoned you?"

"I am hoping you are in need of my experience in military intelligence."

"Exactly so, exactly so. And other factors in your background may make you particularly useful to us at the present time."

Finch nodded. The older man's circuitous approach to the matter at hand was typical of intelligence officers. After time in the field, it became a habit to speak in cryptic ciphers, even when one was certain of the sympathies of one's audience.

When Barton declined to elaborate, Finch hazarded a guess. "Is it my fluency in French that seems useful? Are you seeking additional agents in Paris?"

Barton blinked. "Paris? No, we want to send you to Hampshire."

It was Finch's turn to blink. *"Hampshire?"* Truly, the only place on earth less appealing to him was Badajoz.

"Yes. We've had word that French spies are filtering into England somewhere along the Hampshire coast, possibly as part of a combined espionage and smuggling operation. We'd like you to help us find the chink in England's armor, and gather evidence that will allow us to arrest the parties involved."

Finch tried to keep from laughing—an action that would, under the circumstances, be most inappropriate. Of all the places he had imagined the Foreign Office might send him, Hampshire was the very last. But the opportunity to once again do an honest day's work for his country was too good to resist.

"Finchwood? Are you well?"

He took a deep breath. "Fine. Yes, fine. I am pleased to serve His Majesty's government in any capacity. How should you like me to proceed?"

"The sooner you can establish yourself in Hampshire, the better. I understand you grew up at Gilhurst Hall. It will make a perfect base for your operations, and you will rouse far fewer suspicions than a stranger moving into the area."

"I am practically a stranger. I have not been to Gilhurst Hall since I joined the army, and I was away at school for several years before that." Finch's mind was only half on his words. The other half was busily trying to come up with any alternative to returning to his father's home, cap in hand, begging a place to stay. Unfortunately, no other choices occurred to him.

"But still, your father is a major local figure. No one will question your presence."

"Except my father," Finch muttered.

Barton cocked his head to the side, like a curious puppy. "Don't get along with your parent, eh? Not the first whelp to disagree with his papa, nor the last. Make the best of it. You're the best chance we have. Not only do you have espionage experience and roots in the area, but your knowledge of French may also be most useful."

"Many men know French."

"Yes, but few speak it like a native. With a bit of advance planning, you might even be able to convince any

French agents you encounter that you are one of their number."

Finch doubted that—his French was good but not perfect. But he had no intention of undermining the Foreign Office's confidence in his abilities. If he managed to complete this job to their satisfaction, perhaps they would offer him permanent employment with the Secret Service. For the chance to regain a focus and a purpose in his life, he would do more than equivocate about his language skills.

"One more thing—we will occasionally require written reports." Barton waved toward the stack of files he had deposited on the desk. "You do know code?"

Finch nodded. "Yes, but my hand—"

"—was injured at Badajoz. Yes, we know."

"You seem to know quite a bit about me."

"We're in that business." Barton smiled. "Seriously, however, I know that you are no longer able to write. That is why I am going to give you the authority to engage an aide when you arrive in Hampshire. The more eyes we have, the better."

Finch's jaw sagged. "*Hire* someone? Without training or experience?"

"You need tell this person only what he needs to know."

"Perhaps you would be better to look for an agent who has full use of his hand." The words stuck like rocks in his throat, but Finch felt it was best to be frank. He doubted that his slightly accented French would impede his progress in this assignment. But his inability to communicate with his superiors, save through an intermediary, was another matter. It could jeopardize everything.

He sighed. No matter how dearly he coveted this job, he could not live with himself if he put innocent people—and the country—at risk.

To his surprise, Barton was shaking his head. "No, we

would ask any agent to make an alliance with a local res-
ident, whether the agent could write or not. You yourself
have admitted that you have been away from Hampshire
for many years. You will need someone whose connections are not quite as rusty as yours. Who may have
already heard or seen something suspicious."

"Of course," Finch murmured in a neutral voice, even
as elation coursed through him. Despite his injury,
someone believed he still had something useful to con-
tribute to the world. He would soon escape the pointless
round of routs and card games. Perhaps he might even
feel alive again, as he had not since Badajoz.

When the first rush of joy receded, Finch focused on
the first task at hand. Where on earth was he to find a
trustworthy assistant? Aside from his father, who was far
too conspicuous a local person for the task, Finch could
not think of a soul with the combination of education and
discretion required. However, in all of Hampshire, there
had to be *someone*. This opportunity was far too valuable to
let it slide through his fingers. If he had to live under the
same roof as his father, and comb the fields and byways of
Hampshire for an assistant, these were small prices to pay
to prove his competence once more.

"Thank you for the opportunity," he said to Barton. "I
assume that the documents in that file relate to my assignment?"

"Indeed they do, indeed they do," the older man said,
unwrapping a thin yellow cord from the stack. "Welcome
to the Foreign Office, Finchwood."

TWO

Miss Charlotte Gregory leaned back in her stiff wooden chair, closed her eyes and took a deep breath of the fresh spring air pouring through the small window behind her. The late afternoon breeze was scented with bluebells, and for a moment it revived her. But then she remembered the dismal figures in the account book spread open on the desk. She opened her eyes again and focused on the columns of numbers. No matter which way she combined them, they added up to disaster.

A small, dark-haired young woman poked her head around the corner of the open door. "May I speak with you?"

"Certainly, Jane. Please be seated."

Her assistant settled into a worn velvet chair. "I wished to ask your advice about Anne Symes."

Charlotte smiled. "Is she asking more questions about medical science again? Or Euclidian geometry? Or is today's topic rhetoric?"

"Military strategy, actually."

They shared a wry laugh. Anne Symes was one of their best students: quick, smart and curious. The only problem was that she was interested in everything, including subjects that Charlotte and Jane were unqualified to teach, that bored the other students, and that would horrify the students' parents—if they only knew. Charlotte intended to do everything she could to ensure that the families of her girls were not shocked. She was in no position to be an iconoclast.

"Well, I shall see whether Mr. Grimes has any books on that topic in his library. I certainly would not be qualified to speak to it. And unless you have a secret history of which I am unaware, I am willing to wager that you don't wish to expound on the subject *ex tempore.*"

Jane shook her head. "My knowledge of military strategy is gleaned entirely from articles in the *Post.*"

"Well, we shall do our best to sate Anne's curiosity without taking too much time from the rest of the curriculum. Much remains to discuss before summer. Perhaps she might be willing to take a private lesson on military topics after regular classes? We could ask."

"Would that require an extra fee?"

Charlotte sighed. "I suppose it should, but since Anne is already paying half fees in return for helping in the classroom, I'm hesitant to suggest it. And yet, we can't give her extra instruction and not charge for it, then turn around and levy fees for similar classes on girls from wealthier families." She tapped her fingers against the chipped china cup on her desk. "We shall just have to work the topic into the regular lessons, somehow. Perhaps as part of a larger discussion of history. Let me give it some thought."

The younger woman stood. "Thank you."

"Before you go, may I in turn ask your advice?"

"Certainly." Jane returned to her chair and fixed her employer with a curious glance.

Charlotte nodded toward the open ledger. "This will likely come as no surprise, but our finances are in poor shape."

Her assistant nodded. "I suspected as much, when you had the cracked window in the parlor stuffed with rags rather than asking the glazier to fix it. And then, of course, there was that dispute with the butcher."

"Yes." With shame, Charlotte recalled the discussion at the back door with Mr. Harper. He had claimed she owed him four shillings more than her accounts showed. Ordinarily, she would have paid the extra fee just to avoid a public argument that all her students could easily overhear. But every shilling was important when the school was so close to penury, and she could not give the butcher the benefit of the doubt.

She had prevailed, but the result was that the butcher now insisted she pay cash. As he was the only butcher in Gillington, she had no choice but to comply. She could not simply stop serving meat to her students. They were growing children, and their parents had sent them to the academy in full expectation that they would be well cared for.

Charlotte sighed. "If we do not find a way to increase our profits before fall term, I fear that we will need to trim our expenses even further, or close the school altogether."

"Close the school!" Jane's voice rose in horror. "But you love this place. As do I, and the girls."

"I know, but Mr. Harper is not the only vendor who treats our account with suspicion. More and more businesses are refusing us credit. If we must pay cash for everything, I will surely have to fold. We simply don't have a sack of coins under the floorboards—unless Harriet neglected to mention it to me when she turned over the school."

Harriet Moore had run the Moore Academy for Young Ladies for thirty-six years. Both Charlotte and Jane had been her pupils, and Charlotte had become her assistant at age seventeen. Three years ago, the schoolmistress had received a letter from her niece in Kent, pleading with Harriet to come live with her and serve as governess to her five unruly children.

"At an earlier point in my life, I would have said no without even considering the matter," Harriet had told Charlotte. "But I am well past fifty, and I am finding the administration of this school increasingly exhausting. The opportunity to oversee five children, rather than thirty, is more appealing than I would have ever dreamed."

In the end, the kind schoolmistress had sold the school to Charlotte, with the payments to be made in annual installments over a period of ten years. Charlotte's father had provided a small sum—all he could afford—as an initial investment.

At first, Charlotte had been delighted. She had hired Jane, an excellent student who had been sorely in need of gainful employment. She had engaged tradesmen to repair sticky doors and repoint the aged chimney in the rambling old house. And she had updated some of the curriculum. Miss Moore had been a dear, but rather resistant to changes in educational philosophy. In particular, Charlotte had started rudimentary classes in science, mathematics, and Latin, introduced so gradually that neither the students nor their families found any cause for complaint. Since she and Jane continued to provide instruction in more traditional topics—any student of theirs would be well able to embroider, paint, and play the pianoforte by the time she left the academy—everyone seemed satisfied.

What neither Miss Moore nor Charlotte had envisaged, however, were the hard times brought on by the war on the Continent and a series of crop failures across England. When funds were scarce, the education of girls was the first expense to be trimmed.

"It's not that you haven't been doing a good job, Miss Gregory," sad-eyed parents would tell her as they came to collect their daughters for the last time. "My daughter simply adores it here. But we can only afford to send one child to school, and her brother must take priority."

Charlotte understood their reasoning even as she inwardly chafed against it. Boys needed a formal education in order to earn a living. Girls could manage a household quite well with the skills their family could teach them at home. Education for girls was a luxury. The only reason she had been able to attend Miss Moore's school herself was by working as a junior assistant.

Charlotte returned her attention to the matter at hand. "Don't worry, Jane. I will do everything I can to keep the school open. But what I should like you to do is to think about ways we can further economize. And if you know of any families who might be seeking a school for their daughters, by all means, let me know. I shall write to them myself."

"Certainly," Jane said, a worried frown creasing her high, pale forehead. "I would do anything for you and for the school. You know that."

"I do, and I'm lucky to have you." She stood. "I am sorry to have burdened you with my worries. Now, do you have everything you need for the evening?"

"Yes, it is all arranged. Sarah and Catherine are going to give a little performance for the younger girls."

"Lovely. Well then, I shall take my leave. My father will be expecting me for dinner." The vicar always delayed dinner by several hours on Tuesday evenings, to give his daughter time to fulfill her duties at school and walk home. She hated to keep him from his meal any longer than necessary.

"Enjoy your night at home, Charlotte. Heaven knows, you deserve it."

Charlotte gathered up a bundle of student assignments and tied them together with string, then made her way through the school's drafty foyer and out the front door. She was still thinking about the dismal accounts book as she walked down the drive that curved across the wide lawn. Once on the main road, it was but a ten-minute walk

to Gillington. Her father's vicarage stood on the other side
of the village, a scant ten minutes farther.

The fresh breeze she had noticed earlier ruffled her
skirt. Looking behind her to ensure that none of the
girls was observing, she removed her demure mobcap
and tucked it into the small pocket she had sewn into
her pelisse. On a day like today, she longed to go bare-
headed. She hoped that no one in the village would
think the worse of her for it.

A stray curl escaped from the knot at the base of her
neck and fluttered against her cheek. For a minute, she
felt almost as free as a child.

As she turned onto the main road, she began review-
ing her ideas for bringing the school into solvency. An
advertisement in one of the London newspapers might
bring attention, but that would have to be paid for in
cash. Perhaps the lawn behind the school could be
turned into a market garden. But then where would the
girls take their exercise? Charlotte had learned during
her first year that allowing the girls, particularly the
younger ones, to expend their excess energy was crucial
to peace in the classroom.

Almost without realizing it, she had reached the edge
of Gillington. She passed a row of workers' cottages,
then the mercer's rambling shop. Few people were
about on the streets. It was late, and most had gone
home long ago for their dinner.

Dinner. Was there anything they could make in the
school's antiquated kitchen that might bring in a few
pennies in the weekly market? Charlotte was pondering
the possibilities when she collided with a man who had
just stepped out of the village's lone pub. She caught a
faint whiff of some kind of liquor.

"Sir, I'm so sorry!" she exclaimed, as the bundle of papers she had been carrying fell to the ground. She knelt

to collect the few pages that had worked themselves loose, before they could blow away on the rising breeze.

"No, ma'am, it was my fault entirely. I should have looked where I was going before stepping into the street."

She knew that voice. She had not heard it in years, but she doubted she would ever forget it. Looking up, she stared straight into the face of Viscount Finchwood.

The shock almost knocked her back on her heels. "My lord, I had no idea you had returned to the area. Welcome home."

He frowned, and she knew he was trying to place her. She was not in the least offended. It was only natural that she would remember him. After all, his father was the grandest gentleman—and largest employer—in the area. But there was nothing remarkable in her history that would lead Lord Finchwood to remember her.

"Miss Gregory," she said, eager that he not feel foolish.

"Oh yes," he said, in a rumbling bass. His voice had taken on added depth in the years he'd been away. "The vicar's daughter. Very nice to meet you again." He extended his left hand to help her up from the sidewalk. She debated the wisdom of taking it, then decided it would look odd if she did not.

As his large gloved hand closed around her smaller one, her fingertips tingled and she felt a slow flush staining her neck and ears. How embarrassing. As a girl of fourteen, she had harbored secret dreams about the dashing young nobleman, and she had not been alone. Just about every girl in the village had taken covert peeks at him as he cantered along the high street or dallied in front of the few simple shops. Some had even dared to dream that he would invite them to one of the grand soirees at Gilhurst Hall or for a ride in his father's crested carriage. But although he was always cordial and kind, he lived in a different world, and they all knew it.

That was how it should be. The sons of peers married

the daughters of peers, and the daughters of physicians and vicars married the sons of barristers and country squires.

At the age of four-and-twenty, Charlotte found the memory of her youthful imaginings almost unbearable. She hoped her discomfort did not show on her face.

"Thank you," she said as she regained her feet and dropped his hand. Now that they were almost face-to-face—or as close as they could get, since he was at least two heads taller than she—she studied him more closely.

More than his voice had matured. His features seemed more angular than she remembered, and a small scar above his left eyebrow had not been there before. Tiny lines creased the edges of his mouth. But it was his eyes that drew her attention. From the few conversations they had had years ago, it was his eyes she remembered best. They had always been laughing and full of mischief. Today, however, they were dull and hooded.

A wave of sadness engulfed her. It was his liveliness, as well as his indisputable good looks, that had always drawn the attention of the village girls. It seemed wrong to see him so restrained.

I suppose that's what happens when we grow up, she thought. She was sure she looked much less buoyant than she had a decade ago, when she wasn't weighed down by worries about grocer's bills and leaky foundations.

"How long have you been back in the area?" she asked.

"I arrived just this afternoon." He looked away from her, down the street.

"Your father must be overjoyed to see you again, after so many years."

"I have not been home yet." His gaze remained focused on a point in the distance.

"But of course." Charlotte suddenly remembered the tales her father's neighbor, Mrs. Kane, had told her of

Lord Finchwood's exploits in London. Mrs. Kane subscribed to several London scandal sheets, and her
excitement when someone she actually knew finally appeared in the gossip columns had known no bounds.

"Of course, they always refer to him simply as Lord
F———," she'd told Charlotte in a low, thrilled voice.
"But without doubt it is our own Lord Finchwood. 'Heir
to a rich Hampshire estate, recently returned from the
Peninsula,'" she'd read out. "Who else could it be?"

Charlotte had known it was wrong to listen to Mrs.
Kane's ramblings. Her father did not approve of gossip,
and neither did she. Most of the time. But the temptation to hear news of the exotic young viscount had been
too strong to resist. Charlotte was only human, after all.

But when Mrs. Kane shared her news, it simply de-
pressed Charlotte. Every mention of the viscount involved
a near duel, a liaison with an actress, a contentious wager
at cards, or some story of inebriated excess.

"Just youthful high spirits," Mrs. Kane had said indul-
gently.

But Finchwood was eight-and-twenty, past the point
where many men were married and assuming their responsibilities. Such excesses might be understandable in
a young man just down from Oxford. In a war veteran,
they were . . . unseemly.

It was well known in the neighborhood that the Marquis of Gilhurst was similarly unimpressed with his son's
activities in London. Perhaps the viscount had felt the
need to gather his courage in the pub before bearding
the parental lion in his den.

When he finally turned back toward her, it was evident
from his expression that she had guessed correctly. "My
father does not know I am here. If he knew I was coming, he likely would have made arrangements to be
elsewhere."

Charlotte, who had always shared a devoted relationship with her family, was at a loss as to how to respond. "I am sure that is not the case, my lord."

"You are kind, but I suspect that my sojourn in Hampshire will not be restful." He gazed at her and a slow, lazy smile crossed his face.

Suddenly, Charlotte realized why all those London actresses had been so eager to have their names linked with his in the gossip columns. Despite his weary demeanor, he was as devastating as ever—in a more dangerous way. She swallowed.

"You have changed greatly since we knew each other years ago," he continued, his eyes never leaving her face. "When I left to attend Oxford, you were little more than a gangly schoolgirl." His grin widened. "You are certainly not a schoolgirl any longer."

Charlotte's breath caught in her throat. Was he *flirting* with her? Surely not.

"I am four-and-twenty, my lord, and a schoolmistress rather than a schoolgirl."

"A schoolmistress?"

"Miss Moore sold her academy to me several years ago."

"Ah. The perfect road to security for an educated woman."

Charlotte sighed. "Hardly." As soon as the word crossed her lips, she could have bitten off her tongue.

His eyebrows flew up. "Miss Moore seemed to find it so."

"Times have changed." She hugged the bundle of papers closer to her chest as a stiff gust of wind ruffled her hair. With embarrassment, she realized she was not wearing a hat. What must he think of her? "If you will excuse me, my lord, I must hurry. I am expected at the vicarage for dinner."

"How are your parents?" His voice was polite and interested.

"My father is very well, thank you for asking." She paused. "My mother passed away two years ago."

"My condolences. I know how painful it is to lose one's mother, at any age."

She remembered that Lord Finchwood's mother had died in childbirth when he was but a child. "But more so when one is very young. At least my mother and I had many good years together."

"Yes."

An awkward silence hung between them, yet the viscount made no move to leave.

"I really must be on my way, my lord," Charlotte piped up, eager to be gone. She had thoughtlessly encroached too far on the viscount's privacy with her last remark. "It was lovely to see you again."

His smile returned. "The pleasure was all mine, Miss Gregory." Was it her imagination, or did his grin widen on the word *pleasure*? "I hope we have occasion to meet again during my stay at Gilhurst Hall. School was never my strong point. I suspect there is much you could teach me."

There was no mistaking it this time. His eyes had lit up with a faint trace of their old mischief.

Well, any thoughts he had of a country dalliance would need to be nipped firmly in the bud. Her being seen in the company of such a notorious rake would do nothing to enhance her school's reputation. And that reputation was just about all that was standing between her and financial ruin.

"I think you might find other teachers better suited to your . . . proclivities," she replied, and for the second time in as many minutes she could have cheerfully amputated her own tongue. She had meant to dissuade him from flirting, but she hadn't intended to sound like a prim shrew in the process.

He didn't seem to notice. "I suspect I will have little time for education, in any case." He bowed. "Good day, Miss Gregory." He crossed the street and made his way toward a plain black carriage waiting on the other side. A coachman in nondescript tweeds leaned against the polished wood door. The carriage must have been what had caught the viscount's attention earlier. Charlotte had been so addled by his sudden reappearance that she hadn't noticed it. Or perhaps she had been thinking that the viscount would travel in something rather more spectacular.

She watched as the coachman opened the door and the viscount stepped into the back seat. It was odd that he wasn't driving his own coach, she thought. As a youth, he had been a noted horseman, taking prizes at several events at the village fairs.

Suddenly aware she was staring, she turned her attention to the road in front of her. Father would be worried if she didn't arrive soon. As she hurried away, she thought she saw a curtain twitch in the window of the grocery store. It wouldn't be surprising, she thought. Lord Finchwood's arrival was the most exciting event in Gillington since Christmas. It would be the main subject of conversation for weeks, she would wager, if she were a betting woman.

He would certainly be a primary subject of admiration for her students and a whole new generation of young women in the neighborhood. They would battle with fans and lowered lashes for the privilege of a kind word from him. It wasn't surprising. When he had smiled at her a few moments ago, his blue eyes alight with some of their youthful fire, Charlotte had felt the warmth all the way down to the tips of her sensible boots.

The folly of such thoughts made her chuckle. Fantasies about the viscount had consumed far too much of her time when she was an adolescent. A woman with responsibility for thirty students, an assistant and an aging father had no time for idle speculation.

She pushed all musings on Lord Finchwood's fine countenance aside and made as much haste as she could toward the vicarage, although she could not in all po-

liteness refuse to pause occasionally to chat with the few
other souls who were about at this hour. Mrs. Kane was
eager to share news of her sister's new baby, and Mr.
Drummond urged her to take some of his extra spring
carrots. "I'll never be able to eat them all," he said with
a kind smile, and she knew he had heard of her financial
difficulties and was trying to offer some small assistance
without embarrassing her.

On days such as this, when her worries threatened to
overwhelm her, Charlotte gave thanks that she had been
able to remain in Gillington. Even though the size of the
small village made it impossible for one to keep a secret,
it also made it impossible for one to be in trouble without finding many sources of support and friendship.
That was a comforting feeling.

Another gust of wind threatened to tear the stack of
student papers from her hands. Dusk would fall soon,
and Charlotte was suddenly eager for her father's warm
fireside and a bit of homely chat. These dinners were
always the highlight of her week, and she could almost
smell the roasted joint her father's housekeeper would
have prepared. Mouth watering, she turned into the
lane that flanked the small stone church.

Half an hour later, a few miles from Gillington, Finch
had long since dismissed his encounter with the charming young schoolmistress from his mind. Far more
interesting, at the minute, was the vista that had opened
up before him. He gazed out the window of the carriage
at the grounds of his childhood home.

Even in the gathering gloom, he could see that his father had invested a considerable sum to bring the park
up to the latest standards of landscape gardening. The
simple wooden bridge across the stream had been replaced by a substantial stone crossing. New plantings of

ornamental bushes ringed the small pond. Good heavens, the marquis had even ordered the construction of a small, Gothic-style gazebo—a very fashionable addition, Finch knew, but one that must seem oddly out of place on the grounds of the resolutely classical house.

The coach rounded the last bend in the road and approached Gilhurst Hall. Finch noted that a few dilapidated outbuildings had been removed. But the main house itself, to his relief, appeared unchanged. Three orderly rows of small, square windows glowed in the last rays of sunset, golden eyes in the stark white façade of Portland stone. A small portico still sheltered the entrance, and the front door was still blue. It looked as though it had recently received a fresh coat of paint.

As he often did, Finch marveled that England had changed so little in the years he had been in the Peninsula. It seemed inconceivable that the fires and terror and inhumanity that had swept across Spain had not engulfed the whole world. He was devoutly glad that England had been spared, but sometimes he found it hard to reconcile the memories that haunted him at night with the reality he encountered by day.

The carriage rolled to a stop, and Finch sat up straight and adjusted his neckcloth. Inside his gloves, his palms were damp. He felt almost as he had the day he had first seen battle in Spain.

Chiding himself for his faint heart, he didn't wait for the coachman to come to the carriage door. He wrenched it open himself and leaped lightly to the gravel drive. Lamplight shone through the fanlight above the blue door, but no servants were in evidence. That was not surprising, since he had sent no word of his impending arrival.

A surprising nostalgia engulfed Finch as he ascended the steps of his childhood home. He knew he would feel dread when he returned, but he hadn't expected to feel affection as well. In the years he had been away, he had forgotten how much he had loved this place.

As he stood before the door, he hesitated. Should he knock, or simply walk in? All of this would one day be his, after all.

But for now, it was still his father's home. He raised his right hand, fixed it carefully around the gleaming brass knocker and delivered two short, weak raps on the door. Stubborn fool. He should have used his stronger left hand.

Within a minute the door opened and on the threshold stood Hepworth, the Gilhurst butler since long before Finch had been born. The servant was a little more stooped than Finch remembered, but other than that he was as unchanged as the façade.

"Lord Finchwood!" Hepworth exclaimed. "What an unexpected pleasure!"

His delighted shout—surely the loudest sound Finch had ever heard the old man utter—brought Finch's father striding from the study at the back of the house.

To Finch's shock, his father looked as though more than five years had passed since they last met. He was not yet sixty, but he looked decades older. His skin was sallow and sagging, and purple smudges rimmed his eyes. His hair was noticeably sparser than it had been, and what little was left was snow white.

"Francis." The marquis's voice was flat.

"Father." Finch stayed rooted to his spot by the front door. Despite the bravado he had cultivated in the carriage on the way back to Hampshire, he felt as he had at the age of eight, when his father had caught him stealing apples from a neighbor's orchard.

Truth to tell, Finch would almost rather be back in Spain, facing that crazed French agent who had threatened him with a loaded musket behind a bawdy house in Salamanca.

"The prodigal returns. If you are expecting a fatted calf, I'm afraid you will be disappointed." His father remained in the corridor and made no move to approach or embrace his only son.

"I expect nothing, aside from shelter for a few weeks."

"Been tossed from your rooms in London for lewd and lascivious behavior?"

"If landlords evicted gentlemen for such reasons, half the lodgings in St. James's would be vacant. You know I own a house in Mayfair."

"Right. Yes. Thanks to that meddling uncle of your mother's."

So, the fact that his sizable inheritance from Oncle Guillaume allowed him financial freedom from the Gilhurst estate still rankled his father. Good.

Finch silently thanked his late uncle for his thoughtfulness, as he had so often done in the past, and turned his attention to the matter at hand. "Notwithstanding my house in Town, I have some affairs to attend to here in Hampshire, and I thought I might prevail upon your hospitality."

"What affairs?" His father's voice was laced with suspicion.

"Personal matters."

"Then you should take care of them personally."

If Barton's assignment had not been so tempting, and hadn't hinged so strongly on not arousing local suspicions, Finch would have walked back to his carriage at that moment. Other men served their country and returned to a hero's welcome. It was unjust in the extreme to be treated like a criminal.

He drew in a deep breath. "Will it not look odd, Father, for me to rent a house in the neighborhood, when you are rattling around this enormous building all alone? People will talk."

The marquis scowled, and Finch realized he had

played his hand correctly. As always, his father put his reputation—and that of the estate—above all things.

"I have the funds to do it," Finch added. And then he played his trump card. "Who knows what sorts of activities I might engage in, far from your dedicated supervision?"

His father had always subscribed to a variety of London papers. Finch had no doubt he was aware of the minor scandals that had swirled and eddied around his feckless son in the past year.

The marquis let out a beleaguered sigh. "I have some idea. Very well, if you insist on staying here, I suppose there is little I can do to stop you. The north wing is virtually empty. Take your old room." He frowned. "I see you are as selfish as always. You might have thought to give the servants some warning before landing on our doorstep. The rooms will need to be aired and dusted. The linens will need to be changed."

"It will be the staff's pleasure, I'm sure, to prepare the north wing," Hepworth piped up. His father shot him a quelling look, and the butler said nothing more.

"I will take my meals in my study for the duration of Finchwood's stay," the marquis told the butler. "I suggest you make haste to inform the staff of the new arrangements."

With a nod, Hepworth headed down the corridor.

"How long do you anticipate staying?"

Finch shrugged. "I'm not sure. A month. Perhaps more."

"I shall do my best to stay out of your way. I suggest you make an effort to stay out of mine."

"Thank you, Father." Now that it seemed he would be allowed to stay, Finch removed his hat and stripped off his gloves. As he should have predicted, his father's gaze moved immediately to his scarred right hand. Finch quickly shoved it in his pocket.

For a brief moment, a flicker of warmth showed in the

marquis's eyes. "It would be churlish in the extreme, I suppose, to not say welcome home. So welcome."

It was a small concession, but any chink in his father's frosty armor was worth savoring. Touched, Finch looked down, focusing on unbuttoning his greatcoat with his left hand. "Thank you. I shall do my best not to be an inconvenience."

His words fell on empty space. His father had already disappeared through a side door.

When had the marquis become so harsh, Finch wondered as he laid his coat and hat on a small bench in the foyer. He had always been a bit gruff and reserved, but when Finch was a small boy, there had been much laughter in the house, too. He remembered his father teaching him to ride, a task the marquis had insisted was too important to be left to a groom. Around the paddock they had circled, the marquis showing infinite patience.

After Finch's mother died, the laughter in the house had become somewhat less frequent. But he had still had no doubt of his father's respect and affection, and returned them in equal measure.

The first inklings of deep rancor had appeared when he had resisted the marquis's attempts to mold him into a scholar, Finch thought as he unwound his muffler and laid it on top of the coat. He had been more than ready to leave Oxford at twenty-one, when most of his schoolmates had come down to enjoy the amusements of London. At his father's insistence, he had stayed several more years.

"What is the point?" he had argued at the time. "I will never be able to become a don, for eventually I will need to take over the duties of the estate. And I have neither the mind nor the inclination to pursue years of study."

"Don't pass up the opportunity, for it will not come again," his father had said.

Finch sighed as he opened the door and signaled to

his coachman to bring his small trunk into the foyer. He held the door open as Jenks climbed the steps.

Finch knew the marquis had once dreamed of an academic career. Indeed, John Burnham had never been destined to hold the title. As a third son, he had always expected to make his own way in the world. But when his eldest brother had died in a riding accident, and the second of a fever, he found himself the Marquis of Gilhurst.

And he had always carried out his duties with skill and good grace, Finch had to admit. Only once, late at night, when Finch had been lying awake long after his nurse had put him to bed, had he overheard his parents talking in the corridor and realized that life as a peer had never held much allure for his father.

"I could still be working on the proof for Fermat's last theorem, if the demmed estate and its problems didn't consume all of my waking hours."

"Shhh, John," his mother had soothed. "Mathematics is a noble pursuit, yes, but the work you do here is just as admirable. Many of the people of the village would be without work, were it not for the estate. *C'est vrai.*"

After depositing the case in the hall, Jenks touched his cap and went back outside to drive the carriage around to the stable. At a loss as to how to proceed, Finch wandered into the drawing room and pressed the bell on the far wall before settling onto a blue and cream striped settee. That was new, he noted. Looking around, he realized that most of the décor of this room was unfamiliar. His mother's portrait remained above the fireplace, and the matching picture of his father still dominated the far end of the room. But the walls had been painted a soft, warm yellow, and the Aubusson carpet beneath his feet was new.

When a young housemaid appeared, she dropped a brief curtsey. "What would you like, my lord?" she asked in a small voice. Then she eyed him warily, chewing on her lower lip.

His rakish reputation had obviously made its way through the ranks of his father's staff. He considered teasing her, but dismissed that thought as unkind. She was little more than a child.

"Tea, please," he said. "And a plate of cakes would not go amiss, if one is to be found."

"Yes, m'lord." She disappeared like a frightened rabbit.

He leaned back against the silk upholstery and wondered again about his father's coldness. It had started when Finch had chafed against Oxford. But it had blossomed into full enmity when Finch had insisted on joining the army.

His father had been livid at the thought that Finch would put the inheritance of the estate in jeopardy. "I will *not* see this house and all I have worked for go to that man Seabrook!" he had thundered on more than one occasion.

Henry Seabrook, Finch's gambling *confrère*, was a distant relation—second or third cousin, he could never quite remember which. If anything happened to Finch, Seabrook would inherit the title. The marquis had long harbored a virulent hatred for Seabrook, which Finch suspected was founded mainly on snobbery, since Seabrook's father had earned his wealth in industry.

While Finch found such high-in-the-instep attitudes outdated at best, he supposed he could understand his father's anger at Finch's decision to place himself at risk by joining the army. But he had left on military service years ago, and he had returned in one piece. Well, largely in one piece. Could they not simply forget the past and move ahead?

Perhaps it was as well that Barton's assignment had propelled him back to Hampshire. He had long been searching for a way to make amends with his father while retaining his pride. Judging by his father's evident ill health, he should make the effort sooner rather than later.

The door to the drawing room opened. Finch looked up, expecting the nervous little maid with a tea tray. Instead, he saw a young blonde woman, about his own age, wearing a stylish blue gown and smiling.

"Lord Finchwood!" she exclaimed, rushing into the room and holding out both hands. "What a delight to meet you at last!"

He stood and bowed. Who the deuce was she?

"I am Lady Gilhurst," she said, as if she had heard his unspoken question.

Lady Gilhurst? There is no Lady Gilhurst. Hasn't been for almost eighteen years.

His confusion must have shown on his face, for her bright smile faded somewhat. "Your father's wife," she added in a quieter voice.

THREE

Finch withdrew his gold watch from his pocket and looked at it. Six-thirty. Miss Gregory should emerge any minute now. A few inquiries in Gillington had revealed that she always dined with her father on Tuesdays, and he had encountered her in the street around seven o'clock on the Tuesday just past.

He leaned against a tree at the end of the academy's lane. Waiting had always been his least favorite part of intelligence work, as it always made him restless. In fact, he had left his horse in the village and walked to the school, just for the exercise. Something about the country air had given him more energy than he had had in months. Or perhaps it was just the prospect of beginning his assignment for the Foreign Office.

The sun was warm on his face, and he loosened his neckcloth slightly. His father would disapprove of him being seen in public in anything less than a perfectly tied and starched cravat, but Finch's attire was probably the least of his sins in his father's eyes, at the moment.

Although the marquis had a lot to answer for as well, in Finch's opinion. How could he fail to have informed his son that he had remarried? And that he had done so not six months after Finch left for Spain?

His mind still boggled. No wonder his father had been reluctant to write.

It had been a most interesting dinner that first evening. His stepmother had joined him in the stately dining room, while his father had indeed taken his meal in his study. The new Lady Gilhurst, who had insisted that Finch call her Amelia, had been all that was charming. But when she thought he wasn't looking, he caught a faint shadow of sadness in her eyes.

She was probably just embarrassed by her husband's rudeness. Finch had tried to make the best of the situation, asking about her family and her interests. She was the only child of the late Earl and Countess of Southfield. Apparently, Amelia had spent much of her time since her marriage rearranging the house. "It is one of my extravagant hobbies," she had confessed. "I love trying out new colors and styles, and your father indulges my whims with good humor."

"You have a talent for it," Finch had told her. He had warmed to the gentle young woman, even though he found it hard to believe that he now had a stepmother younger than himself. Amelia, it transpired, was six-and-twenty. She was also quick, well educated, and utterly devoted to the marquis.

If Finch hadn't been afraid that she would share the information with his father, he would have considered asking her to serve as his assistant. But whomever he asked would need to be completely discreet.

The question of how to find a capable assistant had bedeviled him for several days until he had devised a possible solution. He would hire a correspondence secretary. No one would question the fact that a man with an injured hand would need such a person. Once he had engaged a secretary, he would assign that person tasks that required increasing degrees of wit and secrecy. Someone who showed cleverness and sense in such duties might just make a natural agent.

If he was right, Miss Gregory might be the perfect person for both jobs: intelligent, literate, inconspicuous, well connected in the community—and just desperate enough to consider the position.

His inquiries in the village as to her schedule had also unearthed a few details about her financial straits. As he remembered, little was private among country folk.

"She's two years behind on her payments," revealed the mercer. "I likes her well—we all do, and respect her father, too—but soon I'll have to deny her more credit. The only reason I haven't done so before was to avoid scandalizing the vicar."

"Miss Gregory does her best, but that building is slowly falling into rack and ruin," said Mrs. Peters, the doctor's wife. "My Caroline says the children half freeze there in the winter, all the windows are so drafty. I make sure she wears two extra shifts and a flannel petticoat when I send her there. I've often thought of offering a loan so Miss Gregory could repair the windows, but she is proud and I know she would refuse it."

Finch was sorry to hear that Miss Gregory had fallen on hard times, but those hard times suited his purpose admirably. He suspected that he was just the sort of person proper schoolmistresses avoided. In fact, he had seen a look of mild panic in her eyes when he had attempted a little mild flirtation yesterday.

But proper schoolmistresses with debts had an Achilles heel. And if he had learned nothing else in military intelligence, he had learned how to exploit each person's weakness.

The squeal of a door opening on unoiled hinges caught his attention. At the top of the low rise on which the school sat, he saw a figure emerging from a side door. A female voice calling out to someone inside drifted to him on the breeze, although he could not make out the words.

He straightened up and brushed a chip of stray bark

from the blue superfine of his riding coat. The day was unseasonably warm for late April, and he had been able to leave his greatcoat at home.

He realized that, from his position behind the tree, he could see her but she would be unlikely to see him, unless she was specifically scanning the landscape for someone. He watched as she stopped in the middle of the drive. After glancing behind her, she plucked the white mobcap from her head and stuffed it, somehow, into her pelisse. It must be hidden in her sleeve.

Now that he thought about it, she had been wearing neither cap nor hat when he encountered her on the street the other day. Her auburn hair had been tousled from the breeze. Rather fetchingly tousled.

Mobcaps were not in vogue among the glamorous young women of London's *ton*, but apparently they were still the fashion among country schoolmistresses—if not the fashion, exactly, at least the expected garb.

He could feel the corners of his mouth twitching. Perhaps the proper Charlotte Gregory wasn't entirely proper after all.

She was almost upon him before he called out. "Good afternoon, Miss Gregory."

She twitched and turned to face him, then dropped a curtsey. "Good afternoon, my lord."

"We meet again."

"You must have suspected we might. Not many people have cause to lurk about our drive."

He nodded. She was both quick and forthright, despite the difference in their stations. Good. The last thing he needed in an assistant was missish reticence. "*Touché.* I was rather hoping to see you. Would you be willing to walk into Gillington with me? I would have brought my carriage, but I thought you might be averse to climbing into a closed carriage with a relative stranger."

"You thought correctly. Even walking alone with you is

highly irregular," she said, casting a glance back at the school.

"I will make my business brief, and make myself scarce before we come close to the village. But I have a proposition to put to you, and I was hoping to make it in private, rather than at the school or in your father's house."

Her jaw fell open, and he immediately realized how she must have interpreted his words. What an ass he was! If he hadn't been so concerned about preserving her reputation, he wouldn't have made such a mess of his explanation.

"Not that sort of proposition!" he exclaimed, gratified to see some of the color return to her cheeks.

"Well, that is a relief," she said. "I have little experience with propositions of that sort, and I would have been at a loss as to how to respond," she added, with a gleam of humor in her green eyes.

Suddenly, she seemed less governesslike and, well, more human.

He laughed. "Well, now my offer is going to seem something of an anticlimax. But I was wondering whether you had ever thought of taking on some responsibilities outside the school. You mentioned the other day that the academy doesn't provide you with a rich living."

"I am surviving quite tolerably."

The physician's wife had mentioned Miss Gregory's pride, and if her stiff shoulders and averted gaze were any indication, that pride ran deep. He would have to proceed gently.

"I am glad to hear it," he said as they turned into the road to the village. "But you would also be doing me a favor if you would consider my . . . suggestion. You see, I am in need of a correspondence secretary. My right hand was injured during the war, and while I have mastered many skills with my left hand, writing isn't one of them. Even I can't read the resulting scrawl."

"I am sorry to hear about your hand, my lord. I admire your success in reschooling yourself," she said. "Many men would have simply given up."

He smiled and tried to conceal his considerable surprise. For once, it appeared that a woman was going to focus on the things he could do, rather than the things he couldn't.

"Thank you. However, there are many veterans more incapacitated than I, who have made even more astonishing strides. I met one man at a hospital in London who had lost one leg at the knee, who levered himself across the floor on crutches almost as quickly and smoothly as any other man. He had arms like hams from the effort."

"It is remarkable what so many men have given to keep England safe." She paused. "Regarding this correspondence secretary position—would it be something I could do in addition to my duties at the academy? The school must remain my first priority."

"I believe you could handle both. I don't have large volumes of correspondence. One or two evenings a week should be adequate for the task."

"Evenings could be difficult. I have no means of transportation."

"What sort of ogre do you take me for?" He laughed to remove any sting she might impute to his words. "Of course, I would send my carriage around to collect you and bring you back to the school. You do live at the academy, correct?"

"Yes. Either my assistant, Jane Carter, or I am in residence in the school at all times. Many of our students are boarders, so there must always be an adult on hand. I customarily stay at my father's house two nights a week, and Jane spends Saturdays with her parents in Farnborough." She stepped almost into the ditch to avoid a large puddle, while he walked halfway into the road to do the same. "So what sort of correspondence would you need me to write?"

"Most of it is very routine. Letters to friends, responses to my lawyer and other associates in London." He paused. Did he trust her enough to go on? He must take a few risks, or it would take him until Christmas to even hire a secretary. Time was of the essence. "But some of my correspondence is of a rather confidential nature, and whoever I engage for this task must be capable of discretion."

She smiled. "That is one skill I believe I have developed to a quite admirable degree. One doesn't grow up as a vicar's daughter without hearing daily about the evils of gossip. And one cannot run a school for long without realizing that students' business must remain private if the school is to maintain its reputation."

"Just so." It appeared the glowing reports he had received of her character from people in the village had also been correct, although he intended to take no one's word as gospel. A few tests would be in order before he would be confident in entrusting her with any of his missives to Barton.

"I know this is impolite to ask, but it will be a crucial factor in my decision," she said, her eyes on the recently macadamized road. "What remuneration do you expect to pay a correspondence secretary?"

He named a weekly sum that would barely cover his liquor account at White's.

The eyes in the face she turned toward him were wide. "My lord, I asked my question in all seriousness. It is unkind to mock me."

Blast. He had no experience in hiring staff—he counted on his housekeeper and his butler to attend to such affairs. Not for the first time, he wished he had sufficient knowledge of Hampshire, and sufficient strength in his hand, to obviate the need for an assistant altogether. But there was no help for it—he must recant. Clearly, the sum he had offered had been too low.

"I can increase that by twenty percent, if that would make the offer more enticing," he said now, speculating idly that he was not used to negotiating fees with beautiful young women for something as mundane as correspondence services.

The thought brought him up short. Miss Gregory—beautiful?

Perhaps not in the conventional sense, he admitted. Red hair was not at all in fashion, even here in the country, and her face was somewhat plainer than those that appealed to the leading portraitists. But her smile was brilliant, and her threadbare pelisse revealed several enticing curves. Altogether, she was far more appealing than a country schoolmistress had any reason to be.

"Your original offer was enticing enough, if you really meant it," she said.

He started and reined in his improper thoughts, bringing his mind back to less distracting matters. "Don't talk yourself down. That's very poor negotiating strategy." He grinned. "I offered the original fee plus twenty percent. It's yours if you will take the position."

She frowned. He could almost see her weighing the pros and cons of the idea, like a small, muslin-garbed Lady Justice. To his delight, she made up her mind quickly. "I do believe I shall take it," she said.

He released a breath he had not realized he'd been holding. "Excellent. What nights do you visit your father?"

"During the school year, only on Tuesdays. I also help out after services on Sunday mornings."

"Well, shall we arrange for you to start your new position next Wednesday, then? I can have my coachman collect you at seven o'clock, if that is convenient. Will that give you time to supervise dinner at the school?"

"Yes—thank you for taking that into consideration." A

thought seemed to strike her suddenly. "Will it be proper for me to visit you in your home, unchaperoned?"

He grinned as they stepped aside to avoid the encroaching limbs of an untrimmed barberry hedge. "You will hardly be unchaperoned. My father's house is as crowded as the London docks. There are footmen everywhere." He did not add that those footmen would likely be asked to leave the room if anything related to the investigation was to be discussed.

"Besides, my step—" He stopped. The whole idea still felt odd. "My father's wife, Lady Gilhurst, is in residence. Nothing untoward is likely to happen in her presence."

Miss Gregory's narrowed eyes showed she had not missed his stumbling as he mentioned Amelia. Well, if she spent any time at Gilhurst Hall, she would certainly notice that it wasn't a happy household. Better she learn now rather than later.

"Well, it appears you have thought of everything." She stopped as they approached a curve in the road. "We are about to enter the village. I will proceed alone, if you don't mind."

He touched the brim of his beaver hat. "Your servant, Miss Gregory."

She smiled. "I believe you have that the wrong way around. *Your* servant, my lord. And thank you." With a swish of her skirt, she turned and walked away.

He waited a minute, watching her retreating figure with an unholy degree of enjoyment. She might be a small, plainly dressed woman, but she moved like the most elegant Incomparable. He suspected he should feel guilty for staring, but what else could he do? He'd agreed to let her walk through town ahead of him.

No, he didn't feel the slightest bit guilty, he thought, as her rather pleasing form disappeared around the bend.

* * *

What on earth have I done? Charlotte thought as she walked down the lane beside the church and past her father's carefully tended mulberry tree.

Greed was one of the seven deadly sins, and she had given in to it when Lord Finchwood had named the sum he intended to pay her. It would not be enough to meet all the school's debts, but it would keep the proverbial wolf from the door for a few months until she could come up with a more permanent solution. She could pay the butcher and several other creditors. Perhaps even fix the window in the main classroom.

But if she were to be truly honest with herself—and Charlotte was nothing if not honest—she had to admit that greed was not the only deadly sin she had allowed free rein when she agreed to Lord Finchwood's offer. Her knowledge of lust was limited, but she knew enough of what passed between men and women to realize that part of the reason she had agreed so readily to serve as the viscount's correspondence secretary was the prospect of spending time in his company several evenings a week.

She closed her eyes and drew a slow, deep breath. But instead of smelling the freshly turned earth from a nearby field, she recalled the crisp scent of soap, leather, and something indefinable that swirled around Lord Finchwood. It seemed to emanate from his clothes, his skin, his hair. She breathed again, then opened her eyes.

This was ridiculous. She was behaving like a cow-eyed schoolgirl, not a sober schoolmistress of four-and-twenty. If she was to work with the man, she had to focus on the work rather than on him. It shouldn't be such a problem. Over the past four years, she had become an expert at focusing on tasks and responsibilities rather than on personal matters. It was the way she had accepted her mother's death, her fiancé's decision to jilt her, the financial problems at the school. She just thought about each day's duties rather than thinking about things that made her sad or tense or angry.

It had worked admirably so far. She had no reason to believe it wouldn't work again.

She had made the right decision. The fee for this light work would help save the school. To put the academy on a firmer footing, she would have taken on much worse duties. This position appeared to be heaven sent. And, she reminded herself, there was no whiff of scandal about the arrangement. The viscount might be a rake of the first order, but servants could hardly be held accountable for the behavior of their employers. It would cause no tongues to wag if she were to be seen in his presence, once it became generally known that she was his secretary. All would appear proper.

All would *be* proper.

Feeling better about the whole affair, she opened the faded front door of the whitewashed vicarage and stepped into the little vestibule. As she was hanging her pelisse on one of the wooden hooks that lined one wall, she heard her father's voice within. "Is that you, Charlotte?"

"Yes, Father," she replied, coming into the cozy sitting room. Although the evening was warm for April, a fire glowed in the grate. In general, the Reverend William Gregory was very economical with his small living, but he rarely skimped on coal. "'Twill do the parish no good if I die an early death of fever or rheumatism, and they have the trouble of locating another vicar," he often told visitors with a chuckle.

Her father stood. "Welcome home, child."

She kissed him on the cheek. "Good evening, Father. Has your week been a good one?"

"Tolerably so." He sat back down and poured her a cup of tea from the chipped pot on the small table before the fire. "It looks as though we shall need to repair the roof above the chancel. After the storm last week, the leak worsened."

"Will Lord Gilhurst agree to the expense?"

"I expect so, although he will not be pleased. This will be the third major repair to the church this year."

"It is an old building. Such repairs are to be expected."

Her father's eyes lit up. "Did I tell you that I found some old papers in the loft regarding the provenance of the window above the altar?" Architectural history, particularly the history of Gillington's thirteenth-century church, was one of her father's main passions. In his scant moments of leisure, he was writing a treatise on the subject. "Apparently, it dates from the early years of the Restoration—about fifty years earlier than I had thought."

"How intriguing! Perhaps the parishioners wished to give thanks that their church was spared Cromwell's torches."

They discussed the window and other matters for a few minutes, but part of Charlotte's mind was still on her agreement with Lord Finchwood. Now that she was in her father's house, she had begun to rethink her decision yet again. She knew the viscount was exactly the sort of rogue of whom her father strongly disapproved.

Partway through a story about an escaped chicken startling the housekeeper in the kitchen garden, the vicar stopped. "Are you feeling well, child? You appear worried."

She started. "What makes you say so?"

"That little ridge between your eyebrows. Ever since you were a child, you have creased your forehead just so when you are turning something over in your mind."

Charlotte smiled. "Well, yes, something happened as I was walking to the vicarage, and I wanted to tell you about it, but I wasn't certain how you would react."

"Just tell me. I cannot imagine anything you could say that would disturb me unduly."

Her father's confidence both comforted and rankled her. She was comforted that he had such faith in her. But a tiny, half-hidden part of her wondered if, at her age, she had already become so staid and predictable that nothing she could say or do would be remotely out of the ordinary.

"I have agreed to take a temporary position with Lord Finchwood."

The vicar appeared struck dumb for several seconds. "What sort of position?" he finally asked.

"As his correspondence secretary." She outlined their conversation on the road.

"And it would not interfere with your duties at the school?"

"I don't believe so. In fact, it might just be the salvation of the academy."

The vicar leaned back in his chair. "I cannot say that I am delighted to see you associating closely with a gentleman of such poor reputation as the viscount."

"I know, Father, but—"

He held up a hand. "Wait, my dear. I was about to say that while I am not delighted, neither do I think you made the wrong choice." He sipped his tea. "Lord Finchwood's father is a good man, and perhaps the viscount has reasons we cannot understand for behaving as he has—reputedly—since returning to England. One must not forget that he served our country proudly in war, and he has likely seen things we cannot imagine."

Charlotte remembered the chill look in the viscount's eyes she had noted the day they met in front of the pub, and nodded.

"So while I disapprove of his conduct, I think this is a case of hate the sin, not the sinner. He has offered you such a valuable opportunity. I think you were right to take it. Just be prudent, my dear, as I know you always are. I know that the marquis and the marchioness will be at Gilhurst Hall, so I am confident that no harm shall come to you."

Charlotte sighed with relief. "Thank you. I am so glad you understand."

He leaned across the table and patted her hand. "I am just happy that you have found a way to put the school on a more solid footing. It will be good to see those shadows beneath your eyes disappear."

The door to the sitting room opened and the rotund figure of the vicar's housekeeper appeared. "Begging your pardon, Reverend, Miss Gregory. Dinner is ready."

"Thank you, Mrs. Smithson," the vicar said as he stood and sniffed the air appreciatively. "Shall we, Charlotte?" he asked, gallantly offering her his arm.

Together, they made their way to the small dining room to partake of Mrs. Smithson's justly famous spring lamb.

FOUR

"Do you have time to write one more letter for me?" Finch asked. He wanted to give Miss Gregory the opportunity to take her leave if she so desired. The young schoolmistress looked weary. When she thought he wasn't looking, he had seen her rub her eyes with the back of her hand. Candlelight was not the best illumination for long periods of writing—he had learned that to his chagrin on the Peninsula, when he had spent more nights than he could count huddled next to a lantern writing coded dispatches for Lord Holt.

He wished they could do some of their work during the day, but he knew that Miss Gregory's responsibilities at the school would not permit it.

"Of course, my lord," she replied, pulling a fresh sheet of paper toward her and dipping her quill in the engraved silver inkwell. She looked perfectly at home behind the small escritoire in his father's drawing room.

In the far corner of the room, a young footman took a deep, quiet breath. The boy had fallen asleep, and fortunately, Miss Gregory had not noticed. The servant's slumber was well timed, because Finch did not want anyone but Miss Gregory to hear what he had to say next.

"This letter is of a rather unpleasant nature," he warned her, a seed of guilt sprouting in his belly. At first, he didn't recognize the sensation. In his work in military intelligence, he could not afford the luxury of wondering what would happen to his informants and the people he turned over for arrest. He was doing his job and serving his country. What justice was later meted out, by Providence or the British Army, was none of his affair.

But he did feel a twinge of regret for what he was about to do to Miss Gregory. Ruthlessly, he squelched it. Like his activities in Spain, this ruse was essential to the greater cause.

"I am here to write your correspondence, not to judge or censor it, my lord." Her pen was poised above his engraved stationery.

"Very well, then." He cleared his throat. "Dear Kitty."

The room was silent except for the hiss of the coals in the grate and the scratching of the schoolmistress's quill.

It distresses me that I need to ask you once again to cease and desist from all communication with me.

Head bowed, Miss Gregory wrote. One auburn curl that had worked its way loose from her simple knot lay across the back of her long, white neck. It shimmered in the light from the blazing fire and bobbed slightly as she wrote. He felt an odd urge to brush it away from her skin, where it was likely irritating her.

It was only when Miss Gregory raised her head and tilted it that he realized he'd been staring. He cleared his throat.

"I beg your pardon. Woolgathering, I'm afraid."

She smiled, nodded and returned her attention to the letter. He continued his dictation.

I believed we had an agreement, Kitty, one that many paramours would have accepted with gratitude.

The quill stopped momentarily. She swallowed once, dipped the pen in ink again, and continued to write.

He had to admire her fortitude. Such matters were likely distasteful to her in the extreme, but she was determined to live up to her end of the bargain. He felt the tendril of guilt unfurling in his gut again.

"Your repeated requests for more money begin to border on extortion," he continued, drawing on every ounce of cunning he had developed while in Lord Holt's employ. *Demme*, he thought, *if a permanent position with the Foreign Office does not materialize, perhaps I should give some thought into pursuing a career on the stage.*

"Is something amusing, my lord?" Miss Gregory was looking at him again, and her voice was sharp.

Good heavens, he thought, *I am going to have to watch myself very closely indeed. I had not even realized I was smiling.*

"No. I was thinking of another matter entirely. Let me get back to the letter." He shifted on the striped settee, crossing one foot on his knee. "The next sentence should read:

> *I owe you nothing, and your continued harassment is irksome.*"

He paused while she wrote this down.

> *"Any further attempt to communicate with me, either at Gilhurst Hall or at my home in London, shall cause me to meet with my solicitor."*

Her hand swept across the page.

> *"I shall ask him to challenge your right to the house I purchased for you, if you do not leave me in peace. Consider*

whether you really want to find yourself adrift on the streets before writing to me again."

A muffled gasp escaped Miss Gregory's lips. He could not resist asking her what she thought about this extraordinary missive.

"Miss Gregory? Are you distressed?"

She shook her head, keeping her eyes fastened on the paper. "Would you like me to begin a second sheet when I have used up this one, or shall I write crossways?"

"It won't go to a second sheet. I have said everything I have to say to Kitty Sherman. Simply leave a space for my creaky signature."

She did so, sanded the paper, blew away the fine grains, and handed the letter to him.

"I cannot help but think you disapprove of my letter to Mrs. Sherman."

A dull flush crept up her neck from the collar of her plain day dress. "It is not my place to approve or disapprove. I am here simply to write."

"But I am asking you for your opinion." Why was he opening himself to her disapproval—all for a letter that would never be sent, to a person who did not exist?

"I am not the best person to ask for such an opinion. I have never been to London, and know little of its ways." Her voice was low and cool.

"People of the *ton* are like people everywhere, with just a little more time at their disposal and a bit more blunt in their purses."

"I think you exaggerate, my lord. To the best of my knowledge, no one in this village has ever had cause to use the word *paramour* in reference to themselves or anyone else." Her hands were twisting in her lap like puppies in a basket. He suspected she would say much more if she were not afraid of losing her well-paid position.

That tendril of guilt was growing larger by the second.

If this conversation lasted much longer, he'd have a royal oak lodged in his gut.

At that moment, he heard the creak of footsteps in the wood-floored corridor leading from his father's study to the stairs. He looked up just as the marquis passed by the door of the salon. Automatically, he started to speak, intending to wish his father good night. But his voice caught in his throat as his father pinned him with an almost savage glare.

The marquis's glance passed over him swiftly and shifted to Finch's companion, and his aspect softened. "Good evening, Miss Gregory. I trust my son is not keeping you at work too late into the evening?"

She shook her head. "Not at all, my lord."

"And he is behaving himself?" The older man's voice was sharp.

"He has been a perfect gentleman, my lord, just as I expected."

"Humph," his father snorted before turning from the room and making his way to the stairs.

An uneasy silence settled over the room after the marquis had ascended the stairs. His father could not have made the rift between himself and his son clearer if he had printed a notice in the *Post*.

Miss Gregory raised her eyebrows but said nothing.

What must she think of him now, he wondered. Not only was he a man so callous that he would let his discarded lover starve on the street, but one so reprehensible that his own father would not speak to him. Against his better judgment, he felt compelled to explain.

"My father and I disagreed about my decision to enter the army," he began in a rush. "He tolerates my presence here only because it would cause gossip in the village were I to rent a property elsewhere in the neighborhood. And my father, above all else, abhors gossip."

"As do I," Miss Gregory replied. She stood, brushing

the last bits of sand from her skirt. "I believe that was the last letter, was it not, Lord Finchwood?'"

He nodded, abashed at her obvious haste to leave his presence and end the discussion of his poor relationship with his father. Her action left no doubt in his mind that he had become the sort of man respectable women despised. He'd known that already, in his head, but it still pained him to see such obvious proof of the fact. "I shall have my carriage brought round." He moved to the door and signaled his wishes to Hepworth. The elderly butler nodded and walked slowly toward the rear of the house.

Turning back into the room, Finch motioned Miss Gregory back into her chair. "It will take a few moments to harness the horse."

She retook her seat at the desk.

"Thank you for staying until such a late hour," he said, hoping his genuine concern for her welfare would redeem him at least a little in her eyes. "I hope it has not inconvenienced your assistant unduly."

"Jane is well able to handle the school on her own. In fact, since beginning my work with you, I have decided to delegate even more responsibility to her. It is for the best, in the long run. The fee for my secretarial duties will be useful to the school."

"Simply 'useful'?" he inquired.

"*Most* useful," she added. She looked at him directly, without any missish reluctance, her back straight and her head held high. But, probably without even knowing it, she was nibbling on her bottom lip. It was a habit he had quickly come to realize signaled her distress.

The school's debts must be more extensive than he had realized. From their initial discussions, he knew the fee he was paying her was a handsome sum in her world. Evidently, however, it wasn't sufficient to cover all her obligations.

Unless she had developed a sideline in gambling—he

struggled to suppress a smile at the thought—he doubted her debts would make even a dent in his funds. After writing letters to his solicitor and to his bank in London, she would know that as well. His inheritance from his uncle, the rents on the house in London, and a series of investments he had made before leaving for the Peninsula had made him a wealthy man. And when he came into his title, he would be far richer than that.

It seemed obscene to leave her in such desperate straits when he could so easily help her. But would rescuing her from her financial worries mean that she would leave his employ? Finch dismissed the thought as soon as it occurred to him. Through their brief acquaintance, he already knew that she would fulfill the spirit of their agreement even if she no longer needed the salary he was paying her. Charlotte Gregory was a woman of integrity, and she would remain as his secretary as long as he required her.

So could he simply ask the extent of her debts, and give her the money she needed?

No, she would be far too proud to accept such a gift from him. He would have to make his effort some other way. Perhaps a wallet with no identification left in front of the academy? Or a bank draft from an anonymous donor? No, both those stratagems would be too transparent. He would have to give this matter some thought. Deviousness was one of the few skills he had developed in the military that he had found useful in the civilian world.

The silence in the room was beginning to oppress him. He cleared his throat.

"That's a very fetching gown, Miss Gregory," he said, saying the first thing that popped into his mind. The odd thing was, the comment was partly true. It wasn't so much the gown, but the way she wore it, that attracted attention. Although soberly cut, it emphasized her pleasing curves and brought out her green eyes, even in the shadowy candlelight.

She raised her head. "Thank you, Lord Finchwood, but you are too kind. It is an old, plain dress—certainly nothing comparable to the sorts of gowns you must have seen in London."

Was she referring to his infamous liaisons, or simply making polite conversation? Demme, but he couldn't be sure. One thing he did know—he wanted to raise her opinion of him.

"I am not much of a connoisseur of women's clothing, Miss Gregory."

Her eyes glinted, and the ghost of a smile tugged at the corners of her mouth. "Don't play the innocent with me, my lord. I may be a sheltered rural schoolmistress, but even I recognize a rogue when I meet one."

"A rogue? I?" He began to tease her, then realized such an approach would not do anything to raise his stature in her eyes. But before he could change tack, a footman appeared at the door to announce that the carriage was ready. Before the servant had finished speaking, Miss Gregory was back on her feet.

"Until Monday, then?" she asked, moving toward the door.

"Yes. And thank you for your hard work."

"I am pleased to help."

He followed her into the foyer and watched her don her simple cottage cloak. She fastened the button below her chin, and pulled on a pair of cotton gloves.

"Have a safe journey," he said, trying to think of something suitably non-roguish with which to end their conversation.

"Thank you. I suspect I shall. I doubt many highwaymen will be lurking on the two-mile stretch between Gilhurst Hall and the academy." Her gentle smile sent an odd sensation through him, right to the soles of his feet.

What was it about this woman? She was neither stunningly beautiful nor dazzlingly witty, the two attributes that had always seized his attention before. But there was something about her that attracted him.

"Good evening, my lord," she said as Hepworth opened the door and ushered her out into the fresh spring night.

It would not be right to seduce such an upright young woman, of course. Simply raising her opinion of him, however, would be most satisfying.

This public house was even darker and grimier than the first two, Finch thought as he slipped in a side door and scanned the room from under his battered cap. The odors of stale beer, sweat, and sea air filled his nostrils. The soles of the worn boots he'd found in the Gilhurst Hall loft stuck slightly to the wooden floor, letting go with a faint sucking sound with each step as he made his way to the scarred oak bar and asked for a glass of porter.

"What's the story with yer hand?" the barman asked as he placed a cracked mug of the malty beverage on the counter. A rivulet of froth slid down the side of the glass.

"Loom accident." Finch picked up his glass and headed into the crowded room before the barman could question him further. Putting on accents was one of his weaker skills, and anyone speaking to him for any length of time would likely pick up the rounded vowels and precise consonants bred into him during his years at Eton and Oxford.

He wandered without apparent purpose around the edges of the room. Anyone watching would assume he was seeking an empty seat, of which there were few. But in reality, he was listening for the distinctive pitch and cadence of a native French speaker.

Sipping his porter, he maneuvered himself behind a

cluster of men in dingy knitted jumpers. Posing as fish-ermen would provide a good disguise in Portsmouth. After a couple of minutes of listening, however, Finch concluded that these men were genuine sailors. Few Frenchmen would be able to mimic the unmistakable combination of fishermen's slang and ingrained bitter-ness that were the hallmarks of the born-and-bred Hampshire sailor.

He suppressed a sigh. This night was shaping up to be a fool's errand. He had been trolling the pubs of Portsmouth for almost three hours, with nothing to show for his efforts. Fortunately, his rakish reputation ensured that his coachman would think nothing of his adventure. Finch would have to remember to act inebriated when he finally returned to his carriage. Once again, he cursed the fact that he had to travel by carriage rather than riding. But it would have taken him the better part of a day to reach Portsmouth at a gentle trot. Even a carriage could make better time than he could on horseback.

He scanned the room again. Nothing appeared out of the ordinary, even though the coded notes from Bar-ton had indicated that dissidents and suspicious aliens occasionally met here. In particular, a Frenchman with the legal name of Pierre St. Amour and several aliases bore watching.

Pulling his cap low over his brow, Finch gave thanks for the gloomy lighting. In his plain worker's jacket and tweed trousers, hunched over in defiance of every bit of his military training, and with a day's growth of stubble darkening his chin, he suspected that even the marquis wouldn't recognize him.

Fortunately, he had rarely come to Portsmouth as a youth, even though it lay just a few hours' ride from Gilhurst Hall. So there was little chance of encountering anyone he knew. Nevertheless, it paid to be cautious.

He tried to tamp down his unease regarding his attire.

In Spain, his uniform had been his only protection against accusations of spying in the event he was captured. It felt most odd to be eavesdropping and lurking in shadows in anything but regimentals.

Odd, but still wonderful. He had not felt this alive since he had returned to England. It was a treat to use his finely honed senses once again for something more worthwhile than distinguishing varieties of sherry at White's or observing the alluring sway of a woman's hips as she danced at a society ball.

Although he could think of one woman he would be more than intrigued to watch dancing at any sort of function. Did Miss Gregory dance, or did she consider it too risqué a pursuit? Were schoolmistresses allowed any fun whatsoever?

Perhaps the financial aid he had been able to engineer last week would erase some of the worry lines he had noticed on Miss Gregory's forehead the last time they had met. He had come to know her fairly well in the three weeks of their association, and he had noticed her face becoming more pinched with every passing week. With luck, the next time they met, that hunted look would have disappeared. He hoped so.

A movement at the side door of the pub interrupted his train of thought. Three men entered the building and made their way to the bar. The tallest had the finest clothes, although they appeared fine only in contrast to his companions' outfits. His stocky, dark-haired friend matched the description of St. Amour to some extent, despite the fact that he was clean shaven and St. Amour had last been spotted with a thick beard. The discrepancy didn't bother Finch unduly; such changes in aspect were among the easiest for any man seeking to avoid detection to undertake. The third man was the most ragged of the three. From his pocket hung a handkerchief similar to those carried by many sailors.

Unlike many of the patrons at this late hour, the trio neither swayed nor shouted. They appeared relatively sober, and that in itself made them worth watching.

Finch bided his time until the group had bought refreshments at the bar and repaired to a crowded corner. The tall one looked vaguely familiar, so Finch approached the knot of men from the rear. Leaning against a wooden support post, he took a long draft of his porter and tried to appear as though he was following a conversation about horses taking place to his left. His concentration, however, was trained behind him.

If he was correct, the man with the handkerchief was doing the lion's share of the talking. And what he was saying was most interesting.

"Ye have to make this more worth me while. I'm the one taking the risks. Yer just sittin' on yer fancy behinds."

"I'm taking just as many risks as you, so I'll thank you not to think so highly of yourself," came a querulous voice that, given its direction, Finch attributed to the tall man. The voice sounded familiar. Who *was* he?

"Yer not the one livin' in fear of the naval police," came the voice Finch had attributed to the man with the handkerchief. So he was a sailor, likely a deserter. "If I'm caught, it's the gallows for me."

"And you think the punishment would be any less severe for me?"

"Yer a gen'leman, not a deserter like meself."

"But we share one crime in common, and that crime is punishable by death."

Treason.

"Stop yer whinin', Norris."

Norris. Finch wracked his brain for the connection, and soon he made it. Anthony Norris. Minor gentry. Had stood to inherit a small estate near the coast, partway between Portsmouth and Gilhurst Hall. Finch had crossed paths with him several times in his youth. They were of an age.

"Don't call me by name! How am I to stay invisible—"

"If ye keep yer nose clean, ye'll come out of this with not a soul the wiser. But if ye don't close yer mouth—"

"Don't speak to me that way." Norris's voice had taken on an unpleasant shrillness.

"Are ye deaf?" The sailor's voice dropped, and Finch lost the thread of the conversation in the general hub-bub. When he was again able to hear, the sailor was still speaking.

". . . the plan, or ye'll get no more wine."

Wine? This didn't seem the type of establishment likely to serve anything but beer and rum. Norris must be smuggling, which was promising. As Barton had mentioned, illicit trade in people and goods often occurred simultaneously.

Norris and the sailor continued their dispute for several minutes. Finch shifted against the pillar and sipped his porter. To the amusement of his drinking companions at White's, he had actually developed a taste for the rough brew while training in Southampton. But he was drinking it cautiously tonight. He needed all his wits about him.

Finally, he heard a new voice, low and fluid. "Martin," the voice said, pronouncing the word in the French manner.

Finch held his breath.

"Stop baiting Mr. Norris. We need 'im and 'e needs us." The accent was not strong, but it was definite. "Let us focus on the matter at 'and. We must resolve it before the *Neptune* arrives."

"Yer right on that score," replied the man called Martin. "You two will be wise to be ten miles from Portsmouth before the *Neptune* gets here, if ye don't want to find yerselves the newest recruits to His Majesty's service." His laugh was hollow.

Definitely a deserter.

"Is everyt'ing ready, as we discussed?"

Silence. Finch longed to turn around to see whether someone had nodded or shaken his head. He took a deep, quiet breath. Finally, Norris spoke. "I've done my part. Cost me a pretty penny, too. Just hope you two have done yours."

"There's more to tell, but not here. Too many people about fer my likin'. Finish yer drinks, men."

Glasses clinked behind him. Finch looked away as stools scraped back. He counted to twenty, then put his own glass on a low shelf and turned, just in time to see Norris disappear through the front door.

He threaded his way through the crowd and went through the side door. Half a street ahead, he spotted the little group. Norris and Martin walked down the middle of the largely deserted lane, where the light was best. The man he suspected to be St. Amour stayed largely in the shadows cast by the mean little storefronts, as Finch did himself.

It takes one spy to recognize another, he thought.

By regularly flattening himself against doorframes and alley entrances, Finch managed to avoid the backward glances St. Amour occasionally cast behind him. Such maneuvers depended as much on luck as skill. Fortunately, Finch had both on his side.

His thin-soled boots made little sound against the cobblestones. Nonetheless, he hoped no press gangs were about at this hour. He had his discharge papers with him, of course, hidden in the bottom of his right boot. But the Impress Service was not known for its respect for paperwork. And dressed as he was, it was unlikely that the beached officers who ran the service would believe his claim that he was Viscount Finchwood.

After a few minutes, the conspirators reached an intersection and dispersed. Finch suspected they would not stay separated long. Hedging his bets, he followed Norris.

As he had suspected, Norris did not look back once, nor did he make much of an effort to conceal his movements. He half walked, half ran down a series of lanes, each narrower than the last. Finch followed several streets behind.

The area reminded him uncomfortably of the port in a small fishing town in Portugal. He remembered, as though he had seen it just moments ago, the twisted body of a British soldier he had encountered in just such a lane, on just such an evening. Blood had formed a small pool on the paving stones beneath the crumpled form.

Stop dwelling on the past. There was nothing you could have done to stop that man's death then, and there is no point recalling it now.

Up ahead, Norris emerged into a small square. The air was damp and smelled strongly of salt and fish. Finch hung behind in the alley, watching his quarry.

Norris cut across the square toward a long, low warehouse and rapped at a door half-hidden in the gloom. Within moments, the door opened and Norris slipped inside.

Finch bided his time and was not disappointed. Several minutes later, Martin emerged from a side street next to the warehouse. He, too, knocked at the door and was admitted. It must have been almost half an hour later before St. Amour appeared and joined his colleagues in the warehouse.

Finch watched the windows for signs of light, but none came. He doubted, however, that the conspirators were sleeping. He was debating the usefulness of continuing observation when two more figures scurried across the square, skirts rustling. Their large bonnets completely obscured their faces, but other than that they were barely clad. Their skimpy dresses were cut low to reveal a fair expanse of skin, which glowed palely in the waning moonlight.

Intrigued, he watched as the two women were admitted through the same darkened door. Despite their costumes, he would wager his finest horse that they were not Cyprians but were dressed that way in order to travel through the nighttime city unnoticed.

His suspicions were confirmed when the women were still in the building two hours later, as dawn began to tint the eastern sky. Any Cyprian with an eye to profit would have moved along by now, hoping to find at least one more customer before daybreak.

The fact that there were women involved in this operation added a whole new twist to the investigation. Finch was no stranger to interrogating female spies. Indeed, it had been one of his specialties in Spain, and he had developed an arsenal of tactics for extracting information from women. He prided himself on the fact that none of them involved force. The women he interrogated gave up their secrets—and other things—willingly.

As he thought about trying his methods on the two women, should he encounter them again, he felt an unfamiliar reluctance. Surely, after only a year as a civilian, he wasn't going soft?

Unused to analyzing his feelings, he dismissed the hesitation and pushed himself away from the wall where he had been huddled for the past few hours. He stretched his arms over his head and shook out his tingling legs, suppressing an enormous yawn as he did so.

It was time to leave, before the rising sun made him completely visible to his quarry. He had learned quite a bit for one night's work.

As he made his way back to the corner where he'd asked his coachman to wait for him, he made plans for his next actions. He would need to submit a preliminary report to Barton. It was time to decide whether to make Miss Gregory privy to his secret life.

Not one word of his supposed liaison with the fictitious Kitty had reached his ears in the weeks since he had asked Miss Gregory to write the unposted letter. That was a strong sign in her favor. His further inquiries into her character had only enhanced the picture he had sketched of her at their first meeting: a smart, upstanding young woman with no hint of gossip or scandal about her.

The news about Norris, St. Amour and their mysterious companions had to go to Barton immediately. It was time to trust Miss Gregory, at least a little.

FIVE

"What is the matter, Charlotte?" Jane Carter asked as she entered her employer's office.

Charlotte instantly schooled her features into a bland expression. It was a skill she had honed to a fine pitch over years of dealing with fractious children and the equally fractious parishioners of her father's church. "Nothing is precisely wrong. It's just that something isn't precisely right."

"You're speaking in riddles." Jane smiled as she took a seat opposite Charlotte's small desk, her expression taking any sting from her words. "I brought you some tea," she added, proffering a chipped cup and saucer. "Cook said you looked tired, and I thought this might revive you."

Charlotte accepted the cup gratefully, and a quick sip did indeed make her feel slightly less rattled. The tea was good and strong. Cook must be at the beginning of this batch. Within a few days, the oft-used leaves would create a much more tepid drink.

If the school ever found itself on firm ground again, one of the first things Charlotte planned to do was ensure that all tea leaves were used but once. Even a schoolmistress should be permitted some small luxuries.

Thoughts of her financial straits reminded her of the current dilemma. She handed her assistant a letter that had arrived that morning. "What do you make of this?"

Jane scanned the short missive, then raised her gaze to Charlotte's. "This is wonderful news! Three girls, to start immediately, with a generous bank draft to cover their tuition for the remainder of this year and all of the next! It is just the sort of miracle for which you've been praying."

"It is a bit too miraculous, if you ask me."

"What do you mean?"

Charlotte accepted the sheet Jane handed back to her, and pointed to one sentence written in an elegant hand. 'We have been persuaded by a close friend that your academy is the best place for our daughters,' she read aloud. "What sorts of parents decide on a school for their children based merely on hearsay? I have never spoken to these people, Mr. and Mrs. Dean, in my life. They have not visited, nor have they asked me one question about the curriculum, the facilities, or my qualifications. And yet, Mr. Dean claims to be a diplomat of some distinction. That is why he and his wife are in such a hurry to see their children settled—he has been asked to accept a post in Vienna with all haste."

"But does that not explain everything?" Jane settled into the room's lone armchair.

"It would seem to, except that a man careful and skilled enough to be a diplomat would be unlikely to be so careless with his own children." She paused and tapped her fingers on the scarred surface of the desk. "And look at the bank draft. It is for more than double our usual fee."

"Perhaps his acquaintance told him the wrong rate by mistake."

"Perhaps, but this sum would be extraordinary even for tuition at Eton. Surely the Deans would have questioned such a fee."

Jane frowned. "I would never have considered these points, but they make eminent sense."

Charlotte twisted the small locket her mother had given her, which she always wore about her neck. "And that name. Augustus Dean. It seems familiar, but for the life of me I cannot explain why."

Jane shook her head. "I know I have not heard it before."

"Then perhaps there is some connection to the village. Something I heard as a child." Charlotte shook her head. "As you say, I may be too suspicious for my own good. This money does seem providential. Combined with my salary from Lord Finchwood, it will be more than enough to keep our creditors satisfied until the end of term and well into next year."

"Perhaps, soon, you will be able to give up your employment with his lordship." Jane's eyes were worried. Charlotte knew that her assistant was concerned for her welfare. On more than one occasion, Jane had observed her yawning at her desk.

The younger woman had every right to be worried. The position as Lord Finchwood's secretary was seriously impinging on Charlotte's sleep, and not only because she was often at Gilhurst Hall until after ten in the evening.

No, it was the sleepless hours she spent *after* returning to the academy that were the main cause of the circles beneath her eyes. Hours she spent tossing and turning in her narrow bed as she recalled some aspect or another of her evening with the viscount: the way the candlelight brought out the copper tones of his elegantly tousled hair, or the ringing tones of his infrequent laughter.

Charlotte brought her attention back to Jane's question. "No, I shall continue in that capacity as long as the viscount needs me. I made a promise to assist him, and I shall fulfill it."

Jane nodded. "You are right, of course."

But thinking of the viscount, as she held the letter in her hand, engendered an unpleasant suspicion deep in her mind. Was it vain to think that someone as elevated as Lord Finchwood would be interested enough in her affairs to intercede on her behalf? And, if he had, what exactly was she to do about it?

She felt a faint flush of anger stain her cheeks, and her heart hammered in her chest. No one, not even a friend—not even the viscount—had the right to interfere with the academy. She had worked too hard to make the school a success on her own.

Pride goeth before a fall, she told herself. *Turn the other cheek.*

But she seemed incapable of taking that timeless advice to heart. Her thoughts continued to career down less uplifting channels.

If Lord Finchwood had indeed encouraged the Deans to send such an exorbitant sum, he obviously thought that Charlotte was little better than a charity case. And while she had deep sympathy for people who needed charity through no fault of their own, she did not count herself among their number. She was beginning to succeed in extricating the school from its debts, and she did not need anyone's help.

Help, she knew from working with her father's parishioners and benefactors, often came with obligations attached. At the very least, sponsors usually felt they had the right to offer opinions as to how the assistance should be used. They tended to become annoyed when funds went to purposes they did not approve of. And as she had learned to her initial sorrow years ago, when Mr. Binks had cried off, she was far too opinionated and stubborn to tolerate much interference in her affairs.

If the viscount truly was the impetus behind the Deans' mysterious bank draft, she would need to take the matter up with him directly.

Charlotte put that discomfiting thought to the back of her mind. There would be time enough to deal with it later in the week, when she was due to meet with the viscount at Gilhurst Hall. Until then, she had to focus on the school.

Charlotte was feeling much less equable as Lord Finchwood's carriage approached Gilhurst Hall.

In the evening after her meeting with Jane, she had gone to her father's home for dinner, as usual. Over a marvelous roast chicken dinner—Mrs. Smithson truly was an excellent cook, and Charlotte never failed to appreciate her efforts—Charlotte had asked her father if he had ever heard of Augustus Dean of Staffordshire.

"Dean?" Her father had tapped his fingers on the table, deep in thought. "I believe that family has some connection to Lord Gilhurst. Let me look in the parish register. I believe a Dean once stood as godfather to one of the marquis's family."

Together, Charlotte and her father had made their way to the church office. The evenings were lighter later now, and they were able to read the faded script of the register by the golden early evening sun flooding through the small window.

"Here it is!" her father cried, pointing one gnarled finger at an entry dated April 16, 1768. "Before my time as vicar, of course. This is the baptism of the marquis's eldest brother—the one who was killed in the riding accident. I was certain I had encountered some mention of a gentleman named Dean, when I was doing my research about the history of the parish."

"Godfather, Robert John Dean, Medford, Staffordshire," Charlotte read over her father's shoulder. Her heart plummeted to the pit of her stomach. "Good heavens."

"What is the matter, child?" her father asked.

She was reluctant to tell her father of the viscount's apparent interference in her affairs. "I received a letter today from a Mr. Augustus Dean, also of Medford," she explained. "He wishes to register his three daughters at the academy. I was simply curious to learn how he happened to hear about the school. Now that I know the Dean family has a prior connection to the village, it makes sense."

Her father had seemed to accept her explanation at face value, for which she was grateful. If she had been forced to explain her well-founded suspicions about Lord Finchwood, she was not sure she could have controlled her anger at his arrogance. And her father abhorred displays of temper.

In the days since she had made her discovery in the church office, she had tried to keep that fact very much in mind. But she was not the gentle soul her father was. Despite her best efforts, she could not find any way to consider the viscount's deception with anything but fury.

But it would be folly to unleash that fury on the viscount, she admonished herself as the carriage halted and the coachman hurried around to open the door and lower the steps. She had to tell Lord Finchwood what she thought in a calm, professional manner. After all, she needed her salary to keep the academy solvent—particularly since she would be unable to accept the Deans' generous bank draft.

She took a deep breath as she crossed the drive and mounted the steps under the classical portico. Before she could knock, the butler opened the bright blue door and welcomed her into the Gilhurst foyer.

"Lord Finchwood will be with you shortly," Hepworth informed her with a smile as he took her light cloak. "Lady Gilhurst is in the salon and would be happy if you would join her there."

"Of course. Thank you." Charlotte bit back her frustration as she followed the butler. Despite her attempts to rein in her temper, she was eager to see Lord Finchwood and inform him in measured tones that he was not to meddle in her affairs. Ever.

"Miss Gregory! What a pleasure to see you! For once, I am home and not gadding about during your evening call." Lady Gilhurst rose as Hepworth announced Charlotte's arrival and ushered her into the room.

Charlotte curtsied. "Good evening, my lady. I am glad as well to have the opportunity to see you. We missed you at church last Sunday."

To her surprise, the blonde woman blushed. "I was feeling very unwell that morning. My apologies to your father. I do so enjoy his sermons, truly. The vicar in the village where I grew up had no sense of humor at all, but I don't find a chuckle or two unseemly at all during a service. Surely even God likes to smile."

Charlotte herself grinned at her companion's comments. Lady Gilhurst was immensely likeable and not at all pretentious. Charlotte had long hoped that the marchioness could raise the spirits of her somewhat dour husband.

"Indeed, I suspect He does."

Lady Gilhurst motioned her to sit. "Lord Finchwood will be with you in a few minutes. Something he had to attend to in the stables. In the meantime, may I offer you tea?"

"Yes, thank you."

The two women chatted of inconsequential matters and sipped their tea for several minutes until the door opened and Lord Finchwood strode in. Despite her anger with the viscount, Charlotte could not help but note that he looked as polished as ever. He had obviously taken the time to freshen up before joining them. His neckcloth was snowy, as always, and his buff inexpressibles were spotless—and rather well tailored, Charlotte noticed with a quick glance. He wore a plain coat of blue superfine that looked as though it had been molded to his broad shoulders. Without doubt, there wasn't a man in the parish who could hold a candle to him.

Perhaps his looks were the reason he felt himself superior to mere mortals and thought nothing of meddling in their affairs, she thought, then immediately chided herself for her churlishness.

He smiled and dropped into the Queen Anne chair opposite Charlotte, his movements as smooth and sure as a racehorse's.

"Is that tea still warm?"

Lady Gilhurst nodded and poured him a cup. He accepted with a grateful sigh.

"It's a miserable night out there. Windy and cold."

"Whatever were you doing in the stables at this hour?" Lady Gilhurst asked. Charlotte had been wondering the same thing but did not feel she had the right to ask.

He added a lump of sugar to his tea and stirred it before replying. "This and that."

His evasiveness made Charlotte's skin prickle. Not for the first time, she sensed that she was only seeing a small fraction of him, the fraction that he chose to show the world. What was he hiding?

Lady Gilhurst stood. "I know you both have much work to do, so I shall take my leave. Don't keep Miss Gregory too late, Francis."

Lord Finchwood winced. "Please call me Finch."

His stepmother smiled. "I shall try to remember. But since your father always calls you Francis—"

"I can't imagine my father calls me much of anything besides a useless popinjay."

"Really, Finch, you must try harder to make amends with your father."

Lord Finchwood's lips compressed into a thin, angry line. "I appreciate your concern, but this is an affair between my father and me. We shall resolve it in our own time, in our own way."

Lady Gilhurst nodded and walked toward the door. "I meant no disrespect."

"And neither did I." Lord Finchwood smiled. "It seems I am destined to misstep tonight."

"It is no matter. I know that relations between parents and children are rarely perfect, as I expect I shall discover for myself some day." A smile played fleetingly about her lips as she left.

The viscount turned back toward Charlotte. "I am sorry you have been dragged, however inadvertently, into my personal business," he said as he continued to sip his tea. He stretched his long legs out in front of him.

His tailor was to be commended, Charlotte thought. His trousers fit almost like a second skin. She paused only briefly to wonder why his clothing held such interest for her. Coming up with no answer that pleased her, she dismissed the question from her mind.

"It is no matter, my lord. But speaking of personal business . . ." Charlotte suppressed an urge to twist her hands together. Instead, she straightened her shoulders and stared right into the viscount's eyes. However well intentioned he might have been, he had to be told that his behavior was unacceptable. He looked so puzzled, however, that she stopped.

He was her employer. Her father's living depended on his father's whim. Could she afford to offend him?

"Miss Gregory?" He leaned back into his chair, the picture of ease. He truly had no idea that anything he might have said or done could have offended her. His insouciance gave her the courage to go on.

"Lord Finchwood, it has come to my attention that the Dean family of Staffordshire has a longstanding connection with your own."

His face was neutral and bland as he replied, "Yes. I went to school with Christopher Dean."

"He would not, by any chance, be related to Mr. Augustus Dean?"

The viscount's gaze didn't waver. "He would. Augustus is Christopher's eldest brother."

He was not even ashamed of his subterfuge. She tried to ignore a surge of annoyance. Anger, as her father often had cause to remind her, was a sin—one Charlotte had struggled since childhood to control, with varying degrees of success. "And did you convince the elder Mr. Dean to send his three little girls to my academy, sight unseen, at double the usual tuition?"

Lord Finchwood's eyes lit up. "*Touché*, Miss Gregory. You have unraveled my scheme with uncanny speed." He doffed an imaginary cap in her direction.

"Was this a game? Were you so desperate for sport, stuck here in the provinces, that you felt the need to play with my livelihood, and with the lives of three children, for *amusement?*" She had been angry before, but his attitude made her livid. At least she had managed to modulate her voice as she replied.

To her shock, he did not look in the least ashamed. On the contrary, he seemed to be suppressing a smile.

"Are you so skeptical of the quality of your school that you don't think people would be eager to enroll?" he countered.

"Do you think I'm so hen witted that I wouldn't look askance at a rich family with three daughters suddenly applying to me at the end of the school year, complete with a very large bank draft?" she retorted in a too-loud voice, her vow to maintain her temper forgotten.

His faint smile faded. "Of course not, Miss Gregory. I had no intention of questioning your intelligence, which I am coming to realize every day is more and more formidable."

She wasn't certain whether he was patronizing her or speaking sincerely. As she had been raised to always look for the best in people, she decided that the latter was the case. If so, it was flattering. But it wasn't enough.

Charlotte cleared her throat.

The viscount raised an eyebrow.

Into the lengthening silence, Charlotte said, "I believe you owe me an apology, my lord."

Both eyebrows flew up into his tousled hairline.

"Apologize?" he asked, his voice indicating that he had only a passing familiarity with the concept. "For what? For helping you?"

She took a deep breath and tried to see things from his point of view. Of course it was not reprehensible that he had tried to help her. She was simply being proud. Pride was yet another sin. She should let the matter drop.

"You should apologize for not having faith in my ability to solve this problem in my own way," she heard herself say.

Humility was another trait she needed to spend more time cultivating.

"And you should also apologize for making three little girls the pawns in this scheme," she added, feeling on more solid ground. "Did you not give one thought to their welfare? They are to be torn from their parents' home on nothing more than your whim."

"Now that is completely untrue," Lord Finchwood replied with a slight edge to his voice. "Augustus and his wife truly *were* searching for a school for their children, which I found out from Christopher when I paid him a purely social call a few weeks ago. They had examined several schools and found none to their liking, and were becoming increasingly desperate. Augustus and his wife are due to leave for the Continent any day now, just as they told you. Chris wrote to his brother, telling him that I recommended your school highly. Augustus was delighted to find a suitable academy vouchsafed by someone he could trust."

Charlotte struggled to keep her mouth from falling open. "You gave my school a personal recommendation? Why, you have never even set foot inside the door!"

"And I did not give the Deans to understand that I had. What purpose, after all, would a childless man have to visit a girls' school?" He laughed. "I simply said that all the reports I had heard of your character were good, and that I had found nothing to complain of in your performance of your duties as my correspondence secretary. It turns out that Augustus's wife knew a family whose daughter once attended the academy, and a glowing recommendation from them tipped the scales in your favor."

Somewhat mollified that Lord Finchwood and the Deans weren't using the children as pawns, Charlotte suddenly remembered one other salient fact. "But what about the money? Even if the Deans were convinced that the Moore Academy was the right place for their daughters, why did they feel the need to send such an extraordinary sum?"

For the first time in their conversation, Lord Finchwood seemed discomfited. He glanced around the room before replying, as if seeking the answer in the plaster moldings or the rich wool carpet. "Oh, that. Well, I gave them to understand that a substantial premium would be necessary to ensure the girls' acceptance so late in the school year. I, um, well, also offered to pay the difference between the regular tuition and the sum I said would be required. I justified it by saying that I felt obligated since I had, after all, directed them to the school."

This time, Charlotte's jaw did drop. She couldn't help herself. "You paid part of the Dean girls' tuition—all to help me? Why?"

"I'd have just given you the money directly, but I knew you'd be too proud to take it." He reached toward the teapot and refreshed his cup.

"So you thought it would be better to resort to deception?"

"You accepted that money, didn't you?" He replaced the teapot on the table and turned to face her fully. "But your pride would have led you to throw my money back in my face."

"I did *not* accept the money," she said, deeply grateful that she could report this fact. He was right, she conceded. Her pride was perhaps too great. That realization did not stop her from continuing her explanation, however. "I returned everything but the actual fee to the Deans. You shall have to write to them for reimbursement."

He blinked. "You returned it? But would it not have been useful?"

"Of course it would have been useful!" She stamped her foot in frustration. Fortunately, the soft carpet muffled her display of petulance. "It is obvious that you know how much the academy needs the money. I think it unkind of you in the extreme to belabor the point. I myself need no reminders of it."

"Miss Gregory, I did not mean—"

Charlotte heard him, but she was too angry to let him continue. "What I don't understand," she cut in, "is why you felt the need to help me at all. You barely know me."

"At first, I was afraid to help you," he admitted. "I worried that, if the school was on a more solid financial footing, you wouldn't feel the need to continue as my correspondence secretary, and I sorely need help in that regard."

"I made a promise to do that work, and I would not renege on it." Did he think her flighty as well as incompetent?

"I was counting on that. You strike me as a most principled person." His voice was warm and, as far as Charlotte could discern, sincere. She felt her fury abate slightly. At least he did not seem to think her a complete widgeon.

"I apologize for offending you," he continued, leaning forward with his elbows on his knees as if to emphasize the point. "Truly, that was not my intention. I had counted on keeping my ploy a secret from you, but I should have realized that you would uncover it quickly. It appears that I have sorely underestimated your powers of perception." The corners of his eyes crinkled as his lips curved into a small smile.

Charlotte struggled to maintain her indignation. But she could not fault his apology, and she felt the anger seep out of her like water down a drain. When it left, she felt adrift. She had thought she understood the viscount. Now, she was unsure.

In the silence that settled over the room, she could hear the faint tick of the mantel clock.

He continued to regard her with that odd smile, as though she were an intriguing specimen under glass in a museum. Despite herself, Charlotte could not help but relish being the object of his admiring gaze. A strange sort of tingle slipped down her spine. That would not do at all.

Perhaps his seeming sincerity was nothing more than a rakish trick, designed to distract angry women by making them feel admired. If it were just a trick, she had to admit that it was an effective one.

"You still have not answered my question," she finally said in a strained voice. "Why did you want to help me?"

He sighed. "You are very persistent."

"When you work with young children, it's a skill you develop quickly."

"Are you equating me to a child?" He chuckled.

"Are you evading the question?" she countered.

He twitched the cuffs of his jacket, as though he did not realize they were already straight and pristine. "Why did I help you? Simply because I admire you, and I have the wherewithal to help. I know this will sound arrogant, but the money you owe—as large a sum as I know it is to you—is comparatively little to someone like me."

A warm flush crept up her cheeks. "Yes, I know. I remember one letter I wrote for you to your bank manager. The interest on one of your investments alone would keep the school in food for the better part of a year."

He nodded. "It seemed cruel for me to hoard my money, most of which I do not need, when you are doing good work and could make much better use of it." He cocked his head to one side. "Is what I did so much worse than letting your pride stand between the success of the school and its ruin? Would it be better for the students if the school closed, but you kept your *hauteur* intact?"

Someone who could threaten to evict his own . . . ladybird . . . onto the streets of London was in no position to lecture her on morality, Charlotte thought. But such a reaction was a classic logical fallacy. *Ad hominem.* Attacking one's opponent instead of his argument.

With a sigh, she had to concede that he had a point. She usually had little problem putting her students' needs ahead of her own pride. She would have to take care in the future not to turn down more conventional sources of assistance just to save face. "You are right, of course, Lord Finchwood. Although I do wish you had approached me directly, rather than resorting to lies."

"I never lied. I simply never revealed the whole truth." He grinned, and Charlotte almost gasped. The expression made him look ten years younger. All of a sudden, he was the glamorous boy who had held the Gillington girls in thrall, not a weary ex-soldier.

She refused to succumb to his tactics, appealing as they were. "Well, I suppose we both have our sins for which we must repent," she said in the voice she reserved for recalcitrant students. "I must learn to be less prideful, and you must learn to be more direct."

"Directness did not serve me well in the army. I suppose it is something I shall have to practice." He set his teacup on the table. "In the spirit of directness, may I ask you a question?"

"Certainly." The serious look on his face made her wary, but she could hardly refuse to answer after just encouraging him to be more open.

"How did you make the connection between myself and Augustus Dean?"

"It was quite simple, really. The large payment, so fortuitously timed, made me suspicious. I first asked my father whether he had ever heard of the Deans, and he found an old entry in the parish register."

"That's right. Chris's grandfather was godfather to my uncle. I had forgotten that." He smiled. "And that evidence was enough to convict me?"

She shook her head. "I wanted to be certain. A man is innocent until *proven* guilty, you know."

He chuckled. "So I understand."

"A few evenings ago my father and I dined with my sister Eliza and her husband, Mr. Milton. I asked Mr. Milton if he recalled anyone named Dean from his years at Eton—I explained that three Dean children would soon be students at the school. He remembered Augustus and recalled that you and Christopher had been in the same form. He also recalled that the younger Mr. Dean now lives not far from Gilhurst Hall, which meant that you could have arranged all this without using me to write any letters for you. While not incontrovertible proof, all that information gave me enough confidence to at least confront you. When I mentioned the Deans, I could see in your eyes that I was right."

Lord Finchwood nodded. "A most impressive display of investigation and deductive reasoning, Miss Gregory.

I apologize most sincerely for underestimating your powers of perception."

She shook her head, even as a blush crept up her cheeks at his praise. "Thank you, my lord. But I doubt the Bow Street Runners have anything to fear from me. I simply put together some fairly obvious pieces."

"Sometimes that is all that is required to solve a problem." He cleared his throat. "And that leads me, quite nicely, into a discussion of something I had meant to raise with you anyway. Your quick unmasking of my little scheme only increases my resolve to raise the issue."

Whatever could he mean? She nodded to encourage him to continue.

"Would you mind if we dismissed the footman and closed the door? I know it is highly unusual." He walked across the room and picked up something she could not see from the mantel. Crossing the carpet, he leaned over her chair and deposited a small bell on the table next to Charlotte. He was so close she could feel the warmth emanating from his skin. She pushed her spine further back in her chair.

He straightened and nodded at the bell. "My stepmother is across the hall. I assure you that you are in no danger from me, but I'm giving you this as concrete proof. If anything untoward were to happen, you could ring the bell and shout, and Lady Gilhurst would be here in seconds."

Charlotte had the extremely improper thought that if anything untoward were to happen, the last thing she should want to do would be to ring for Lady Gilhurst.

"Thank you for your concern for my welfare," she replied on a rush of breath. "Please feel free to dismiss the servants and proceed as you see fit."

When the footman had left, closing the door to the salon behind him, Lord Finchwood retook his seat. Suddenly, Charlotte was more conscious than ever before of his sheer physical presence. He seemed to fill the room, which had also shrunk in her mind to encompass just their two chairs and the scant space between them. She could hear her blood rushing in her ears.

Silently, she willed herself to be sensible. What on earth did she think he intended to do, with his stepmother across the hall?

She realized she didn't have the slightest idea, but she was most curious to find out.

"I have asked some questions in the village, and it appears that no one—not even the ever-curious Mrs. Kane—has heard a murmur of gossip about my supposed ladybird, Kitty Sherman." He crossed his arms and eyed her.

Charlotte frowned. She didn't know what she had expected him to do or say, but that certainly wasn't it. "Supposed? But was she not the lady to whom you wrote several weeks ago, imploring her to leave you alone?"

"We wrote the letter, yes, but it was never posted. You see, Kitty Sherman does not exist."

Charlotte could feel her brow furrowing. "It appears, Lord Finchwood, that you make something of a career out of spinning lies and half-truths and prevarication." She felt a glimmer of despair. A part of her longed to admire him as she had years ago, when they were little more than children. But the more she learned about the adult viscount, the more she realized that he was not as simple and straightforward a creature as he once had seemed. Indeed, he had more twists and turns than the ivy that snaked along the south wall of the academy— and seemed just as impenetrable.

"You are more correct than you know," he said.

"Again, I must ask: why? Why did you have me write such a letter? Were you testing my stomach for distasteful correspondence?"

He ran a finger along the edge of his neckcloth. "In

part. But I had a larger motive in mind." He took a deep breath. "I wanted to assess your capacity for discretion."

Charlotte bristled. "I assured you that I could keep a secret."

"Yes, and I believed you. But in my line of work, one must not rely only on verbal assurances."

"Your line of work?" She had understood from everyone—from Lord Finchwood himself—that he had few daily responsibilities. She felt the crease between her brows growing deeper.

"Yes. This is why I have dismissed the footman." He leaned forward, and once again she was conscious of his almost overwhelming physical presence. "Do you know what I did in the Peninsula, Miss Gregory?"

"I know as much as anyone in Gillington knows, I suppose. You were with Lord Wellington's army in Spain. You served with Lord Holt, I believe, and were wounded at Badajoz. Other than that, I am the first to admit that my knowledge of military hierarchies and responsibilities is slight."

"My responsibilities were uncommon ones." He paused. "I must ask explicitly for your discretion regarding the rest of this discussion."

A pinprick of fear tickled the back of her neck. Whatever could he be about to say? "You have my word."

He nodded. "I served Lord Holt for several years as a military intelligence officer."

Charlotte frowned. "What is that?"

"It is a relatively new position in the British Army. In plain terms, I was a spy."

Charlotte sagged back against the chair cushion. "But surely that is exceedingly dangerous work?"

"No more so, really, than riding into battle. War is dangerous for everyone."

His offhand dismissal of the danger didn't fool Charlotte. She had seen the way his hand clutched the arm of his chair more tightly, the way his eyes had taken on a faraway look. Sensing he would rather not pursue this line of conversation, however, she asked the other question that was uppermost in her mind.

"What has that to do with our working relationship?"

"The Foreign Office has asked me to put some of my military skills to use here at home." He lowered his voice. "The government suspects that a ring of French agents is operating here in Hampshire. That is why I have returned home. To investigate the situation."

"Oh." For once, Charlotte was stunned into silence. Again, she wondered what this could possibly have to do with her. Before she could ask the question, he answered it.

"I can carry out the vast majority of my duties without the full use of my right hand. But I must report back to my superiors in London, and to do that I need to write letters. In code. And for that, I need your help." He placed one hand on the table where he had set the bell a few minutes earlier. His gaze was intense as he spoke. "I do not want to ask you to do anything you feel uncomfortable with. But it would be a great help to me—and to England—if you would take on this task."

She was silent for a moment or two. Who would have believed that she—a schoolmistress in a rural village—would have the capacity to serve her country in such a way?

"Before you make up your mind, I should warn you that the task might involve more than writing letters." Lord Finchwood stood suddenly, and began to pace before the fire as if he needed to expend excess energy. "I believe there are at least two women involved in the spy operation. Sometimes, women find it easier to glean information from members of their own sex than men do. There are more opportunities for them to encounter each other casually. And women arouse less suspicion in certain circumstances."

Charlotte's throat went dry as she considered the implications of Lord Finchwood's extraordinary proposal. He wanted her to become a *spy*?

SIX

"The requirement for field work is the reason I did not choose the other people I considered for the position of my assistant," Lord Finchwood continued. "I need someone inconspicuous, nearby, discreet and, preferably, female."

He continued to pace before the fire, ticking off points on his fingers as he walked. "My father is too visible and would, I fear, consider my activities an extension of my somewhat risky employment in Spain, of which he strongly disapproved." A brief, humorless laugh escaped him. "Christopher Dean lives too far away for us to communicate quickly. My stepmother would be likely to share anything she learned with my father. So you see, Miss Gregory," the viscount concluded, as he sat and spread his hands wide across his knees, "you are my best hope."

Charlotte's head felt as though it were filled with angry bees. When she arrived, she had expected to admonish Lord Finchwood for intervening with the Dean family, and then to settle down to write some innocuous letters to bankers and lawyers. Her worst fear had been that he would ask her to write another letter to Mrs. Sherman.

Contrasted with his suggestion that she consider joining the ranks of England's spies, writing one—or ten—letters to a gentleman's discarded ladybird seemed positively appealing. She did not share this thought with her employer, however.

"I am flattered, Lord Finchwood. But I don't believe I am the person best suited for this position." That was an understatement of the first order. How could she explain to him what seemed so obvious to her? "I am not a worldly person. Indeed, I have never set foot outside Hampshire. Would you not be better to approach a woman of your own station?"

Another mirthless chuckle escaped him. "Perhaps, except for the small complication that I have met not one other female with the combination of local knowledge and innate sense that you display."

She restrained herself from dwelling on the cheering fact that he thought her sensible. If she were sensible, she would not even be giving this ridiculous proposal a moment's consideration.

But to her astonishment, she was considering it.

"I have responsibilities, at the academy—"

"Admittedly, it would be more convenient if you did not. But I have no intention of asking you to curtail your involvement with the school any more than is absolutely necessary. Not only do I realize how important it is to you, but I know how odd it would appear if you were suddenly to distance yourself from your duties. Doing one's best to avoid raising suspicions is one of the keys to intelligence work."

He seemed to have a ready answer to her every concern. That in itself made her nervous. Students with glib responses were usually hiding something, she had learned over the years.

She thought for a moment about his outlandish suggestion that she, Charlotte Gregory, work closely with him in an attempt to capture spies. Did she have the resources within herself to carry out such a task?

Resources she might have, but she had few skills beyond the ability to find information in books and teach nine-year-olds how to sew a straight seam. "I have no experience in such matters," she said.

"Few people do. Espionage techniques were not on the curriculum at Eton or Oxford when I attended, and I rather suspect that they are not a standard subject at Miss Moore's Academy either." His smile was strained.

"So then, how did you become involved in such matters?" It seemed wise at this point to turn the conversation away from her and toward him. At the very least, doing so would give her time to think. "Not every man who joins the British Army does so with the intent of becoming an intelligence agent, I assume?"

His smile became more relaxed. "Hardly. Every soldier was encouraged to bring his particular skills to the fore, however. I am fluent in French and, thanks to the tutelage of my mother, speak the language with almost no accent."

"Of course. I sometimes forget that your mother was French. I was very young when she passed away."

Lord Finchwood was silent for a moment, then continued as though Charlotte had not spoken. " I'm also reasonably competent in Spanish. I learned it on my own while at Oxford. I have always had an interest in languages. And once you know French and Latin, it is relatively simple to acquire the rudiments of other Romance languages. I know a smattering of Portuguese and Italian as well."

"So it was your facility with languages that brought you to the attention of your superiors?"

He nodded. "There were few men, even in the officers' ranks, who could speak both Spanish and French."

Charlotte touched the side of the teapot. It was cool, and she decided against pouring herself another cup, despite the fact that she could have used a sip of something bracing to continue this conversation. "But surely there is more to the job than knowing many languages?"

"Yes."

When he said nothing more, Charlotte sighed. He seemed eager to engage her cooperation, but frustratingly vague about the nature of the job.

"It appears that brevity is also a characteristic of a successful spy," she said, reaching for the teapot after all. Cool tea was better than nothing.

"In matters related to the way we operate, yes, it is." He nodded toward the teapot. "Don't suffer through that brew, Miss Gregory. When we have finished our discussion, I will ring for fresh tea."

She refused to be distracted from her point with discussions of refreshments. "But if I am to join your ranks, I must know what is involved in order to make a wise decision."

"I will tell you what I know, but I am somewhat in the dark myself. Espionage here in England will differ somewhat from intelligence work in the Peninsula."

She waited for him to continue, but he did not. She twisted a fold of her skirt in an effort to channel her frustration.

"Yes, without doubt. But if you cannot supply some details on the sorts of things I shall be required to do, my imagination will fill them in for me. And, I must assure you, I have quite an active imagination." Even as she said it, her mind raced ahead to envision secret letters being exchanged behind trees and whispered conversations in shadowy forests. The thought of skulking through a shadowy forest with Lord Finchwood most certainly had appeal. She gave the skirt fabric between her fingers a sharp twist. Clearly, she had been wasting more time than was wise reading fantastical novels.

"If you could simply tell me a bit about your activities in Spain, it might give me some idea of the *sorts* of things I might be expected to do here at home," she said.

He looked away. "I am not sure I should speak of such things."

Charlotte puffed out her breath in exasperation. "Do you not consider me trustworthy, even after the tests you have given me? If you do not trust me, I doubt we will make worthwhile partners in your efforts to trap the French spies."

He turned back toward her and expelled a long breath. "You are right, of course. Trust is the most valuable commodity among spies—well, at least among spies who are all working for the same side." His smile was faint. "But it is not lack of trust that makes it difficult to talk about Spain."

She nodded but said nothing. From years of dealing with tongue-tied students, she had learned that there was nothing like silence to encourage others to talk.

Finally, he adjusted his neckcloth, brushed a minute horsehair from his jacket, and began.

"The main aspect of my duties in the Peninsula involved reconnaissance. I rode deep into enemy territory, usually at night, to learn what I could about encampments and troop movements. Occasionally, I was asked to eavesdrop in public places, and to draw people who had attracted our notice into conversation." He stopped and eyed her, as though daring her to question him.

Perhaps this was another test, Charlotte thought. Perhaps he wanted to ensure that she had the ability to charm people into talking. He obviously had no idea what it took to encourage a recalcitrant nine-year-old to read aloud.

"And how did you draw these people into conversation?" she asked.

"In various ways. Often, a few glasses of sherry would loosen the tongues of witnesses who were otherwise unwilling to share information on troop movements in neighboring villages. Sometimes the quarry would be more receptive to compliments—" Again, he stopped.

"Compliments? It seems odd that a man—" It was Charlotte's turn to stop in mid-sentence. With a start, she realized that not all of the informants Lord Finchwood had charmed into talking had been male.

She could certainly understand how any female he chose to charm would find it hard to resist him. His slow grin as he watched her face should have annoyed her, but instead it warmed her as though she were standing before a roaring fire. She twitched in her seat as unfamiliar sensations prickled along her shoulders and back. Yes, she could quite see how that grin could be devastating in the field.

She should be shocked at what he had implied about his activities on the Peninsula. She *was* shocked. But if Charlotte were to be truly honest with herself, she had to acknowledge that a small, secret corner of her mind was unabashedly curious. When would she, a sheltered gentlewoman, ever get the chance to find out about such things again?

"I see you have divined the nature of some of my work in Spain," he said in a low, lazy drawl.

"You need not be so proud of yourself," she snapped, more as a defense against his lethal smile than out of anger. She was far, far out of her depth with the viscount, and the last thing she needed was for him to realize how greatly he affected her poise. "I already knew you were a Casanova. Any person with access to the London newspapers would know as much."

"I thought you did not engage in gossip, Miss Gregory." His grin, if anything, had grown wider.

"Some men's deeds are so remarkable that even those who wish to close their ears to them cannot help but hear a little." *Oh, very good, Charlotte. The man already had a high enough opinion of his charms, without you stoking the fire.*

As she had feared, her remark did little to dampen his

amusement. "Remarkable, eh? I had no idea my fame in such matters had spread as far as Hampshire."

"Don't play me for a green girl, your lordship. You knew exactly how much we had heard. For one thing, you knew that your reputation was partly to blame for your father's enmity. Second, if you are the intelligence agent you claim to be, you would have determined the lay of the land before even arriving in Hampshire."

His smile turned from lazy to admiring. "The last thing I would play you for, Miss Gregory, is a green *girl.*"

For a moment, Charlotte was at a loss for words. Men simply did not flirt with her. They never had, and it was highly unlikely that one would start doing so now.

Of course, she realized. Taking advantage of her shock and confusion, Lord Finchwood was doing an almost perfect job of deflecting the conversation away from his activities in Spain.

The gentleman was very, very skilled.

"Getting back to the Peninsula, Lord Finchwood," she said, in her most stentorian schoolmistress tones.

"Must we?"

"Yes."

"What else would you like to know?"

The first few questions that occurred to her were indelicate in the extreme. So she settled for something vague and basic that might get him talking. "So, your job was to gain information from sources that could aid the British cause?"

He nodded. At first, she thought he would say nothing more, but then he added, "Few people, even in the army, knew what I was really doing in Spain."

"How did you keep it from them?" She found it difficult to believe that anyone as vibrant as Lord Finchwood would be able to skulk about the ranks unnoticed.

"I used a combination of ruses, aided and abetted by my superiors. Sometimes I claimed to be traveling behind the lines to check on the supply wagons. In other cases, my commanding officer told people he had sent me to deliver a message to another regiment."

"I doubt that any of those excuses would hold much water were I to offer them to my students."

He laughed. "Likely not. But if you decide to join me in this work—which I very much hope you will—I can help you devise explanations that are not too far from the truth. You would, I assume, be uncomfortable with serious untruths?"

She nodded.

"I suspected as much. Most admirable." He paused. "There is not much I can really tell you about the day-to-day work. I expect it will consist largely of eavesdropping on conversations and staying alert for anything odd."

"Odd?"

"It's . . ." He shrugged. "It's hard to explain. It's all a matter of noticing things that aren't usual. Someone who is usually gregarious who suddenly becomes tight-lipped. A half-forgotten road that overnight shows signs of heavy use. That sort of thing."

"And will there be any need to encourage wily Frenchmen to . . ." Charlotte could not think of any word to explain her fears. "To . . . dance . . . with me?"

The viscount hooted with laughter. "No, Miss Gregory. I will not ask you to do anything that would injure your reputation. Of course, if you determine on your own that such actions are necessary and undertake them independently—"

"I don't think you need fear that."

He chuckled again. "I suspected as much. You have my word—I shall only ask you to do that with which you feel comfortable. I suspect I will be able to handle any male suspects on my own."

Charlotte felt a knot of tension in her shoulders dissolve. Perhaps this would not be so difficult. It would be foolish of her to dismiss the opportunity to serve her country out of some misplaced missish fears.

And yet, something else was worrying her. She bit her bottom lip.

"Miss Gregory?" His face was concerned. "What else would you like to know?"

She nodded toward his gloved hand, but hesitated to voice the question on her mind. She hated to pry, but she needed to understand the physical as well as the social risks she might be courting.

His shuttered expression did nothing to encourage her, but she plunged ahead anyway. "Did intelligence work lead to your injury?"

"Indirectly. It happened in Badajoz." He stood and crossed the room to the bell pull near the door. "I believe I offered to ring for more tea."

Every instinct of politeness—indeed, of self-preservation—urged Charlotte to stop her inquiry. But the cold, dead look in the viscount's eyes prompted her to continue. She sensed the moment of his injury still haunted him. Perhaps, by discussing it, he could diminish its power to hurt him.

She waited until he had pressed the bell. A faint chime echoed in some distant part of the house. The viscount returned to his chair, dropped into it and fixed her with a chilling look.

Charlotte felt her stomach twist. But if she was to fall in with Lord Finchwood's mad plan, she would likely find herself in other situations just as unnerving. And she truly did believe that discussion might help him. It certainly helped many of her father's parishioners, when they came to the vicar to discuss their fears.

"Would you like to talk about it?" she asked in a soft voice.

"It isn't relevant to our discussion of intelligence work. It happened in broad daylight, with no hint of espionage." He was looking at her as though she were a stranger. "It isn't relevant," he repeated, as if trying to convince himself as much as Charlotte.

There was a scratch at the door, and a young housemaid came in. She bobbed a curtsey to Lord Finchwood. "Yes, my lord?"

The viscount didn't speak for several seconds, then seemed to focus on the girl. "We should like some more tea."

"In a few minutes," Charlotte added without thinking.

He raised his eyebrows.

"I am not thirsty now, but I am sure I will be as the evening wears on," she explained, hoping he would accept her flimsy excuse for overruling him. "If it is all right with you, my lord, I should like to wait a few minutes, so that the tea does not become cold."

She watched as he obviously debated whether it would be unseemly to dismiss a woman's express wishes, even if only before a servant.

Finally, he gave the housemaid a curt nod. "I rang in error."

"Very good, my lord," chirped the maid as she scuttled away, closing the door behind her.

Lord Finchwood gave Charlotte a considering glance. "Do you make it a habit of contradicting people in front of their staff?"

She flushed, and felt a bead of sweat trickle down behind her ear. She had not meant for this conversation to become contentious, but she would not turn back from her purpose. "I am sorry, Lord Finchwood. But you had ordered the tea mainly for me, and I truly am not thirsty."

"Was that the only reason you counteracted my—request?" She had a strong suspicion he had been about to say "orders." He might have left the army, but the army, it appeared, had not fully left him.

"No," she admitted. "I did not want to be interrupted by

the tea tray, for a few minutes at least. Until we had had a chance to conclude our discussion of . . . your injury."

He frowned and said nothing. She let silence hang between them and felt uncomfortable. Her behavior was passing the bounds of politeness, she knew. But somehow, she just could not shake the notion that he needed to talk. Resolutely, she fixed him with her best schoolmistress stare.

"You can try that look all you like. It didn't work for my masters at Eton or for the dons at Oxford, and it won't work for you. I'm immune to your schoolteacher tricks." His laugh was uneasy.

"I don't want to force you to talk about it, but I have the feeling you would like to tell me the story."

He groaned and tilted his head against the back of the chair, staring at the plaster ceiling. "Why do you care?"

"Because you're my friend." As she said it, she realized that in an odd way it was true. She still did not know him very well. And formally, he was her employer rather than her friend. But he had tried—albeit in an arrogant way—to help her out of her financial woes. Just because the execution had been awkward did not mean that the sentiment had not been genuine. The least she could do was respond in kind.

He smiled. "I count very few women among my *friends*." The words might have come across as challenging, but his voice was rueful.

"It is a night for firsts, my lord. You have asked me to take a risk this evening—"

"—which you have not yet agreed to take—"

"—so I'm asking you to take a risk with me."

He let his right arm drop to his side, over the edge of the chair, so that she could not see his hand. She suddenly realized how often he concealed his hand—in gloves, in pockets, behind doorframes—whenever any reference to his injury came up. Clearly, the events of that day—and their aftermath—still disturbed him.

Almost without thinking, she stood up and crossed the room. She approached him as she would a bird that had fallen from a tree or a child that had stumbled on the roadside. As she knelt beside his chair, she registered his startled look.

If she stopped to think, she would be startled by her forwardness herself. But she didn't allow herself to stop and think. If she did, she knew she would never break through the wall he had constructed around himself.

She took a deep breath and reached beside his chair. Gripping his hand in hers, she raised it. She could feel a thick line of flesh along his palm. It must be a scar.

Never had she touched a man this way. What would he think of her?

Stop thinking, she told herself. *For once in your life, don't worry about propriety.*

Placing his hand firmly on the arm of the chair, she covered it with her own. The back of his hand bent at an unnatural angle, but it was warm nonetheless. It heated her palm like spring sunshine. She closed her hand around it.

"Miss Gregory—" the viscount began.

"I know, Lord Finchwood," she interrupted. "This is highly irregular. But I needed you to know that I cared, and I could not seem to make you believe that from the far side of the room."

He nodded.

"In no way do I want to force you to talk. But if you wish to, I am happy to listen." She paused. "Sometimes, talking about a nightmare makes it seem less real. I never really accepted my mother's death until I discussed it, months later, with my sister."

He nodded again, and lowered his gaze to their clasped hands. Charlotte felt momentary embarrassment at her forwardness, but she would not retreat now. Instead, she gave his twisted hand a brief squeeze, willing him to release some of the sorrow he carried with him.

The viscount took a deep breath, then slowly released it.

"It was not a particularly heroic injury," he began, shifting his glance to the fireplace grate. "In the melee, I was thrown from my horse and momentarily stunned. While I was lying on the ground, a frightened horse trod on my hand. As well as breaking a number of small bones, the impact also drove a discarded musket blade deep into my palm."

Charlotte suppressed a flinch. She had pressed, so she couldn't complain when he told her. And, given the tautness in his voice, he was concealing some of the most lurid details.

"The physicians acted quickly and were able to avoid amputation," Lord Finchwood continued. His eyes seemed unfocused on the elegant room around them, as if he were seeing that battle taking place again in his mind's eye. Beneath her palm, she felt his hand tense. "However, they did not set the bones properly. My hand will always be gnarled and almost useless. But at least I still have it."

Anger seeped through her. "It is appalling that men must be maimed in such brutal ways, all for the so-called glory of war."

He twisted in his chair and stared at her for several moments. His fierce expression made her wonder whether she had been wise to encourage him to remember his experience. "War is far from the glorious endeavor our historians and journalists would have us believe. Anyone who witnessed the sacking of Badajoz would agree."

Lord Finchwood yanked his hand from beneath hers and jumped to his feet, then strode to the far end of the room. When he reached the wall beneath his father's portrait, he turned. "Would it have been better to sit back while Boney marched into every country in Europe and imposed his will, his laws and his ways?"

That was not what she had meant to imply. "You are right. It is vital to stop France's attempts to rule us all," she said carefully, looking at her hands, still lying on the arm of his chair.

She had made a hash of everything. She had hoped to help him but had only made him angry. "I just wish that there were some other way to stop Napoleon than by sacrificing our young men in foreign fields far from their homes," Charlotte said, desperate that he should understand. She had always felt thus, but she believed it now more strongly than ever before. She could still feel the terrible ridge of his unseen scar beneath her fingertips—gruesome evidence of the sacrifice he had made for his country.

"There is another way." The passion in his voice made her raise her eyes. Even half hidden in the shadows, he looked more alive than she could ever recall, more vital even than he had in his glamorous youth. "We can work here, in England, to prevent the French from getting information, money and supplies. Breaking this ring of spies could save uncounted men from death in France. We can't be certain how many, but every effort makes a difference." He paused. "We need your help. *I* need your help."

Charlotte hesitated. A month ago—a week ago—she would have known what to do. She would have declined Lord Finchwood's outlandish proposal. She did not court risk, nor did she enjoy games of deception.

But she did not want to refuse. She wanted to aid the war effort. She wanted to justify the viscount's faith in her abilities. But there was something more to her desire to help, and it had nothing to do with patriotism or honor.

As a girl, she had daydreamed of adventures with the

handsome viscount. So had every other girl for miles in any direction. The allure of fulfilling some of those youthful fantasies was almost irresistible.

Perhaps she was being foolish, to take such a risk just in the hope of a kind word or a warm smile from a peer who had not even remembered her existence until they had re-encountered each other outside the village pub. If she were sensible, she would thank the viscount and take her leave.

But she had spent her whole life being sensible. She would spend the rest of her life being sensible. It seemed—well, foolish—to let such an opportunity to taste a different sort of life pass her by.

"There is something to consider that I urge you not to take lightly," the viscount said in a strained voice. "I will do my best to ensure your safety at all times. But truth to tell, no one can guarantee another's safety with absolute certainty in a situation such as this. For that reason, you must consider this idea very carefully, and do not feel under any pressure to say yes, or even to decide right now. I fully realize the scope of the task I am asking you to undertake."

She nodded as she moved back from her position next to his chair and sat down on the settee.

"Let me explain in more detail what you may be called upon to do." He crossed the room and leaned against the substantial marble fireplace. "First of all, I expect that I will frequently draw on your knowledge of local society."

"*My* knowledge of local society?" Charlotte tried, and failed, to keep the skepticism from her voice. "You are far more grandly connected than I."

"Perhaps, but my connections are old and rusty, and extend mainly into other aristocratic houses. Between your school and your father's church, you know many more people from all parts of society's spectrum."

He tapped his fingers against the mantel. "Between us,

we should be able to engineer invitations into a variety of local houses of interest. The work should not be dangerous if we are careful."

Despite herself, she felt an illicit thrill at his use of the word *we*.

"I am not exactly a belle of the ball in these parts," she felt compelled to point out, in case he was under the impression that she spent every weekend primping for soirées and dinner parties.

"No?" He didn't sound concerned.

"I receive many invitations—" she began.

"That's excellent."

"—but I am usually too tired to attend. Supervising thirty girls all day long can be exhausting work." As soon as she said it, she wished she could swallow the words. To a man who had spent five years in exotic locations facing unspeakable situations, her life must sound dreary and her complaints petty.

If the viscount thought so, however, he couched his opinions with diplomacy. "I fully understand how weary you must be," he replied. "Looking back, I often wondered how our masters at Eton coped without going mad."

"Oh, it is not an unpleasant life. I truly enjoy my occupation. It is just that it leaves me little energy for social engagements. And when I do go out, I prefer small gatherings where one can talk and actually hear oneself think. Large gatherings are noisy, and I often feel overwhelmed."

He continued to tap on the mantel. "That could be a drawback. Large events will probably provide our best opportunity to observe without being observed. Do you think you could learn to enjoy—or at least to tolerate— major soirées?"

"I suppose I could. If I can teach myself military strategy, I should be able to teach myself anything."

"*Military strategy?*" His voice was laced with good-natured amusement.

She shrugged. "One of my students expressed an interest in the topic. I always try to nurture the girls' curiosity, when I can."

"So how, exactly, are you teaching yourself military strategy?"

"I availed myself of a few books in Mr. Grimes's library. He is a friend of my father's, and they are both amateur historians. Mr. Grimes's particular interest is the Punic Wars."

A smile tugged at the corner of Lord Finchwood's mouth. "So your knowledge of army tactics is—how shall I phrase this—slightly outdated?"

She could be offended by his obvious amusement, or simply join in. She chose the latter course. It would be odd, really, to be telling students about Roman warriors in chariots when, just a few hundred miles from home, a much more relevant fight was being waged. Perhaps she should rethink her approach. It was just that the current conflict seemed so much more, well, painful.

She laughed. "If you don't think my knowledge is *au courant*, you shouldn't have asked me to be part of the fight."

He sobered. "I wouldn't have asked you if I wasn't convinced you had the courage and intelligence for the task. Don't underestimate yourself, Miss Gregory. I certainly do not."

This declaration set the bees in Charlotte's head buzzing at an even greater volume. She reminded herself that he was an accomplished flirt—and worse. His casual compliment should not have set her hands trembling. "I have lived my whole life within fifteen miles of my birthplace," she said, making light of his remark. "I have never taken any risks or done anything heroic."

"Some people have the seeds of courage inside them, and only need to face a test to show their true colors," he said. "Others are weak-hearted from birth, and crumble under fire. Those people one can usually pick out because they are not up to scratch in other matters. They lie, they cheat, they tell tales, they have no self-control and no discipline. In Spain, I became adept at distinguishing the strong from the weak. It was a survival skill. You are one of the strong ones."

"Oh," was all she could say.

"I have told you as much as I feel I should, before you have committed yourself to helping me. I hope you understand that this is not a matter of personal trust. My superiors have instructed me to play my cards rather close to my chest."

"Of course, Lord Finchwood."

Charlotte leaned back in her chair and closed her eyes. Truly, in her wildest imaginings, she could never have dreamed of being placed in such a situation. Such things simply did not happen to vicars' daughters in Hampshire.

And such an opportunity will likely never arise again, a small voice in her head whispered.

Suddenly, Charlotte saw the rest of her life mapped out for her as a long, straight road, filled with quiet joys and successes but no surprising detours. Working with Lord Finchwood would be about the only event in her life she would not be able to predict twenty years before it happened.

She opened her eyes and leaned forward. "I don't need any extra time to think, Lord Finchwood. I would be honored to accept this opportunity, and I thank you for considering me worthy."

He smiled. "Your decisiveness alone proves you are more than up to the job." He tilted his head to the side. "It is customary to seal such an agreement with a handshake since, of course, no written contract can be exchanged." He extended his gloved right hand. "I know that my grip is not particularly firm with this hand, but it somehow feels less official to shake with my left."

Tentatively, she put her hand in his. Her cheeks flamed as she remembered her earlier boldness.

"Don't worry, Miss Gregory. My hand does not pain me now, and the simple act of shaking it won't hurt."

Hurting him had not been the reason for her hesitation. She suspected he knew it and was trying to help her save face. As his warm hand closed around her smaller one, she reveled in the crackling sensations that traveled up her arm and seemed to radiate throughout her body.

To her embarrassment, she realized that she had been gripping his hand for a few seconds longer than necessary. With a tiny gasp, she withdrew her hand and dropped it into her lap.

"We are agreed, then, Lord Finchwood," she said, using her briskest schoolroom manner.

"We are," he said, an odd light in his blue eyes.

A spy, it appeared, rarely missed anything. She would have to remember that fact in the future.

"We have not discussed your fee," he continued, and she silently thanked him for not teasing her for her obvious discomfort.

"My fee? But we have. We discussed it the day you first mentioned the secretarial position to me."

"But the duties I am now asking you to perform will be far more onerous than writing a few letters, and will take up much more of your time. I suggest that we double your fee." He held up a hand as Charlotte began to protest. "This is not charity. I intend to wrest every penny's worth from you. That reminds me. How much time will you be able to commit to this project, without neglecting your responsibilities at the academy?"

"I had considered that. Fortunately, the school year is almost over, and Jane is quite capable of handling most of the day-to-day responsibilities. Indeed, she has frequently mentioned that she would like to learn more about the administrative aspects of the school. I may share some of my extra fee with her—without telling her whence it comes—as compensation."

He nodded. "That is most convenient."

"More vexing is the fact that I will be unavailable to you during the day on school days, and on Sundays. I might be able to forgo dinner with Father occasionally, but he will miss me greatly on Sundays, as I help him with a great deal of church business."

"I don't think that will be a problem," the viscount replied. "Somehow, I suspect that our quarry will be the type to lie very low on Sunday mornings, when the roads are alive with respectable people."

"So do you have any idea who in the neighborhood could be involved in this scheme?" she said. The hairs on her neck prickled as she realized that a traitor might have sat behind her at church or wished her good day in the Gillington high street.

"I do, now that you ask." He lowered his voice, and she suspected that was more out of habit than out of any fear that Lady Gilhurst might overhear. "What do you know of Mr. Anthony Norris?"

Charlotte blinked. "Mr. Norris? Not a great deal, but nothing untoward. He seems a friendly man, and he is well liked in the area. He often attends assemblies in the Gillington hall."

"The assembly that is held every second Thursday?"

She nodded.

"Then so must we. You will not arouse suspicion if you go?"

"Perhaps a little, but nothing untoward. I do attend occasionally, particularly when my school duties are light. The assemblies are most respectable."

"Good. Then it is settled. We shall dance for our country, and keep an eye on Mr. Norris in the process."

Charlotte nodded again. The thought of carrying out her new duties in full view of the village had left her dry-mouthed and tongue-tied. And the thought of seeing Lord Finchwood in full evening dress robbed her of what little speech she had left.

Really, she admonished herself. *If you are going to become an espionage agent, you are simply going to have to stop behaving like some buffleheaded girl.*

Resolutely, she moved to the small escritoire and took her seat. "Now that we are agreed on that matter, Lord Finchwood, are there any letters you would like me to write this evening?"

His blue eyes crinkled as he grinned. "All business. I like that."

If he only knew that the thoughts rioting through her brain were anything but businesslike. She yanked a piece of stationery toward her with rather more force than she intended, and uncapped the silver inkwell.

SEVEN

"It is such a pleasure to see you back in Gillington, Lord Finchwood," Mrs. Kane burbled as she sawed the air before her round, flushed face with an enormous fan. It was deuced warm for late May, and the small Gillington assembly rooms were crowded.

Finch could have done without the heat generated by the packed assembly, but the thronged rooms suited his purposes. With most of the population of the village assembled, his attendance—and Miss Gregory's—would create less of a stir.

"I am pleased to be home," he replied without forethought, and then realized that the sentiment was partly true.

Granted, he was still not comfortable sharing Gilhurst Hall with his father, who had made no move to thaw the ice between them. But he was enjoying the chance to revisit some of the haunts of his childhood and to renew old acquaintances.

In particular, he was enjoying his renewed acquaintance with the intriguing Miss Gregory. It had been so long since he had dealt with a woman on equal terms that he was finding the whole experience most gratifying.

They weren't exactly equal, of course. He was her employer and held the purse strings. But in a truer sense, their association was well balanced. He respected her in-

telligence, her wit and her courage. The fact that she
had decided so quickly to join the cause had impressed
him deeply. Most of the women he knew in London
would have vacillated for days before making a choice.
Miss Gregory had been completely rational and businesslike about the whole affair.

He smiled. He had to stop thinking in absolutes when
it came to Miss Gregory. Just as they were not exactly
equal, neither was she completely businesslike. Her startling move across the salon to seize his hand had been
anything but rational. She was fortunate that he had
been raised to be a gentleman. When she had held his
hand between her two small ones, she had called up
emotions in him he had thought long dormant. For one
mad moment, he had been tempted to lean toward her
and brush his mouth across her full, tempting lips.

That temptation was understandable, if unfortunate.
What he found harder to explain was the way he had
talked to her at such length about Badajoz. He had
barely spoken of the battle since the day he had been
carried off the field. Yet he had been able to discuss it
with Miss Gregory at length. Why she had succeeded
where so many others had failed was a mystery to him.

Perhaps it was his physical attraction to her that broke
down his reticence, although his mistresses in London
had never had such an effect on him. He shook his
head. It was a puzzle.

At least the odd sensations between himself and Miss
Gregory appeared to be mutual. When he had shaken
her hand at the end of that evening and she had
snatched it away with that funny little cry, he knew that
she felt the same odd spark around him that he felt
around her. Nothing would come of it, of course. They
came from two different worlds, and she was no actress
or dancer he could tumble for sport. But it was good to
know that he wasn't the only one whose thoughts often

turned in directions that had nothing to do with the investigation.

The investigation. He must not lose his focus on his purpose here. In five years in Spain, he had never once let thoughts of a woman distract him from his greater purpose, and he didn't intend to begin now.

With one ear cocked to Mrs. Kane's extended monologue, he began to scan the room, occasionally murmuring *yes*, or *of course* whenever his voluble companion paused for breath.

No sign of Norris yet, although he had overheard one young woman telling her companion that she had seen Norris in the village a few days previously and he had assured her he planned to attend the dance. With luck, Norris had not merely been being polite.

Miss Gregory had arrived a few minutes ago with her sister, Mrs. Milton. Anyone observing the two women would see immediately that they were related, although Mrs. Milton was but a pale copy of her elder sister. Where Miss Gregory's hair was as bright as an autumn leaf, and her eyes a vivid green, Mrs. Milton's coloring was much more conventional—and unremarkable, in Finch's opinion.

He spared them a few brief glances as they made their way about the room. Anything more than that might attract attention and cause casual bystanders to suspect that his relationship with Miss Gregory was more than a simple arrangement between employer and secretary. Such suspicions could be dangerous to both Miss Gregory and the operation. He did notice, however, that the sisters seemed to know every person they encountered and were welcomed warmly by all.

Finch continued to survey the room in a methodical fashion. There was no sign of the bitter ex-seaman or Pierre St. Amour, a fact that did not surprise Finch. It would be the height of folly for either of them to appear in public, if they hoped to move about the area in secrecy later.

"—don't you agree, my lord?" Mrs. Kane's voice pierced his thoughts.

"Yes, certainly," he said, hoping he had not concurred that England was ripe for revolution or some equally preposterous idea.

"Oh, look, there is Mr. Norris!" she exclaimed, saying the only thing she had uttered in the past twenty minutes that was remotely interesting. He followed her gaze to the door of the main assembly room, where a tall man was doffing his hat to a beleaguered-looking servant.

He was definitely the same man Finch had seen in the Portsmouth public house. If he wasn't mistaken, the idiot was even wearing the same coat. That fact alone gave Finch confidence that at least some of the players in this scheme weren't habitual criminals. That would make them easier to catch.

"I promised his sister that I would give her my cook's recipe for sugar biscuits." The older woman dug into her reticule and extracted a folded piece of paper. "If Mr. Norris brings it to her, it will save her the cost of the letter. Please excuse me, Lord Finchwood."

He bowed as she departed. She had made an admirable cover, but he could not say he was sorry to see her go. Her facility for chatter was extraordinary, and he was longing for a moment of silence.

It was not to be, however, as he was waylaid immediately by a trio of equally vocal females. "Lord Finchwood!" exclaimed the eldest, a thin woman whose mobcap barely concealed a mop of unruly gray curls. "I am so pleased to renew our association."

"Ma'am?" he asked, trying in vain to place her while keeping one eye on Norris's movements.

"Oh dear, how rude of me. It has been so many years, of course I should have thought to jog your memory. I am

Mrs. Carruthers. From Upper Swinton? Your mother and I were great friends. Well, perhaps that is putting too fine a point on it, but she was always most gracious to me when we encountered each other at church. Such a lovely woman she was. Such fine manners. You may not remember my daughters, as they were just out of the schoolroom when you left for the Peninsula. May I introduce them?"

Finch nodded, but barely registered that the plain young women were called Harriet and Cassandra. Or were they Henrietta and Clarissa? As he bowed over each giggling girl's hand in turn, he squinted toward the corner of the room, where Miss Gregory was in conversation with Norris. She was quick.

Mrs. Carruthers, meanwhile, put Mrs. Kane to shame as a conversationalist. Mrs. Kane, at least, paused occasionally for breath.

"Henrietta is a most accomplished dancer, my lord. All the local gentlemen say so. But Cassandra is equally noted for her skills on the piano. Aren't you, my girl?"

The shorter of the two sisters nodded.

"Mrs. Carruthers!" interrupted a shrill voice. Finch's stomach clutched as he saw yet another matron with a young woman in tow. "I did not realize that you and Lord Finchwood were acquainted. You must introduce us."

For the next half hour, Finch was deluged by swarms of avid females of all ages. How could he have forgotten how eagerly ambitious mamas anticipated the arrival of any new gentleman in a rural district? Even though he was not technically a newcomer, he had been away so long that his presence and his purse were bound to attract attention. Even in London, his arrival from Spain had made him the target of much interest at Almack's and Vauxhall. But that interest had been a pale shadow in comparison to this onslaught. Apparently, eligible young men were particularly rare birds in Gillington this year.

Silently, he thanked Barton for having the foresight to

suggest he hire a local assistant. Miss Gregory was creating much less of a furor than Finch himself was. If they were to learn anything from Norris tonight, she would likely be the one to divine the information.

As the crowd of young women continued to vie for his attention, he realized that the only way he would find any peace at all would be to ask one of them to dance. When the small ensemble on the dais at the end of the room wheezed to a finish, he seized his chance.

"Miss . . . Richmond?" he hazarded, addressing the female closest to him, a slim blonde with a circlet of rosebuds in her hair.

"Richardson. But no offence taken, my lord," she said with a pleasant smile.

He breathed a silent sigh of relief. His random choice appeared to be one of the moderately sensible ones.

"May I have the pleasure of the next dance?"

She smiled and turned pink. "I would be honored, my lord."

He nodded to the rest of the group. "It has been a pleasure chatting with you, ladies," he said with a slight bow. Offering his arm to Miss Richardson, he turned from his admirers. It was all he could do to keep from bolting toward the dance floor.

Once there, he noticed Miss Gregory further down the line, paired with Mr. Norris. Had she been conversing with him all this time? Good. Very good. It had been wiser than he knew to hire a female assistant. Heaven knows, *he* was unlikely to have attracted a dance invitation from Norris.

He grinned at the thought. Who would lead, and who would follow?

Finch returned his attention to Miss Gregory. She looked different tonight, somehow. Perhaps it was that her hair was more artfully arranged than the plain twist she usually favored. He supposed that her schoolroom duties made the pretty curls she wore tonight a useless luxury.

That was unfortunate. They softened the lines of her face and made her look . . . what was it exactly? Less worried and strained, he supposed.

The musicians launched into a rousing tune and the line of dancers bowed and curtsied to each other. Finch extended his hand to Miss Richardson. Fortunately, she was the quietest woman he had met all evening, which meant he could spend part of his time during the dance observing Norris and Miss Gregory.

They appeared to be carrying on an animated conversation as they moved through the complicated figures. Norris, he was strangely pleased to note, was an awkward dancer. He headed in the wrong direction at least twice, and accidentally trod on the hem of Miss Gregory's green gown. Finch hoped the clod hadn't torn it. He suspected that his assistant didn't have a closet full of festive dresses to serve as replacements.

He was captivated by her easy grace as she wove among the other dancers. At one moment, she looked directly at him and then glanced away, stumbling slightly.

Good heavens, he had to be careful. He didn't want to make her nervous by staring at her. He had taught her the basics of intelligence observation. Now he needed to leave her to do her work, without hovering over her like a nervous mother cat.

"Lord Finchwood?" Miss Richardson's voice was so soft he almost did not hear it.

He looked up to see that she was holding out her hand to him. Obviously, he was just about to miss a figure. He extended his gnarled right hand to her, grateful as always for the glove that concealed his ugly scars.

It was rare for him to become so distracted by his surveillance work that he failed to attend to his companions. Resolutely, he turned back toward Miss Richardson and asked her whether she had any interest in Lord Byron's poetry. It was an odd choice of conversational gambit, as Finch knew about as much about poetry as he did about embroidery. Fortunately, Miss Richardson knew more, and her reply to his question sustained them for several minutes, until Miss Gregory and Norris moved into the position of top couple.

When his assistant and their quarry finished their turn at the top of the line and turned to walk to the end, Miss Gregory glanced at Finch over Miss Richardson's head and nodded. It was a perfectly polite move that would not arouse the least suspicion—as long as no one noticed the grin and the wink that accompanied it.

The conversation must be going well. But he would have to warn her not to risk an expression as obvious as a wink again.

Nevertheless, it had given him a queer and not unpleasant feeling to have the proper Miss Gregory winking at him as if he were a schoolboy. If he hadn't known better, he could have pretended she was flirting.

That idea struck him as so funny that he chuckled, prompting Miss Richardson to ask what amused him.

"Nothing of importance. I'm just recalling something I saw earlier today," he replied, as he gripped his partner's elbow and guided her across the row. Miss Richardson was a competent dancer, but he found himself wondering how different it would be to be partnered with Miss Gregory instead.

He supposed it wouldn't hurt to find out at some point. It would not be unseemly for him to dance with her, even though he was her employer. As a vicar's daughter, she was perfectly respectable, if not marriage material for the future marquis of Gilhurst.

Within a few minutes the tune ended, and Finch returned a blushing Miss Richardson to her ecstatic mama. With a pang, he realized that his choice of the young woman for his first dance would be the talk of Gillington the next morning.

Suddenly, he longed for the relative anonymity of London, where viscounts more social and personable than he were relatively thick on the ground.

"Lord Finchwood."

He turned to see Reverend Gregory, bowing in welcome.

"Reverend. It is good to see you again. I have barely had a chance to exchange more than a word or two with you after services since I returned."

The older man laughed. "On a Sunday morning, when all the parish has some personal matter they are eager to discuss, I am almost as popular as you have been here tonight."

Finch chuckled. "Believe me, sir, it is a form of attention I could do without. I had forgotten how persistent a mother with a marriageable daughter can be."

The vicar's smile dimmed somewhat. "Such mothers are often blinded by a plump wallet and a handsome face."

"Are you implying, sir, that they are blinded to my less than admirable character traits?" Finch smiled. It seemed that almost everyone in Hampshire was determined to consider him the worst scoundrel in England, even though he had been as scrupulous as a deacon since he had left London.

The vicar shook his head. "Not at all. I apologize if I gave offence." He sighed. "It is just that, well, one hears things . . ."

"About my life in London, you mean?"

The older man nodded, biting his lower lip. Finch realized that the vicar's daughter did exactly the same thing when she was nervous or uncomfortable. He hated to cause Miss Gregory's father any distress, but neither did he wish to engage in an extended discussion of his private life—which was, in the end, his own business.

"Such stories sell newspapers," Finch said. "Do you

come often to the assemblies?" The change of subject was not as smooth as he would have liked, but it would do.

Reverend Gregory shook his head. "Seldom. But as Charlotte and Eliza were attending, I thought it would make a nice family outing." He chuckled. "I come mainly for the conversation. As my daughters would be the first to tell you, I am no dancer."

Finch chuckled in return. "There are other more useful skills in life."

"I'm sure you are quite accomplished, though."

"My talents are adequate." Where was all this leading?

"I suppose you spent a great deal of time dancing at social events in Town."

Ah. The vicar, apparently, was as tenacious as his daughter when he wanted to pursue a subject. Finch wondered whether the older man would kneel before him and take his hand, as Charlotte had done.

The memory of Charlotte's actions brought him up short. Never had he met a gentlewoman who had dared to be so forward. She had taken quite a risk in approaching him thus. He had realized, hours after she left, that she must have more trust in him than she let on. She would not have touched a man she believed to be a true rake. That thought had warmed him through the long, rather sleepless night—almost as much as the sensation of her hands clasping his had warmed him in the Gilhurst Hall salon. Such an innocent touch from Miss Gregory had sparked something deep within him that far more licentious actions from London's most talented courtesans had failed to evoke.

"Lord Finchwood?"

How embarrassing—to be caught ruminating on the charms of the vicar's daughter while in conversation with the vicar himself. Finch cleared his throat. "My apologies, Reverend. I was woolgathering. I was just about to ask you whether you expected a good crop of apples this year." Miss Gregory had mentioned that her father was an avid gardener.

His companion nodded. "My two trees have bloomed wonderfully this spring." He paused. "I confess, I would feel lost in any home where I was not surrounded by growing things. Do you have a garden at your house in London?"

So they were back to London. Finch stifled a groan. It was clear that the vicar had something on his mind, and he would continue his gentle verbal probes until he was able to satisfy his curiosity.

"I don't have a garden at my Mayfair house, even though I would like to. My property is quite compact." He looked directly at Reverend Gregory. "I sense there are other things you would like to know about my Town affairs." He let the unspoken question hang in the air, deciding that he would provide that opening but no more. If the cleric wished to know something specific, he would have to ask outright.

Reverend Gregory shook his head miserably. "It is truly none of my business, my lord. It is just, well, my daughter must be . . ." Again, his lower lip disappeared between his teeth. Then he squared his shoulders and took a deep breath. "All Charlotte has is her reputation. Without it, her school will fail and she will have no source of income aside from my modest living. And when I am gone, she will not have even that."

"I understand, sir. I would never do anything to harm your daughter's reputation or her livelihood." What sort of bounder did people think he was?

It wasn't that he hadn't had a few stray thoughts about the fun he could have with the schoolmistress. However, he had no intention of acting on them.

The vicar was now staring at the polished oak floor. "I know you would never do so intentionally, my lord, but, well, I just wanted to ask you—respectfully—to be careful. I know you are a good man at heart. I remember you as a boy, and I know there is no ill will in you."

A feeling stabbed through Finch that was so unfamiliar it took him a moment or two before he could identify it. Regret.

How had he become the sort of person that made upstanding souls like the Reverend Gregory nervous? He recalled the frightened little housemaid who had fetched him tea the night he had returned to Gilhurst Hall, and he flinched.

But after a moment he banished his regret, consciously replacing it with his customary *sangfroid.* He was the person he was because of the experiences he had had. He had seen things on the battlefield no human should have to see: horses writhing in agony, friends broken and bleeding, women and children in enemy forts quivering with fear as the conquering armies marched in. If he sometimes indulged in a bit of drinking and gambling, and a few amorous liaisons, in an attempt to block those pictures from his mind, he would not apologize for it. That was who he was, and he thought it unlikely that he would change soon.

The fact that his antics had put him beyond the pale for kind, respectable people like the vicar was unfortunate, but he could not change the past. It was just one more regrettable consequence of his decision to enter the army.

He realized he had not replied to the vicar's comment, and he cleared his throat. "I appreciate your faith in me, sir. I assure you, it is not misplaced, and I will conduct myself with the utmost care while in Hampshire."

Miss Gregory's father looked up and smiled weakly. "Thank you, my lord. I have been dreading this conversation, and you have made it very painless."

Finch smiled in return. It had been a long time since he had conversed with anyone as open and guileless as the vicar. It made for a refreshing change.

* * *

On the other side of the crowded room, Charlotte was seeking a way to escape Mr. Norris's company. Lord Finchwood had warned her that spending too much time with any one person could lead to suspicion.

She had tried several times to extricate herself. She had even escaped to the ladies' withdrawing room, but he had appeared at her side as soon as she returned, proffering a glass of ratafia.

Fortunately, Eliza had caught her panicked glance and joined them, her husband Darby in tow. Charlotte sighed in relief. With her sister and brother-in-law in the group, Charlotte's extended conversation with Mr. Norris might not attract as much notice from the rest of the assembly.

"Good evening, Mrs. Milton, Mr. Milton," Mr. Norris said, extending his hand to the new arrivals. "I was just applauding your sister's efforts to attend more social functions."

Eliza's eyes snapped with humor as she looked at her older sister. "I will add my voice to that cause. I am always telling Charlotte that she works too hard."

Charlotte smiled. "But I enjoy what I do."

"Yes, but you should not have to do it all the time," Eliza countered.

It was an old argument between the sisters, and one that they pursued with good humor.

Mr. Norris interjected. "If you are serious about making more time for social engagements, I would be honored if you would join me for a small dinner I am giving at Cliffholme next Monday night." He glanced at the Miltons. "You would be most welcome as well, of course."

"Thank you, Mr. Norris, we are honored. But we have a previous engagement that evening, to attend a musicale arranged by Mr. Milton's sister."

He nodded. "Another time, perhaps, I hope the timing will be more fortuitous. And you, Miss Gregory? Are you available that evening?"

Charlotte's mind was racing. Why on earth was Mr. Norris suddenly inviting her to dinner at his home? They had known each other for years, as acquaintances. He attended her father's church, and one of his young cousins was a student at the school. But he had rarely conversed with her for more than five minutes at a stretch. Did he know that she was somehow linked to Lord Finchwood's investigation?

While she was turning these possible explanations over in her mind, he added, "And perhaps you might tell me whether Lord Finchwood would be interested in attending? I know that you are working as his correspondence secretary, so I thought you might know whether he has another commitment that evening."

Charlotte relaxed. She should have suspected that his interest in her was solely as a conduit to the viscount. Mr. Norris was a known parvenu. It was only a matter of time before he tried to attract the attention of Lord Finchwood. He likely hoped that the viscount would reciprocate in kind, and that he would be invited to all manner of aristocratic soirees.

While despising his open ambition, Charlotte realized that it represented an excellent opportunity for her and Lord Finchwood to explore his house and property for signs of smuggling—or worse. "Thank you very much for your invitation, Mr. Norris. I would be pleased to attend, and I shall mention the event to Lord Finchwood."

"Please don't trouble yourself," her companion replied with an eager smile. "I shall dispatch written invitations to you and the viscount with all haste. That is the more proper avenue, is it not?"

She agreed that it was.

"Then that is what I shall do." With a slight bow, he

bade the group farewell and strode back across the dance floor.

"That was most odd," Eliza commented as she watched his retreating back. "I do not believe that Mr. Norris has ever shown the slightest interest in our family before. Indeed, I had always believed that he held vicars' daughters in only slightly higher esteem than scullery maids."

"Eliza! That is unkind."

Eliza shrugged, her grin unrepentant. "You have always been the kind one. I, however, have no compunctions about plain speaking."

Charlotte grinned in return. Her sister was one of the few people in the world who knew how hard Charlotte struggled to live up to their father's ideals of goodness. "You have likely divined the reason for his sudden fascination with me?"

Darby Milton piped up. "It seems closely related to your new employment in Lord Finchwood's household. Odd, is it not, how association with the local aristocracy can bring a sudden shine to one's hair and make one's conversation more sparkling?"

Charlotte and Eliza both laughed. "You mean I am not scintillating all on my own?" Eliza asked, batting her eyes at him in an extraordinary manner.

"You know that *I* find you captivating," Darby said, looking at Eliza with a warm light in his eyes. "In fact, I find *all* the Gregory women fascinating," he said with a gallant wave of his hand. "But, as you know, I am a man of rare taste. Mr. Norris, it appears, does not share my sense of discernment."

"You are a silly widgeon," Eliza said, rapping his arm with her folded fan. But she gave her husband a small, secretive smile, and Charlotte felt a rare rush of envy.

She had never begrudged the fact that her younger sister had married before she had, and she had never swooned over Mr. Milton, although she got along famously with her wry, sensible brother-in-law. But, occasionally, she did envy the Miltons' warm, loving relationship. How lovely it would be, she thought, to have a partner to share the joys and sorrows of the day with.

She shook her head. If she had wanted to be married, she could have been more accommodating to her erstwhile fiancé. She had chosen the high road, however, and it was a little late to complain about the places it had taken her.

As her sister and brother-in-law continued to engage in their light-hearted teasing, Charlotte stole a moment to glance around the room. Finally, in the corner, she spotted Lord Finchwood's tousled head, towering above a sea of matrons. She suppressed a smile. She really should go over and rescue him.

Then again, she had just spent almost an hour listening to Mr. Norris wax on about the people he knew in London, the new agricultural techniques he was employing on his farm, and the excellent tailor he had discovered in Portsmouth.

No, Lord Finchwood would simply have to cope on his own. He seemed an eminently capable man.

Capable, indeed. She thought again in wonder of all the skills he had re-taught himself since his return from Spain. He might not be able to write or to comfortably ride, but there was little else he could not manage.

She remembered the surprising strength in his injured hand when they had shaken hands. The memory still had the ability to make her blush.

As so often happened when she was around Lord Finchwood, she realized she was staring. There would be time enough for such folly when they met tomorrow to discuss what they had learned here tonight.

Resolutely, she turned her attention back to Eliza and Darby. But somehow, she sensed when Lord Finchwood left the room.

* * *

"This arrived in the post this morning." Lord Finch-wood tossed a buff-colored letter on the low table before the settee in the Gilhurst salon.

Once again, he had dismissed the footman, and they were alone in the room. Even though she knew that the investigation was the sole reason for that privacy, and that the Gilhurst servants were so discreet that no word of the household's private affairs was ever heard in the village, Charlotte could not suppress a tiny *frisson* of unease mixed with excitement. The situation felt so, well, illicit.

"I know. I received one as well." Charlotte sat back in her chair, eagerly awaiting the viscount's reaction. He had to be pleased that they would both have access to Mr. Norris's house.

"Don't you think it's a bit obvious—and dangerous— for us both to be invited to dinner with Mr. Norris?" His voice was cool.

Charlotte blinked. "But I thought you would be pleased."

"How, exactly, did you engineer this? Did you say anything untoward to Mr. Norris? Make any promises?"

"Promises?" She was confused. "No. What sorts of promises could I possibly make that would result in a dinner invitation? We spoke at the assembly and he mentioned the gathering. I said I would be pleased to attend."

"Do you not think it odd that, although he has known you for years, this is the first time he has seen fit to invite you to his home?"

Annoyance crackled through her mind. Certainly, she wasn't as elevated a personage as the viscount, but she had a small measure of standing in Gillington society. He needn't talk as though the mere thought of her in a gentleman's house was preposterous.

"I must assure you, my lord, that I did not agitate for this invitation in any way." She knew her voice sounded stiff, but she could not help herself. "The only reason I received an invitation was because Mr. Norris wanted to increase his chances that *you* would accept yours. He thought that if he included me in his select little gathering that I would be so gratified that I would encourage you to attend as well."

"I? I barely know the man." The viscount, as usual, seemed oblivious to her irritation. "I'm pleased to have the opportunity to explore his house, of course, but a bit perplexed as to why he would go to the trouble to invite me there."

For an intelligence agent, Lord Finchwood could be amazingly obtuse. "Do you really not see that you are the most interesting and influential person to arrive in the area for some months?" she asked. "Mr. Norris is a parvenu who loves to mix with the high and mighty. I imagine he has been looking for a way to encourage you to visit since the day your carriage first passed through Gillington. He was just seeking the most advantageous opportunity, and my unusual attendance at the assembly was it. Of course he would use me to get to you."

"You're certain that is all it is? Social ambition?" Her employer's expression remained skeptical.

Charlotte sighed. Despite his stated desire to rely on her local knowledge, he seemed remarkably reluctant to listen to her opinions. "I cannot be certain. I do not possess magical powers that allow me to see into other people's minds. Perhaps that is something they taught you in military intelligence."

He smiled. "*Touché.* I did not mean to be harsh. Go on."

His brief apology mollified her somewhat. "But ambition is characteristic of Mr. Norris. After you left the assembly, I spent a few minutes chatting with Mrs. Kane."

"You mean listening to Mrs. Kane."

"You are in a judgmental mood this evening." She leaned over the table to examine a selection of sweets on a gold-rimmed plate. Such treats were rare frivolities at the academy.

"Sorry. I keep forgetting I am not in London any more, and that cynicism in the country is more of a vice than a virtue." As he said this, the viscount reached for a lemon biscuit, just as Charlotte plucked a gingersnap from the plate. His gloved hand brushed her knuckle, and she snatched her hand back as though she had been scalded by a wayward splash of tea. The last thing she needed was for the viscount to think she was brash. She had already far overstepped the bounds of propriety the last time they had met in this room, when she had boldly taken his hand.

"Returning to the subject of Mrs. Kane," she said quickly, placing the gingersnap on her saucer and dropping her hand into her lap. "I was able to refresh my memory of some useful aspects of Mr. Norris's history by asking Mrs. Kane a few pointed questions. She reminded me that he had once courted the daughter of Sir Robert Sherrill. And I had forgotten that he tried—unsuccessfully—to curry favor with the Earl Crossley, by campaigning for the earl's son when he ran for election as a member of Parliament." She smiled. "Unfortunately, the candidate lost, and that was the end of Mr. Norris's association with the earl."

"And you had forgotten these events? They must have been prime topics of local conversation."

"It's the school. It takes so much of my attention that I often miss much of the affairs of the day." She retrieved her gingersnap and nibbled at one corner. The taste brought back such memories of a carefree childhood that she longed to cram the entire biscuit into her mouth. Of course, that would be gluttonous as well as unladylike.

"A woman who does not consider gossip the lifeblood of her existence?" Lord Finchwood asked, cocking his head to one side. "Truly, Miss Gregory, you are a lady outside the realm of my experience."

What on earth was she to say to that?

Fortunately, the viscount did not seem to require a response, as he returned without pausing to the subject of Mr. Norris. "Have you been able to discover a reason for his ambitions?"

She nodded, then wondered whether it would be wise to elaborate.

"Well?"

It was clearly going to be difficult to be a principled spy. "My parents always strongly impressed on me the dangers of trading hearsay," she said carefully. "False information can cause irreparable damage to sterling reputations, particularly in a village as small as Gillington."

"But you just told me about Mr. Norris's escapades with Sir Robert's daughter and the earl's son." Lord Finchwood frowned.

"Yes, but I had seen him with the young woman in question, and I knew that he had campaigned for the earl's son, although I did not know the reason why." She chewed on her lower lip. "But Mrs. Kane told me something last night that is purely speculation. There may be not one grain of truth about it."

The viscount sighed. "It appears to be just my luck to have selected as my assistant the only woman in England who does not enjoy spreading innuendo." He spread his hands on his knees and leaned toward her over the small table. She tried not to lean away, even though his sudden proximity made it somewhat difficult to concentrate on his words.

"Your principles are admirable, Miss Gregory," he continued. "But if you insist on sticking to them to the letter, you will make our investigation deucedly difficult. I can assure you that anything you say to me will remain in the strictest confidence. We must share all the information we have, however questionable."

"I suppose." Despite her best efforts, she could not help but think that intelligence work, so far, sounded little different from an exchange of *on-dits* on the village green.

"You suppose?" He raised his hands above his knees as if attempting to slap them, then appeared to think better of the impulse. He brought them to rest, instead, on the arms of his chair, but his arms remained taut and his brow furrowed. "Do you realize the seriousness of the affair with which Mr. Norris may be involved? If spies are coming ashore on his property, with his blessing, he could be charged with treason. These are very serious matters, and I don't think this is a time for maidenly scruples."

"Scruples, of course, being things that rarely burden you." The words escaped her before she even had time to think. When his eyebrows drew together and he fixed her with a rather quelling stare, she wished devoutly that she could retract her hasty riposte.

"How, exactly, do you have any knowledge of my scruples—or purported lack of them—if you are as immune to gossip as you like to claim?" His voice was even lower than its usual bass timbre, the words spoken almost in a whisper.

She could feel a blush suffusing her face right to the roots of her hair. "I never claimed to be immune to gossip, my lord. I'm only human, and sometimes Mrs. Kane shared the contents of her London papers with me." She paused. "I remembered you as a boy and I always . . . had an interest in . . . news of you." If temperature were any indication, her cheeks must be scarlet by now.

How had this happened? How had a discussion of Mr. Norris turned so quickly into a conversation about Charlotte's interest in the viscount's affairs? What a disaster this was. Not for the first time, she reflected that she was on foreign ground when it came to sparring with Lord

Finchwood. She had practically confessed to her girl-hood *tendre* for him. How mortifying. He would never consider her a worthy assistant if he suspected she still harbored missish fantasies about him.

"Well, of course, whatever you say," he blustered, his obvious discomfort proof that he had not missed the im-plications of her confession. Charlotte wished she could fade right into the elegant striped upholstery.

"About Mr. Norris, my lord—"

"Yes. Right." He cleared his throat. "Now that we've es-tablished that you are not immune to gossip in a good cause—" his grin was knowing "—shall we agree that un-substantiated rumors about Mr. Norris or anyone else involved in this investigation are fair game for discussion between ourselves?"

She nodded. Thank goodness the conversation had fi-nally moved into less embarrassing waters.

"Good. So tell me what else you learned from Mrs. Kane." He leaned back in his seat and smiled. "Remem-ber, it shall not go further than me."

Charlotte nodded. This all felt so alien, but she had to remember that it was all in service to a higher cause. She had promised to assist Lord Finchwood to the best of her ability, and she would.

"Mrs. Kane had heard, from someone who knows Mr. Norris's banker in Portsmouth, that Mr. Norris has been in dire financial straits for some time," she said in a rush. "Apparently, he invested in some canal scheme that went awry."

The viscount nodded. "That would explain much. A man facing the workhouse is strongly motivated to make choices he might not make otherwise."

Charlotte felt compelled to bolster his concession that Mr. Norris was not evil at heart. "I must admit, it did seem odd to me that Mr. Norris would be involved in anything criminal until I learned of his possible financial problems. He may be a parvenu, but I would never have suspected him of any serious wrongdoing."

"Consider it another lesson in intelligence work," Lord Finchwood said. "For everything there is a reason." He paused to sip his tea before continuing. "Are you ready for further lessons in espionage?"

She laughed to conceal her lingering nervousness. "It feels peculiar to be the student instead of the teacher."

"It feels just as odd to me to be the instructor. Academic studies were never my forte. Fortunately, this sort of instruction involves little philosophy or composition, and a great deal of intuition and wit. Are you ready?" He grinned, and a queer tremor fluttered across Charlotte's skin. He suddenly looked so much more approachable.

More than approachable, she had to concede. His rare smiles bewitched her much as candlelight must dazzle a moth.

Charlotte took a deep breath. She had no business thinking about bewitching smiles. Not only was the thought of anything more than a business relationship between herself and the viscount ridiculous, she was here to do an important job.

"I'm ready, my lord," she said in a steady voice. "I need all the instruction you can give me before this dinner party."

EIGHT

Charlotte took a deep breath and wiped her damp palms on the skirt of her second-best dress. What on earth was she doing here?

She looked around the drawing room. Everyone seemed focused, to a greater or lesser degree, on Eleanor Oakes, who was accompanying herself on the pianoforte as she sang an aria for the entertainment of the assembled company.

Unfortunately, Miss Oakes was more confident than accomplished. It would have been much more entertaining for Charlotte to listen to Sarah and Catherine, two of her more talented students, playing folk songs and encouraging the younger children to join in. As a bonus, she would have been able to catch up on some work at the same time. As the term was drawing to a close, she wanted to spend more time giving her students detailed comments on their papers.

Yet she was sitting here with a forced smile on her face. She stifled a yawn. It looked as though this would be another late evening. Tomorrow would be another exhausting day.

It wouldn't be so bad if she felt her presence at Mr. Norris's party had accomplished anything. But nothing of seeming importance had been discussed at dinner. Even though Lord Finchwood had warned her that people were unlikely to begin divulging state secrets over the dinner table, she had still hoped that she would be able to observe something of import.

Perhaps she just wasn't looking in the right places or asking the right questions. She glanced over at Lord Finchwood, seated on a low settee on the other side of the room. They had purposely avoided sitting together and had exchanged only basic pleasantries over the course of the evening, to Charlotte's relief. It was much easier to concentrate when he wasn't nearby.

She was becoming entirely too fascinated by the viscount, she reflected as Eleanor launched into yet another verse of the song. Despite Charlotte's best efforts, she felt herself slipping into the same sorts of unrealistic daydreams she had entertained as a girl. It was no more likely now than it had been a decade ago to think that anything lasting could develop between herself and Lord Finchwood. Not only did they come from different backgrounds, but they also approached life from different perspectives.

Charlotte's first priorities were her family and her students. The viscount cared more for excitement and intrigue than he did for his own family or his estate, if his frosty relationship with his father was any indication. Once this investigation concluded, he would be back to London before the dust had settled. Back to his glamorous life. Even though Kitty Sherman had been a fiction, Charlotte suspected that there were many other flesh-and-blood women who would be only too happy to see Lord Finchwood return.

That was assuming that this investigation would ever conclude. To Charlotte, their progress seemed almost nonexistent. They had found nothing to link Mr. Norris more closely to the smuggling scheme, and she had seen no sign of the men the viscount had described seeing with Mr. Norris in Portsmouth. Patience had never been one of her strong suits.

Lord Finchwood, on the other hand, did not seem in the least bit perturbed by their lack of progress. If anything, he looked more relaxed than she had seen him in days. His arm was flung across the back of the settee, and his long legs were stretched out in front of him.

He reminded her of a greyhound she had once seen sleeping in the shade near the racecourse of a country fair. Even in repose, the animal had looked taut, graceful and alert, as though just a snap of its owner's fingers would send it bounding across the village green.

At that moment, he turned to say something to a lady sitting next to him. As he did so, he obviously caught sight of Charlotte staring at him. Before she could look away, he shook his head slightly before returning his attention to his companion.

Yet again, she had been caught out. She had to start behaving more circumspectly. She recalled their conversation of a few days ago, when she had admitted that she had kept up with news of his doings in the London newspapers. She could have bitten off her own tongue when she saw the light of amusement in his blue eyes. How pathetic must she look, a sheltered rural schoolmistress fascinated by the rakish doings of a rich man's son?

If she couldn't even hide her thoughts from Lord Finchwood, what hope did she have of hiding her intentions from Mr. Norris and his associates?

"You look worried, Miss Gregory. Are you all right?" asked Mrs. Kane, who was seated beside her. Her friend had been most solicitous all evening. Charlotte knew that most of her interest was genuine, but a tiny bit was prompted by the hope that Charlotte would share details of her relationship to the viscount. Just the news that she had accompanied him in his carriage this evening was enough to raise the older woman's interest.

In truth, Charlotte had been apprehensive about accepting Lord Finchwood's offer of transportation. Not only would it underscore the relationship between them, but it would also mean traveling in close quarters with the viscount. Given how overwhelming she found his presence in a room, she thought that forty minutes in a closed carriage would be inadvisable indeed.

Lord Finchwood had overruled her hesitation, however.

"Everyone knows that you and I are working together, and that you have no personal means of transport," he had said as they had discussed the matter in the churchyard on Sunday in low tones. "It would look deuced odd for you to be scurrying about the village trying to arrange a ride, when I have a perfectly fine carriage and will pass right by the academy on my way to Cliffholme. Besides, it will give us an excellent chance to refine the elements of our approach without fear that my father's footmen will overhear."

"What about your coachman?"

Lord Finchwood had grinned. "Pains me to say it, because Jenks is devoted, but truth to tell, he's not terribly quick. He barely listens to *me* unless I make a concerted effort to get his attention. That would have made him a wretched agent, but it's an excellent quality in a coachman."

And, despite Charlotte's fears, the trip to Cliffholme had not been as fraught with tension as she had feared it might be. In fact, once she was firmly ensconced in one corner of the carriage, her skirt spread wide about her and her reticule on the floor between herself and the viscount, she had rather enjoyed herself. After discussing their strategies for uncovering useful information about Norris, Lord Finchwood had regaled her with a series of funny stories about his life in London. She sensed he was censoring some of the more ribald elements for her benefit, which both amused and touched her.

It was only when she had accidentally brushed against him as she alighted from the carriage that she had felt any discomfort. Well, discomfort was not the precise word.

"Miss Gregory?" Mrs. Kane's voice was sharp. With a start, Charlotte realized that she had not answered her friend's polite enquiry.

"I am fine, thank you for asking," she said, turning to look the older woman in the eye. "I am just a bit tired."

"Would you like to go home? I could offer you a ride in my carriage, if you don't want to bother Lord Finchwood."

"No!" Charlotte exclaimed with a bit more force than was necessary. Her friend blinked.

"No, I mean, I wouldn't want you to leave early on my behalf. And it isn't often I get the opportunity to attend such an event, so I am loath to cut my time short."

Mrs. Kane, satisfied, returned her attention to Miss Oakes's musical endeavors.

Charlotte bit her lip. She had to be more careful and avoid drawing attention to herself. If Mrs. Kane—a dear soul, but not known for her powers of observation—had noticed that Charlotte looked perturbed, her emotions must be visible to others in the room as well.

Bother. She knew she should take a page from Lord Finchwood's book and simply relax, but she couldn't. She was convinced people were watching her, eager to find some way to point out that she was at this elegant event under false pretenses and would be much more at home among her books and papers. What if she ruined Lord Finchwood's investigation entirely? She was no spy. Why had she ever thought she could do this?

She took another deep breath. Perhaps she should

approach this the way she taught her students to approach projects that unnerved them: stop thinking about the task for a few minutes, and then return to it with a fresh perspective.

Thus resolved, she stood and repaired to the water closet, as much to find a quiet place to think as for any other reason. On her way down the corridor, still lost in thought, she almost collided with a woman wearing a low-cut blue velvet gown, complemented by winking diamonds at her ears and throat. Only by flattening herself against the wall did Charlotte avoid bumping into the other woman, who seemed as distracted as she.

"I'm sorry!" Charlotte exclaimed as the lady stumbled. "I should have been looking where I was going."

"Du . . . no, please, it was my fault," the elegant guest replied. Charlotte wasn't sure, but she thought she detected a slight accent in the woman's voice.

Charlotte observed her more closely. She was short, with a mass of dark curls and wide-set brown eyes. Charlotte was certain she had not been at the dinner table, nor among the number of other guests who had arrived after dinner to enjoy the entertainment. Charlotte would have remembered someone as fashionable as she.

Without another word, the woman slipped past Charlotte and continued along the corridor.

Quickly, Charlotte slipped into a doorway that led into what appeared to be a small office. But instead of closing the door completely, she left it slightly open and peered through the gap.

To her surprise, the stranger did not rejoin the group in the drawing room. Instead, she cast a glance behind her—Charlotte slipped even further into the shadows of her hiding place—and then turned into a side corridor Charlotte had not noticed before.

Charlotte waited a moment or two, then quietly slipped out of the office and retraced her steps. Trying her best to appear casual, in case a servant or another guest should spot her, she strolled by the side passage just in time to see the stranger open a door at the far end. A gust of damp air blew down the short corridor as the woman slipped out into the rainy June night.

It seemed odd that the dark-haired lady had asked the butler for neither cloak nor umbrella, and that she was leaving alone. Cautiously, Charlotte followed her quarry's footsteps to the plain wooden door. Holding her breath, she cracked the door open, praying that the stranger had not stopped on the other side.

She had not. In fact, the woman was running away from the house as fast as her elegant dress likely allowed.

Charlotte shivered, and not only because of the drops of rain pelting her bare arms. Something was most certainly untoward here.

Should she go back and find Lord Finchwood? She had no idea how she would extract him from the gathering without drawing attention. And by the time they returned, the woman would in all likelihood have disappeared.

Charlotte's heartbeat was thudding in her ears as she opened the door all the way and stepped outside. If her palms had been damp before, they were dripping now, and her breath rasped against the back of her throat.

With effort, she quelled her fears. It was much like the first day she had stood up in front of a classroom of boisterous students. Believing she could do something was the most important step she could take toward actually doing it.

Thanking Providence that she had worn a dark gown and that the night was moonless, she stepped away from the door and onto the lush lawn that surrounded Cliffholme. She would have to move quickly to keep up with the stranger, who had already crossed most of the green expanse.

Charlotte ran as fast as she could, her progress impeded by her damp skirt. As she slid on the slick grass, she cursed the fashionable slippers Jane Carter had insisted on lending to her, and wished she had worn her sensible half boots instead.

The rain was coming down harder now, pelting against her forearms like cold, tiny nails. She shivered as she reached a tree and leaned against it to catch her breath, keeping the other woman in sight as she did so.

The Frenchwoman—for indeed, Charlotte had assumed she was French—reached the road. Charlotte expected her to turn left, which would take her back to Gillington. Instead, she turned right, toward the sea.

Charlotte moved out from behind the tree and ran toward the edge of the lawn. Just as she was looking for the break in the hedge that the Frenchwoman must have used to gain access to the road, she felt a strong hand on her arm. Another hand covered her mouth to stifle the startled cry on her lips.

"What are you doing out here alone? Are you deranged?" Lord Finchwood's familiar voice whispered close to her ear.

She almost sagged against him with relief. Although only his hands were touching her, she could feel the heat from his body behind her through the thin, wet silk of her dress, and she knew he was close enough that she could lean back against him. For one wild moment, she entertained the thought of doing just that. Of sinking back against that broad chest. Of leaning her head against his shoulder.

Fortunately, at the last moment, common sense prevailed. She wrenched herself out of his hands and turned to face him.

"I'm doing the job you hired me to do," she muttered. She hoped her brusque tone would conceal the discomposure she felt at their closeness. "And if we don't hurry, we will lose sight of her entirely."

"Who?"

Charlotte pointed toward the road, where it was just possible to make out a figure scurrying along the verge. "I bumped into her in the corridor. She was not a party guest, and I believe she was French. She left by a side door with no cloak or umbrella, which seemed odd. So I followed her."

Lord Finchwood pushed a lock of rain-damp hair from his forehead as he looked in the direction Charlotte indicated. "What did she look like?"

Briefly, Charlotte described her. He nodded, as if the information fit perfectly into some puzzle he was constructing in his mind's eye. She would have to ask him about it later.

"Well done," he said with a quick smile. "I shall take over from here."

Something in his peremptory tone rankled Charlotte. Even though she knew he was being sensible, she heard herself saying, "I will come with you."

He shook his head, but he wasn't looking at her. His attention was focused on the rapidly retreating woman. "Don't be foolish. One can move more quickly than two. And I can't keep an eye on you and on this stranger at the same time."

"I don't need to be minded like a child." A gust of wind rustled the hedge, and she shivered.

He turned and raised his eyebrows. "Really? Right now, you're behaving like one. You're likely to catch a fever out here in the rain, and then what use will you be to me? Please, Miss Gregory, go back inside."

As he spoke, he began shrugging out of the greatcoat he wore over his evening clothes. "I think you need this more than I do," he said, pulling it off his shoulders and draping it about her. It was warm. But more than that, it gave off a comforting fragrance of horses, leather and soap. Suddenly, she felt somewhat as she had when she had imbibed a little too much sherry at Eliza's wedding. Lightheaded and flustered.

"I suggest that you go to the barn or somewhere else inconspicuous until you can dry off, to avoid raising suspicions about where you have been. You can leave my coat with Jenks. He won't tell anyone."

Mulishly, she resisted. How was she to help him if he did not let her learn? She moved toward the hedge and began looking for the break.

With one smooth movement, he vaulted the low hedge and turned to face her. "Do you understand? I mean no offence, but you will truly slow me down. You are not dressed for reconnaissance work. I am."

Already, he was striding away from her. He turned back to add one more comment. "We have no idea where this woman is heading, or why, or who might be waiting for her when she gets there. In my experience, people with a fondness for clandestine meetings often show a marked predilection for firearms as well."

Charlotte had thought her skin felt cold and clammy before. At his words, however, a chill deeper than the wind and rain took hold of her.

"Then you shouldn't follow her either."

He shrugged. "I've done it before." Then he reached into his pocket and withdrew something that shone dully even in the meager light. "And, unlike you, I can defend myself."

She was so shocked at the sight of the small gun in his hand that she was momentarily speechless. She had been afraid when she left the house, but her fear had revolved mostly around being detected. Not once had she been seriously afraid for her physical safety.

"Go inside, and ask Mrs. Kane to bring you home,"

Lord Finchwood said, his face intent. "I do not want any harm to you on my conscience."

"But what about you?" As she realized that he was in serious danger, her heart contracted with panic. She should have just stayed inside the house and let the wretched Frenchwoman go.

"This is my job." He looked behind him. "I don't have time to debate the finer points of intelligence work with you. You can either stand out here and develop a fever, or you can go inside and continue to be alert for information we need. Please give Norris my regrets, and ask Jenks to wait for me at the end of the lane."

She knew he was being logical, and she felt abashed at keeping him from his work. "Be careful," she felt compelled to add as he turned away.

"I always am," he said, his reply almost lost on the wind. "If I weren't, I'd have been dead and buried years ago in Spain."

Without a backward glance, he sprinted across the road, where the shadows cast by the trees would make him invisible to the woman now far ahead of him on the road. With graceful, loping strides, he began diminishing the distance between himself and his quarry.

Despite the drenching rain, Charlotte watched the viscount until his dark form disappeared over a small rise. Perhaps he should have hired a man for this job after all, Charlotte thought as she turned back toward Cliffholme—someone he did not feel he had to shelter like a mother hen. Her stomach twisted as she thought of him facing armed traitors alone.

Finch glanced behind him. Thank heavens. Miss Gregory was finally making her way back toward the barn. Stubborn woman.

He allowed himself a brief sigh of relief before turning his attention back to the road. The unidentified woman, who was likely one of the two supposed Cyprians he'd seen entering the warehouse in Portsmouth, had almost reached a fork near the end of the road. From his reconnaissance ride here earlier in the week, Finch knew that the shore lay about a quarter mile from the divide. As he expected, she took the right fork, which led toward the coast.

The rain had let up slightly, giving him a better view of the countryside. He spotted a sturdy-looking oak on the small ridge that marked the point where pastureland gave way to coast. Despite what he had told Miss Gregory, he had no intention of coming face to face with Norris's cronies if he could help it. Playing the hero was rarely a wise choice in intelligence work. Much better to hide in the shadows and live to work again the next day.

His once-polished Hessians squelched in mud up to the ankles as he entered what appeared to be an empty cow pasture. The wind was sharper, now that he had left the shelter of the trees that lined the road. He thought briefly of his greatcoat, which had served him well on many a similar night in northern Spain. But he was glad he had given it to Miss Gregory.

She had courage, he had to give her that. Not as much sense as he would have liked, but she would be an ally he could trust to act with honor if the occasion ever required it. He sensed the same selflessness in her that he had discovered in David Tate.

With luck, that selflessness wouldn't lead her to the same end Tate had met. Closing his eyes, Finch willed away the memory of his fellow spy's death at the hands of a French patrol. Just because he hadn't been able to prevent his friend's capture did not mean that he would be unable to protect Miss Gregory from harm. He had to keep her safe, as he didn't think he could live with himself if she were endangered.

He shivered, and it wasn't due just to the gust of wind that sliced through his damp shirt and jacket. His concern for Miss Gregory was understandable, but troubling. Understandable because it was solely due to him that she was involved in this investigation at all. Troubling because agents could not afford to become too attached to their colleagues. Intelligence work required focus. If he allowed unreasonable concern for his assistant's welfare to cloud his judgment, he could jeopardize both Miss Gregory and their assignment.

A flash of lightning cracked the sky and Finch threw himself down behind a box hedge. He would stick out like an archery target, exposed on the ridge in the bright light. As he dropped to the ground, he extended both hands in front of him to break his fall. His right hand crumpled under him and he twisted to one side.

Damn. It looked as though he would never learn not to put any pressure on it. Wincing, he sat up and shook out the gnarled hand. No serious damage done, but it throbbed.

There was another reason to avoid meeting the suspicious Frenchwoman face to face. He had spent hours teaching himself to fire a pistol with his left hand, and he was an adequate shot. But if he encountered a situation requiring any dexterity, he would be in serious trouble. He just prayed that if he ever found himself in such a position, his quarry would be unaware that he was shooting with his weak hand.

He crawled on hands and knees behind the box hedge to cover the remaining couple of hundred feet to the tree. Scaling the wet bark was not a simple matter in the dark, but Finch's years of pillaging apple orchards as a child finally came in useful. Within five minutes, he was wedged between two sturdy limbs, well hidden by leaves. He pulled two flexible branches apart and peered between them.

At first, he saw nothing, not even the mysterious Frenchwoman. He scanned the beach, separating it mentally into quadrants. Finally, he spotted a small rowboat emerging from a sheltered cove. Only an insane person—or a criminal—would be out in such a small craft on a night like this.

Two criminals, actually. The person in the bow was small. Likely the woman who had run from Norris's house. The rower in the stern was larger.

Damn the rain. He could not tell if either of them was among the group he had followed in Portsmouth. If he were to wager, he would guess that the man in the back was Martin, the ex-sailor; St. Amour had been a slight man, and the rower looked burly. But at this distance, it was almost impossible to tell anything.

Finch kicked his boot against the tree in frustration. If he had been able to get here a few minutes earlier, he might have overheard something useful. Instead, he had wasted precious minutes standing in the rain arguing with Miss Gregory.

Perhaps it had been a mistake to hire her after all. He had never worked with a woman as a partner. In his experience, women were more use as sources than as colleagues. And this particular woman was too fond of speaking her own mind. That alone would be a hindrance. He has fully expected her to defer to his experience.

The fact that she had looked more appealing than she ought to have, standing in the rain, hadn't helped him argue logically, either. There was a very good reason women carried umbrellas and wore warm coats when they gadded about in the rain, in Finch's opinion. The results if they did not left far too little to their companions' imagination. That dress had clung to her as though it were made of cobwebs. He had noted her pleasing curves before but had tried to pay them as little heed as possible. Dripping wet, she had presented a spectacle that was hard to ignore. His insistence that she take his coat had not been entirely selfless.

Yes, Finch was definitely starting to question his wisdom in hiring Miss Gregory.

But he had to give credit where credit was due. If it hadn't been for her, he would be nosing around—probably fruitlessly—in Norris's barn. That's where he had been when he spotted her dashing across the lawn. At least now he knew what point on the beach the conspirators were using as a landing spot. In daylight, when the weather cleared, he would make his way back to the shore and see whether he could uncover anything incriminating in the cove.

He watched the boat for a few more minutes until it was little more than a speck on the dark waves. After scanning the beach once more to make sure no one else was about, he shinnied back down the tree.

Once back on the ground, he surveyed his clothing. A ragged tear drooped from one knee of his trousers, and his jacket was studded with leaves and twigs. He was clotted with mud from head to toe. If only the belles of London could see him now.

Chuckling at the thought, he squished across the swampy pasture and climbed over a stile. As he stepped down on the other side, a piece of paper impaled on a thorn bush caught his eye. He bent down and worked it free.

It was torn and damp, but he could just make out the words "*contrôlée*" and "*cognac.*" A French brandy label. He suppressed a wave of envy as he stuffed it into the pocket of his trousers. To be drinking cognac instead of Italian grappa would be a treat indeed. The label was just another bit of evidence showing that Norris was engaged in smuggling.

The rain had decreased to a light patter. He hoped Miss Gregory had remembered to leave his greatcoat with Jenks. Once inside the closed carriage, he would be able to exchange his drenched jacket and shirt for the coat. Fortunately, his coachman would ask no questions. Jenks was a man of few words and meager intelligence. For those reasons, he would have made a poor assistant, but he made an excellent coachman.

Miss Gregory, on the other hand, could be trained to become a useful assistant, if he could just curb her tendency to question his decisions. She had the intelligence, the tenacity and the thirst for justice one needed to do the job. Maybe he should suggest a change of occupation. His grin widened. Miss Gregory was far too committed to hearth and home for the life of an intelligence agent. Just yesterday she had told him that she had never even ventured outside Hampshire. Her small circle here provided all she desired.

In an odd way, he envied her.

He turned a bend in the road and Cliffholme came into view. At the end of the lane was his carriage. He offered up a silent thanks to Providence.

Just the sight of the carriage made him realize how chilled he was. The thought of his greatcoat, damp as it probably was, spurred him to trot the last few hundred feet to the barouche. He nodded to Jenks, who was huddled under an enormous umbrella atop the coachman's box.

"Yer lordship," Jenks began, but Finch barely heard him. He'd already wrenched open the door and was shrugging out of his soggy jacket. He jumped into the carriage and promptly collided with a damp bundle wrapped in a large, plain towel.

The bundle turned out to be Miss Gregory, whom he appeared to have awakened from a sound sleep.

"Did no one ever tell you to look before you leap, Lord Finchwood?" she said, rubbing her shin where his boot had collided with it.

"My apologies, Miss Gregory. But I had no idea you would be in here." He was suddenly conscious of his drenched, clinging shirt. Would he look as exposed as she had earlier? Swiftly, he reached for his jacket.

"Good heavens, don't put that sodden thing back on!" She reached behind him to close the door. Finch heard Jenks cluck to the horses, and the barouche lurched into motion.

She handed him a towel. "Do dry off, then exchange your shirt for your greatcoat. It isn't completely dry, but it is much more serviceable than the clothes you are wearing."

"What are you doing here? And where did you get the towels?"

"When I got back to the barn, it became quite apparent that I could not rejoin the party without raising intense suspicion. Even if I could get completely dry—and that seemed doubtful—my coiffeur looks like a bird's nest."

For the first time, he looked closely at her hair. It was difficult to see in the dim light, but he thought it looked rather fetching, although he had to concede that it wasn't appropriate for a drawing room. One long auburn curl had come loose and trailed down her back, and the tight cap of curls around her face was now disheveled.

He wondered what she would look like with her hair completely undone. The image that filled his mind had little to do with the proper, sober image he associated with Miss Gregory. Dash it, he *had* to stop letting his mind wander in this manner.

"I was sure there would be pointed questions about my appearance, and I have no skill in prevarication," she said. He gave silent thanks that one of them, at least, was focusing on the matter at hand.

"Drawing attention to myself seemed like the worst

thing I could do," Miss Gregory continued. "So I simply thought it wise to leave a note with a footman, saying that I was feeling ill and that you had kindly offered to drive me home. Since I had already told Mrs. Kane that I was tired, it seemed like the most plausible excuse." She paused. "Besides, I knew I would not sleep tonight until I was certain you had returned safely."

He declined to comment on that. It had been so long since someone had cared about his whereabouts, other than in a strictly professional capacity, that he was not sure how to respond. Instead, he asked, "But what about the towels?"

Her smile was sheepish. "I came in the same side door through which I had left and crept up the servants' stairs. It did not take much hunting to find a well-stocked linen cupboard."

He felt a matching smile crease his own face. "But Miss Gregory, stealing is a sin."

"But I am certain Mr. Norris would have offered the towels if I had asked him. In a way, I was doing him a favor. By helping myself, I made certain that he would not miss a note of Miss Oakes's performance."

Finch's laugh stretched right down into his belly. "I doubt he would thank you."

"Some people have no manners."

He laughed again. "Did anyone ever tell you that you have a lovely, but dormant, sense of humor?"

She fixed him with her best schoolmistress stare. "Did anyone ever tell you that you are likely to catch a dreadful cold—or something worse—if you sit around in sopping clothes?"

"I did worse in Spain."

"I'm sure you did, but there's no need to be a martyr tonight. Here's a towel. Your greatcoat is on the bench beside you."

So it was. But a sticky problem presented itself.

"Miss Gregory, I cannot possibly change my clothes in front of you."

She looked out the window. In the darkness, he couldn't be sure, but he'd be willing to wager a tidy sum that she was blushing. He wished he could see it.

"I hardly think that signifies. I can hardly let you sit and shiver just to protect my sensibilities." She turned back toward him. "I shall simply close my eyes, and you can tell me when you are respectable again."

"But Miss Gregory—"

"Earlier this evening, you set your foot down and ordered me back to the house. Now it is my turn to get my way."

"But you did not obey those orders."

"So you can show that you're the better man. I'm closing my eyes now. Be sensible, for heaven's sake."

She screwed up her eyes theatrically and crossed her arms over her chest.

There was no doubt about it. The woman was stubborn.

He sighed. It would be more comfortable, he had to admit, to be wearing a dry coat. Quickly, he undid the buttons at his throat and wrists, and tugged the hem of his shirt out of his waistband.

He would leave his trousers on. There were some points past which even a rake did not go.

As he pulled the shirt over his head, he cast a covert glance at Miss Gregory though the neck of the garment. To his intense amusement, she had cracked one eye open and was observing him through lowered lashes.

It appeared that even schoolmistresses and vicars' daughters had a curious streak.

With difficulty, he resisted the strong temptation to preen. Being the subject of her observation was strangely invigorating. For a brief moment, he wished they were different people, in different circumstances. For an even shorter moment, he permitted himself to wonder what it would be like to observe Miss Gregory if she were the one changing into dry clothes, and not the other way around. A lightning bolt of heat shot through him at the idea.

This train of thought was preposterous, he told himself. In London, he could choose from countless widows and actresses whose charms and attentions would come with none of the complications that would ensue if he acted on this unseemly attraction to his assistant. He needed to finish this investigation and return to Town as quickly as possible, and to stop allowing his imagination to run rampant. He was eight-and-twenty, for heaven's sake, not some randy schoolboy.

Quickly, he dried his chest and arms and pulled on his coat. For good measure, he dug a muffler out of an inside pocket and wrapped it around his throat, stuffing the ends carefully into the collar of the coat. Finally, he took the towel and vigorously rubbed his hair.

"I am quite presentable now, Miss Gregory," he said, his voice sounding raspy even in his own ears.

Slowly, she opened one eye, then both. "Good. I would hate to see you shivering all the way home." She smoothed her hands down the front of her skirt, then grimaced and reached for the other towel. "Still damp," she explained.

"You could always borrow—" He had been about to offer her his coat, but she interrupted.

"I'm fine, truly. So tell me—did you learn anything interesting about the stranger?"

Quickly, he summarized what he had seen. She nodded.

"There are a lot of fishing boats along that stretch of the coast, and even a small boat abroad at night might not raise suspicion." She frowned. "If Mr. Norris is smug-

gling, do you think he is keeping all the liquor for himself?"

Finch shook his head. "Particularly if he is in financial
straits, as we suspect, he is likely selling it to someone
with exotic thirsts and blunt to spare. Can you think of
anyone who fits that description?"

"Besides you? I suspect you have a rather wide knowledge of intoxicants." Her smile removed any sting he
might have imputed to her words.

He grinned in return. "I doubt Mr. Norris is about to
approach me to inquire as to whether I'd like a case of
cognac. Anyone he does sell to is probably privy to the
scheme."

"Let me give it some thought. Perhaps some subtle
questions among my older students may yield something
interesting."

"What sort of school are you running, Miss Gregory?
Are you telling me that girls of fifteen are indulging in
a few glasses of wine before retiring for the evening?"

"It might calm them down at night," she said, winding
her fingers absently through her disheveled hair as if in
thought. Her eyes sparked with mischief in the light of a
small candle burning in a holder beside the door. "Perhaps it's something I should consider. But, no, I meant
that perhaps their parents, or friends of their parents,
have liquor cabinets that are particularly well stocked."

"How would you discern this?"

"I haven't the faintest idea." She concealed a yawn behind her hand. "But let me think about it. I've wormed
tougher secrets out of my girls before."

He had no doubt that she had. The more he grew to
know Miss Gregory, the more he realized that she was
difficult to resist when she put her mind to something.

So how was he going to keep her from following him
the next time he headed into a dangerous situation? He
suspected that he'd be placed in that situation sooner

rather than later. With so much on the line—money, liquor, reputation, their necks—the conspirators would be bound to take desperate actions. Finch would be right in the line of fire when they did, but he'd be damned if he'd bring Miss Gregory into it with him.

"Miss Gregory—" he began, then stopped. In the few seconds that had elapsed since she finished speaking, his assistant had fallen fast asleep. She leaned against the wall of the carriage, one hand curled beneath her ear.

He suppressed an urge to brush away a stray curl that was hanging in her eyes.

For the first time since he'd known her, the formidable Miss Gregory looked vulnerable. Seeing her thus made him realize that some small, secret part of him had always been slightly awed by her, just as he had always regarded his tutors and dons with a unique respect. Seeing her thus also increased his resolve to keep her far from the most dangerous aspects of this investigation.

As the carriage creaked along the road, he set his mind toward that task.

NINE

Charlotte shifted slightly in her chair to adjust her skirt, which had become twisted beneath her. It was a relief to be back at the academy, and back in her usual simple garb. Enjoyable as it had been to put on a fine gown for dinner at Mr. Norris's home the other night, she felt much more herself in plain clothing. She had spent the evening at Cliffholme half distracted, fretting that her neckline was too low or her skirts too high. At least she had until she ran out into the rain. After that, she had looked like a wet kitten and had ceased to worry about appearing the fashion plate.

She shuddered as she realized how she must have appeared to Lord Finchwood. Accustomed as he was to being surrounded by grand London ladies, he must have thought she looked the perfect country mouse.

He, on the other hand, had cut an undeniable swath through the crowd. Women's eyes had followed him wherever he walked. And his good looks were based on much more than fine tailoring, she thought with a guilty smile. She hadn't been able to see much in the dark of the carriage when he exchanged his damp shirt for his greatcoat, but what she had seen had been most intriguing. A flash of broad shoulders. A dusting of curly hair on a broad chest.

Things she had no right to see.

But since it seemed unlikely she would have few similar chances, with Lord Finchwood or any other man, the temptation had been far too great to resist. Thank goodness the carriage had been so dim. The viscount could not possibly have seen her observing him. And she couldn't say she was sorry she had broken her promise not to look. She suspected the viscount wasn't exactly shy. So no one had been harmed. And she hadn't been so entertained in months.

Her skin tingled as though a cool breeze had blown over it, even though the day was warm and close.

With a sigh, she refocused her attention on the accounts book. She was adding up the income from the eggs laid by the school's new chickens when Jane Carter stuck her head in the door. "Charlotte, I'm sorry to disturb you, but are you ready to take over the history class now?"

Charlotte glanced at the small carriage clock on the mantel. "Good heavens, of course! I completely lost track of time. You need to make haste if you are to be home before nightfall to help prepare for your sister's wedding." She smiled as she stood up from her desk. "Are you ready?"

"Yes. My satchel is packed, and my father's carriage is already out front."

Charlotte hugged her assistant. "You have been such a help to me over the last few weeks—well, ever since I hired you, but especially lately. Go and enjoy the festivities, and wish Maria every happiness for me."

"I will." She inclined her head in the direction of the main classroom. "I have given the older ones a section of Pliny to translate, and Anne Symes is listening to the younger ones read aloud, but those activities won't keep them occupied for long. I estimate it will be fifteen minutes at most before someone gets bored."

Charlotte grinned. "Can't say as I blame them. I always disliked Pliny, myself. Pompous old bore."

Jane was already hurrying toward the front door. "Thank you for letting me leave early!" she cried as she went out.

Charlotte cocked an ear to the parlor, but heard no signs of incipient insurrection. She should be able to take a minute or two just to finish adding up the egg money before facing the history lesson.

She had just finished her task and closed the accounts book when a rap at the window startled her. Looking out, she nearly fainted when she spotted Lord Finchwood standing knee deep in delphiniums and staring in at her, a rakish grin on his face.

Fortunately, he was wearing both a shirt and a jacket.

She darted toward the door at the far side of the office. "What on earth are you doing here?" she whispered as she ushered him in.

"I had some things I needed to discuss with you, and I didn't think it wise to wait until next week." He removed his hat and stepped further into the room, which suddenly seemed cramped and poor.

"Well, this isn't an opportune time. I have to teach a lesson."

He frowned. "But you looked to be doing paperwork."

"I was just finishing one last task before heading into the classroom."

"Surely you can take a few more minutes to discuss this with me?"

She moved to the main door of her office and cocked an ear for signs of trouble in the parlor on the other side of the house. She heard a few muted giggles. Something thudded as it hit the floor.

"Unfortunately, I cannot. I'm sorry, my lord, but you will just have to come back another time."

His glare reminded her for all the world of Margaret Hitchens, a particularly recalcitrant nine-year-old who had joined the school this fall. Charlotte suspected that, like Margaret, Lord Finchwood was not used to having his wishes questioned or thwarted.

Oh well.

A squeal echoed across the small foyer that separated the parlor from Charlotte's office.

"It is your choice," she said. "You can let me go to my girls, or you can attempt to conduct your business with me while the school burns down around our heads."

He looked startled, and she relented.

"Well, that's not highly likely, but it's possible. One of the younger girls has a disturbing fascination with candles."

"How long will the lesson take?"

She glanced at the mantel clock. "About half an hour. It is the last session of the day. When we're done, my junior assistant will supervise the girls outside in the garden. I always try to ensure they have some time outdoors every day, particularly when the weather is nice." Another peal of laughter filtered down from the parlor.

"Why don't I wait until you're done, and we can have our discussion when the girls are in the garden?" he suggested. "I can watch from the back of the room while you work."

Charlotte blinked. She could think of nothing that would make her more nervous. "It might seem highly irregular. How will I explain your presence to the students?"

"Say I am here to supervise the education of the Dean girls. It seemed to cause you a great deal of distress that their parents did not inspect the school in advance. I shall do it for them. I doubt any of the girls will question it."

He was right of course. The story was watertight, as she always encouraged the girls' parents to visit the academy whenever they wished. The only reason to deny him was that she would barely be able to concentrate on the logistics of the battle of Trafalgar.

Her heart sank. Not only was he to watch her teach,

but he was also to watch her teach a subject about which she felt less than confident and about which he would know much more. After he had teased her about her plans to teach the strategy of the Punic Wars, she had done her best to educate herself on tactics currently in use on the Continent, and that was the course of instruction she had been pursuing with the girls since yesterday. Why could it not have been a class on poetry or botany? Even politics would have been much more palatable than military strategy.

But they had promised Anne to cover the topic before the end of the school year, and Jane had already told the students that it would be the next lesson.

Charlotte squared her shoulders. She and Jane had prepared this lesson carefully, and she had reasonable intelligence and teaching skills. She could do this, as long as Lord Finchwood did nothing to distract her.

"Very well, then. I'm certain you will be bored to pieces. Do feel free to come back to my office if you like. I have a few magazines on the shelf over there that may amuse you while you await my return."

"Oh, I doubt I'll get bored." His eyes snapped with mischief. She devoutly hoped he wasn't planning anything disruptive. Her students didn't need any encouragement in that area.

She walked past him, motioning for him to follow. As she crossed the hall, she could hear the soles of his boots clicking on the cracked marble floor of the foyer behind her.

The noise in the classroom had increased substantially in the few minutes Charlotte had spent debating with Lord Finchwood. It subsided to a dull murmur when she entered. Anne signaled Hannah to stop reading aloud, and both girls took their seats. When the viscount entered the parlor a moment later and leaned up against the small doorframe, the room became completely silent.

Well, peace and quiet was an unexpected bonus. She supposed the viscount's presence here would not be completely without advantages.

Charlotte cleared her throat. "Some of you already know our guest, Lord Finchwood." The few girls who weren't already gazing with rapt eyes toward the back of the room turned to look. She took a deep breath. What she wasn't about to say wasn't a falsehood, exactly. It just wasn't the main truth. "He is a friend of the Dean family, and he is visiting today to see how our little school works. We hope he will give us a glowing report."

"Of that I have no doubt," he replied, an odd light in his eyes.

She turned her attention back to the far less intimidating sea of young female faces. "Before we begin, we'll review the lesson from yesterday. We'll need those facts close to the top of our heads before we discuss the battle of Trafalgar."

The girls nodded and looked up at her expectantly, their hands in their laps.

"Who restarted the naval blockade of France in 1803?"

"Vice-Admiral Cornwallis," the girls chorused.

"Who became prime minister of Britain in 1804?"

"William Pitt."

Charlotte spent another few minutes on a dry recitation of names and dates. This was her least favorite aspect of teaching, and she knew the students disliked it as well. But it was essential to ensure they had the facts well ordered in their heads. Without facts, an intelligent discussion of events was impossible.

Finally, the review was over and she moved into a more substantive discussion of the battle of Trafalgar. From time to time, she glanced at her notes, placed in an inconspicuous place on a small Sheraton desk. She felt Lord Finchwood's gaze on her like a beam of sunlight.

She frowned. He couldn't just stare at her throughout

the whole lesson. The girls would notice. More to the point, Charlotte doubted whether she could get through an entire half hour on the history of the battle of Trafalgar with him watching her every move.

"Admiral Nelson used a cunning tactic to trick the French and Spanish commanders," she said. This much she remembered hearing about, even though she had only been sixteen at the time of the battle. "He divided his fleet in two. At the helm of the *Victory*, he led half the ships, while Cuthbert Collingwood led the other ships from the *Royal Sovereign.*"

The girls nodded, but several of the older ones were much more interested in sneaking glances at the viscount than in any discussion of Nelson's military genius.

"This tactic allowed the British ships to weave among the enemy vessels, creating havoc," she added.

"Nelson had an evocative name for it," Lord Finchwood's deep voice rumbled. Instantly, every girl's head swiveled to the back of the room.

"He called it 'pell-mell warfare,' which is a pretty good description of any kind of military engagement."

"Are you a war hero, Lord Finchwood?" Hannah asked in a breathless voice.

He chuckled. "No. I went to war, but aside from Admiral Nelson, there aren't many heroes in a war."

"What was it like?" another girl piped up. "Did you see Napoleon?"

He shook his head. "No, but I did meet the Duke of Wellington several times. There's another hero. He was the leader of our army in Spain."

"*I* know who the Duke of Wellington is," Hannah said proudly. "He's the man they named the boots after."

Some of the girls laughed, but the viscount looked the small girl straight in the eye. "You're exactly right. And fine boots they are, too." He held up his own booted foot as an example. "These ones served me well for many months in Spain." He looked over at Charlotte. "But I fear I'm interrupting your lesson."

Charlotte shook her head. She'd seen the light of interest in the girls' eyes at the opportunity to talk to a real war veteran. They could always finish their discussion of Trafalgar another day. Besides, the viscount seemed to be enjoying himself, and it was much simpler to let him deal with the girls than to try to hold their attention with him in the room. He had managed to hold his own among Napoleon's agents in Spain, but how would he fare in a room of thirty girls for almost half an hour? Even though she knew it was mischievous, Charlotte couldn't wait to find out.

"I think you will bring a new perspective to the students." She smiled as she saw a look of uncertainty flash in his eyes. So even the ever-confident Lord Finchwood had an Achilles heel?

Good.

"Come up to the front of the room, Lord Finchwood," she said, moving aside and taking a chair to give him the floor. "How fortuitous that you decided to join us today."

His look as he came to the front of the room could have split wood. By the time he had turned to the students, however, he had schooled his face into a bland expression.

As Finch looked out over the sea of expectant faces, he could have cheerfully ripped out his own tongue. Why hadn't he simply sat in Miss Gregory's office until she returned?

Well, the answer to that question was simple. He had been curious to see her at work. Interestingly, she was nothing like the severe schoolmasters he remembered from his youth. She encouraged the girls, smiled at their answers, and freely admitted when she didn't know the answer to a query. Here, in her own milieu, she seemed more relaxed than she had either at his home or at the Norris party. On the other hand, he hadn't felt this nervous since he had galloped toward the breach in the town walls at Badajoz.

What had possessed him to chime in with that comment about pell-mell warfare?

Whatever it was, it had landed him here, and he had to make the best of it. His experience of girls in the schoolroom was limited. To be honest, it was nonexistent.

And aside from that strange, dreamlike evening when he had told Miss Gregory about Badajoz, he had not discussed the campaign once since he had returned to England. He hated talking about the war.

He wondered how quickly he could beat a retreat.

The girls looked up at him, faces shining with anticipation. Off to the side of the room, he could see Miss Gregory smirking.

Smirking. At *him.*

Finch looked directly at the young minx who had made the comment about Wellington's boots and tried his best to appear serious. She gave him a gap-toothed smile.

Perhaps seriousness wasn't the correct approach. "What would you like to know?" he asked, turning his palms upward in surrender.

"Was the war exciting?" asked one of the smaller girls. "Nothing ever happens in Hampshire. I imagine that something happens all the time in Spain."

He grinned. "I thought that too, when I joined up. And yes, it was exciting. I met men from all over England. All over Europe, in fact. And we were able to see places I had never visited before. We saw oranges growing on trees. We saw places where it hardly ever rains, where the soil is like dust beneath your feet. And we saw palaces built hundreds of years ago by men from Africa, inlaid with beautiful tiles." He paused, lost for a moment in memories of ugly battlefields far from this spring-scented schoolroom. He shot a glance at Miss Gregory, and she gave him an encouraging smile. Then she took one of her hands in the other and squeezed, looking him straight in the eye.

There was no mistaking her meaning. She was trying to remind him of the evening at Gilhurst Hall, when she had persuaded him to speak of his injury. A rush of gratitude filled Finch as he remembered her gentle support that night. He took a deep breath and returned his gaze to the children.

"In Spain, we needed to think quickly," he explained. "We needed to work together. And we needed to do things we never would have been required to do in peacetime. Things we never thought we could do." He shrugged. "So yes, I suppose you could say it was exciting."

He pondered his answer. He hoped he had not made war sound glamorous, because military life was many things, but glamorous was not one of them. But they had asked him a question, and he had never believed in being dishonest with children. He remembered how much he had hated it himself, when he was a boy. At least there was no risk that these girls would run off to buy themselves commissions.

He raised his eyebrows in question, silently hoping that the students had sated their curiosity.

An older girl asked in a quiet voice, "Why did you come home?"

"I was injured."

"Where?"

He had forgotten just how curious children were. "My right hand."

"How?" This from one of the older girls. "Was it terrible?"

What to do now? It was so much easier to show people

the injury than to describe it. He tugged slightly at the fingertips of his right glove, looking at Miss Gregory as he did
so. She appeared to hesitate for a moment, then nodded.

He drew off the glove and held up his right hand. One
little girl covered her mouth, which had formed a word-
less *O*. The others were silent, their eyes wide.

Dash it. He hadn't meant to scare them.

"It's all right," he assured them in what he hoped was
a friendly voice. "My hand is ugly, and I know it. Sometimes I even frighten myself."

A couple of the girls smiled.

"Sometimes, I'll be tying my neckcloth, and I'll look
in the mirror and think, 'My . . . goodness. Who stole my
hand and gave me this crumpled old tree limb in exchange?'"

Another few smiles broke out around the room, and a
strange lightness enveloped him. He was actually poking
fun at his injury. For more than a year, the knowledge of
it had hung around his neck like an anvil. Suddenly, he
felt unyoked and unburdened. He chuckled.

He had never laughed at his disability before.

"Does it still hurt?" the gap-toothed child asked.

He shook his head. "Not often. Sometimes when it
rains." He held his hand out. "You can come and take a
closer look, if you like. I don't mind."

Shyly, a couple of the girls approached him and
looked at his hand from a distance. One of the youngest
students reached out and touched the ridge of angry,
puckered flesh along his palm.

Now the questions flew thick and fast.

"Can you still ride a horse?"

"Can you use a knife and fork?"

"Are you able to write?"

"Your teacher, Miss Gregory, kindly helps me with my
correspondence. As for the other tasks, I can manage most

of them." He smiled. "Using a knife and fork was one of the first things I learned. A gentleman likes to eat!"

The girls laughed. Perhaps this wasn't going to be so dreadful after all.

They chatted for a few minutes about inconsequential things. Then an older student who had not spoken before spoke so softly he could hardly hear her.

"My uncle is in the Peninsula," she said. "He has been there for a year. Is he in a great deal of danger? My mother worries about him very much. Sometimes, I hear her crying when she reads one of his letters to my father."

A hush fell over the room. This was just the sort of question he had been dreading. He took a deep breath.

"Frightening things happen in any war," he began. "The war on the Continent is no different. Tragically, people die. You must simply trust in Providence that your uncle will come home safely."

Trust in Providence. He wondered when he had last thought of Providence in anything but bitter terms. Perhaps those Sundays spent in the pews at Reverend Gregory's church were having a salutary effect on him. Or perhaps it was just that he was drawing on the thoughts and phrases of his own childhood because he was confronted with a room full of young faces.

The student who had asked the question nodded. "Why do men go to war? Why do they put themselves at risk of dying, instead of staying home with the families who love them?"

Ah, thought Finch, if he had the answer to that question, he would be hailed as a wise man instead of feared as a rake.

"Sometimes, men—and boys—sign up because they think war is going to be an adventure. But if they think it will be fun, they will be sorely disappointed. The only legitimate reason to go to war is to protect the people and things that you love. That's why most men fight." He looked around the room. How often had he dreamed of a quiet, safe, sheltered place like this during the long, cold nights in northern Spain, with only a drafty tent to shelter him from the wind and the rain?

"Sometimes a threat to all we hold dear comes along, and brave men risk their lives so that others may live in safety. With luck, most of them come home again." Suddenly, he was assailed by memories of the many men he had served with who would never come home again. A witty captain from Lancashire who had been felled by a stray bullet in Cádiz. His first batman, a serious but fiercely loyal young lad from the London streets who had joined the army as a way out of crushing poverty. He had died of dysentery the week before the battle of Oporto. There were so many more who would never feel the quiet of a room like this, who would never get the chance to make peace with their families.

For spending much of the past year hating his father and drowning his sorrows in brandy, Finch felt a gnawing sense of unease. He fought against it. What was done was done, and regrets were pointless.

He glanced at the clock on a shelf behind Miss Gregory's head. "I believe Miss Gregory said that our little session was due to end right about now. Surely you'd rather be out enjoying this fine day than sitting indoors listening to me bore you with old war stories?"

They assured him that they had enjoyed his talk very much, but they began shifting in their seats and gazing out the windows.

"You may go outside to enjoy the garden," Miss Gregory told them, and they jumped to their feet before she had finished the sentence. The smallest ones were at the door within seconds.

"Stay on the property, girls," Miss Gregory called after them. "Anne, please keep an eye on the younger students for me. I will join you in a few minutes."

As the students filed out, Finch overheard one say to another in an excited undertone, "Miss Gregory has a *beau*! And my mother says he's famous in the scandal sheets!"

"Shh, Marianne!" someone else hushed her. "Wait until we are outdoors."

His face flamed and he turned away from the exiting students.

"Children imagine things all the time, and forget those imaginings just as quickly," Miss Gregory murmured from behind him. So she had heard. How much more uncomfortable could this day become? He was beginning to heartily regret his impulsive decision to visit her at school.

"Don't put any stock in it. I don't," she added.

He turned to face her. "I suppose I'm not used to the way young girls talk. Young boys do not pay the slightest heed to such matters. I apologize if I have caused any smear on your reputation."

She shook her head. "People may believe what they like of you, based on the stories of your exploits in Town, but your conduct has been all that is proper while you've been in Hampshire. It would be foolish of me to cut you based on a few inches of ink in the newspapers." She shrugged, clearly eager to put the students' embarrassing suppositions behind her.

"You did marvelously with the children," she continued. "I am glad to see that you did not attempt to hide the truth of war from them. Too many people coddle children, but I believe it dulls their curiosity to constantly have their honest queries deflected."

Finch exhaled in relief. He had not even realized he had been holding his breath, waiting for her assessment of his conduct in the schoolroom. It was gratifying to learn that she had approved of it.

When had he come to hold Miss Gregory's opinion in such high regard? He barely knew the woman.

And yet, he felt as though he knew her as well as some of his most trusted soldiers. He knew she was smart, fearless, loyal, and proud.

What would it be like to be her *beau* in reality? As though seeing her through an improved set of spectacles, he suddenly became aware of things about her he had barely noticed since he first encountered her on the street in front of the pub several months ago.

Such as the curve of her hip beneath her utterly proper muslin gown.

And the few tendrils of reddish hair that had escaped from her eminently practical bun and were curling along the base of her long, white neck.

And the way that her eyes sparkled with admiration for his meager attempts to amuse and educate her students.

Who would have suspected that a rural schoolmistress could be as enticing as the most skilled courtesan in London? Certainly not he. He felt as though a band of iron was pressing across his chest, and his palms were suddenly damp.

"Thank you, Miss Gregory," he replied to her compliment in a strained voice. Speaking seemed to dislodge the odd web of fantasy he had been spinning in his head. For fantasy it was. It was idiocy to even think of Miss Gregory as anything else but his secretary and his assistant. He had no intention of staying in Hampshire, living at daggers drawn with his recalcitrant father. Once Norris and his associates were caught, Finch intended to be back in his cozy London townhouse. Perhaps, if he succeeded in this task, the Foreign Office might have other assignments that would keep him from sliding into boredom and rakish pursuits. And the odds that the next assignment would bring him to Hampshire were very small indeed.

No, while his father lived, there was nothing for him in Hampshire. And for Miss Gregory, committed as she was to her school and to her father's parish, there would be nothing anywhere else. Starting something he could not finish would be the height of folly.

He watched her as she moved about the room, picking up fallen papers. She moved almost as gracefully when she walked as she had when he had watched her dancing with Norris the other night.

The height of folly, he repeated silently, as he forced himself to remember the reason he had come to the school in the first place. He needed to tell her of some information he had managed to unearth about Norris.

"Is there somewhere private we may speak?" he asked.

"Certainly. I wanted to attend to some papers in my office anyway."

Once they were seated in her small, shabby office, Finch came right to the point. "I've found out that Norris has a friend in London who may be useful. An actress."

She nodded.

"Remember that letter we wrote to Sue Brightman?" he continued.

"Yes. She is one of your friends in London, right?"

He deliberated telling her just exactly how he knew Sue, then decided it would add nothing to the discussion and could lead to some embarrassing questions. "Yes. Anyway, she found out that a theatre singer named Betty Lincoln is a . . . particular friend . . . of Mr. Norris. Sue and Betty, well, know each other—" Demme, when had he become so mealy-mouthed?

To his surprise, Miss Gregory laughed. "Please don't mince words on my behalf. I suspect that Mrs. Brightman is also involved in the theatre?"

"Yes. She's an actress."

"And that you know her in more than a theatrical capacity?"

To his astonishment, he felt a flush seeping up behind his ears. "Yes. Well, I did. That is to say—"

His assistant's brows came together. "You're not going to tell me that she is another London woman you've threatened to evict into the street?"

"No! I mean, we have parted, but on amicable terms—" He hurried to explain until he saw that Miss Gregory was smiling.

"I am certain that you did. If I had known you as well when you wrote to the fictitious Kitty Sherman as I know you now, I would have realized that your letter was a hoax. I don't believe you are capable of treating any woman poorly."

He blinked in surprise at this twist in the conversation. "Why, Miss Gregory, are you impugning my reputation as a rake? I will barely be able to hold my head up in White's if such opinions become widely circulated." He was enjoying this conversation much more than he had expected, due mainly to Miss Gregory's easy approach to a somewhat embarrassing subject.

"I promise to keep my ideas to myself. So, to review, your former . . . friend . . . Mrs. Brightman knows Miss Lincoln, and Miss Lincoln is a *friend* of Mr. Norris." Charlotte pursed her lips. "Is Miss Lincoln loquacious?"

He grinned. She had immediately divined the direction of his thoughts. "I have never met her, although I have seen her several times on the stage. But she is apparently most talkative, according to Sue, especially when a bottle or two of gin is involved."

"So will you ask Mrs. Brightman to find out anything she can about Mr. Norris?"

"Indeed. You can help me compose the letter when we next tackle our correspondence."

"I'd be happy to," Miss Gregory replied. "And, since you are here, I can share some news of my own that may be useful."

"Excellent!" They finally appeared to making progress. "What have you learned?"

"I know one person, at least, who might be buying Mr. Norris's wine." Charlotte grinned like a child contemplating a plate of biscuits.

"Who?"

She glanced out the window behind her. All the girls were quite a distance from the house, but nevertheless, she lowered her voice. "Henry Seabrook. One of my students, Emily Templeton, is his niece, and she mentioned that he had supplied a cache of fine liquors for her upcoming debut."

"Seabrook? My cousin?" Finch tried, but failed, to keep a note of incredulity from his reply.

Her smile faltered. "Oh goodness. Of course. I had forgotten the distant connection between you."

"It is distant, but also strangely close. Seabrook stands to inherit Gilhurst if anything happens to me."

"Yes, I remember my father mentioning that to me once. He is very interested in the genealogy of everyone in the parish. He traced the line of inheritance for me to quite an extent. I must admit, with shame, that I did not attend to his explanation as closely as I might have."

Finch shook his head. "Seabrook may be buying Norris's wine, but I doubt he is more closely involved in the espionage scheme than that. I played cards with him at White's a few days before I left for Hampshire." He smiled as he remembered Seabrook's inebriated stumbling. "My cousin is a professional dandy. I can't imagine him being interested in international politics—he's much more concerned about finding shirt points of just the right height. Brummel has him wrapped around one baby finger."

Charlotte shrugged. "Just because a man is a fashion plate does not mean that he has no interest in other matters. If you are going to solicit my advice and input, my lord, I would appreciate it if you would consider it seriously."

Dash it, he hadn't meant to denigrate her efforts! "It was a good thought, Miss Gregory. We must pursue every possible line of inquiry, and this information would have sounded most promising to anyone who did not know my cousin." As he spoke, Finch wondered whether he was being too hasty. Perhaps Seabrook's image as a fop was a carefully cultivated disguise.

As quickly as the thought occurred to him, he dismissed it. He had known Seabrook casually since childhood and had never had cause to think him anything but a lightweight. On the few occasions when the Seabrook family had visited Gilhurst Hall, young Henry had spent most of his time inveigling biscuits from Cook, crying to his mama about some imagined slight, or reading in the library. When Seabrook had joined the army, Finch—and just about anyone else who knew the dandy—had been astonished. Sadly but not surprisingly, Seabrook's foray into military life had been short and painful. Not six months after arriving in Spain, he was grievously injured at Talavera and lost his left eye. To Seabrook's credit, Finch had to admit, he was always sanguine about his impaired sight. But aside from that one bit of stoicism, military life seemed not to have toughened Seabrook one whit. His current dandyism was no invention.

Miss Gregory's voice roused him from his musings. "No offence taken, Lord Finchwood. We are working as a team, and the members of a team must feel free to share all thoughts."

Her use of his title, for some reason, grated on him. "If we are to be a team, perhaps it would be helpful to dispense with strict formality. I would be pleased if you would call me something less imposing than 'Lord Finchwood' or 'my lord.'"

His assistant's eyes widened. "What should I call you, then?"

"Finch would do."

She shook her head. "I don't believe I could call a gentleman by a nickname. It would be most improper."

"Would it be, even though I have invited you to do so?" To his surprise, he was avid for her to agree. Diminishing the walls between them seemed an important enterprise.

"But what would you call me?" She nibbled on her bottom lip in a way that almost distracted him from her question.

"I should continue to call you Miss Gregory, of course, unless you expressed a different preference."

She appeared to be turning the matter over in her mind. "If you agree to call me Charlotte, I shall call you—whatever you like."

He laughed. "That seems only fair, Charlotte." Her name felt natural and sweet on his tongue. "Equals, after all, should address each other on equal terms."

She nodded. "That's as may be, but I must confess that it shall take me some time to get used to the idea. Perhaps because we are equals in this enterprise only."

"We are equals in more ways than that. Titles and birth alone do not define a person." Her eyes widened, and he realized he had revealed a bit more of his regard for her than he had intended. He cleared his throat and continued. "At the pace this investigation is proceeding, I suspect we shall have more than enough time together to adjust to whatever form of address we select."

Just a few short months ago, he would have groaned at the thought of being trapped in Hampshire for months or more while they unraveled the chain of conspirators surrounding Anthony Norris. But now, if he

were to be truly honest with himself, he had to admit
that the idea of a few more months in Miss Gregory's
company would make the boredom of the countryside
much more bearable.

TEN

If nothing happened tonight, this was the last evening Finch planned to spend up a tree on Norris's property.

He shifted a bit so that he could stretch his numb left leg. A riot of pins and needles traveled up and down his limb. The discomfort gave him a momentary burst of alertness, at least.

It must be at least three in the morning by now. Finch had not bothered to bring a watch—on a moonless night like this, he had little hope of reading its face anyway. He smothered a yawn. Staying awake on watch had always been difficult.

"Two times two is four. Three times two is six. Four times two is eight." His voice reverberated in his own head as he resorted to a trick he had used many times to stay awake on the Peninsula, when lingering warmth had threatened to lull him into slumber on a quiet Spanish evening.

As usual, he became bored with multiplication tables by the time he reached seven times nine. His mind drifted to Charlotte, as it did so often of late. He wondered if she was enjoying her weekly visit with her father. He hoped so. She had been looking very tired this week. He supposed he had only himself to blame for that.

He sighed. Obsessing about his assistant would only serve to distract him. It had been idiotic to encourage more intimacy between them by asking her to call him

Finch, but it had begun to seem ridiculous to trust his secrets to someone he couldn't trust with his own name. If he wasn't careful, though, his growing fascination with the schoolmistress would cause him trouble. He had learned in the army that it was never wise to become too attached to one's comrades.

Resolutely, he willed himself to stop thinking of Charlotte and moved on to recalling the monarchs of England in chronological order. He usually became confused around the War of the Roses, but this time he managed to keep his Yorkists separate from his Lancastrians. He had managed to progress as far as the Restoration when a dog's nasal whine drifted over the stiff breeze.

Finch stiffened. Casting a wary glance over the marshy field below the tree, he saw no sign of the beefy man he had evaded earlier, by diving beneath a privet hedge when the man and his menacing mastiff had passed along the road leading to the beach.

Despite the fact that the dog was likely a half-mile away, its cry distorted by the wind, Finch found himself hoping once again that his dark greatcoat and black trousers were enough to conceal him from sight. About his scent, he could do little. If the dog picked it up, all the stealthy clothing in the world would not hide him.

He scanned the field again and listened intently for a few more minutes, but heard no more from the dog. With relief, he shifted his glance back to the shoreline—and saw a flicker of light that had not been there minutes earlier. He judged it to be about a quarter of a mile away, although in the darkness it was difficult to be certain.

Quickly, he glanced out at the ocean. So faint he almost missed it, he saw a light wink in response. A ship.

Looking below him to make sure the dog and its owner had come no closer, he twisted to the edge of his perch and thudded to the ground. It would have been more elegant to lever himself down branch by branch, but he could never rely on his right hand being strong enough for the task. Getting up the tree had been difficult enough.

His leg was still stiff, but he shook it out and struck out in the direction of the cliff edge that faced the beach. Keeping low to the ground, he made slow progress toward the shoreline, stopping frequently to take cover in the local shrubbery. His heart slamming against his rib cage, he straightened so that he could vault over a low wooden fence. On the other side, his boot slid in something soft and slimy.

He grimaced. He'd obviously leaped into a field used for sheep, if the odor that assaulted his nostrils and the remnants beneath his feet were any indication. Fortunately, the sheep themselves were nowhere in evidence. The last thing he needed was a fluffy, bleating mob announcing his presence.

His location could turn out to be a blessing, he reflected. The fence would provide a useful hiding place, and the odor of sheep dung just might conceal him from that blasted mastiff, should the dog and its owner return.

With one ear cocked for sounds of pursuit, he eventually reached a small ridge overlooking the strip of beach from which the light appeared to have originated. Peering between two slats in the fence, he noticed nothing on the shore. But, about ten yards beyond the fence was a worn strip of grass that could be a path to the water's edge.

There was no one in sight. Far off on the ocean, Finch thought he spotted a lantern, but it could just be that peculiar glow that oceans always emitted at night.

Could he have imagined the lights?

Possibly. But since they were the only things of remote interest he had encountered all night, he decided to wait and see whether anything transpired in the next hour.

It didn't take an hour. In fact, within ten minutes he spotted a small rowboat pulling slowly for shore, just east of his observation point. It was riding low in the water, and seemed to contain an inordinate number of passengers. Too many for a fishing boat, if indeed any fishermen were foolish enough to be out at this odd hour.

Within a few minutes, the little craft was at the shoreline. Half a dozen men leaped out to pull it the last few yards to dry land. Finch held his breath. They were so close that he could have called out to them, if he'd wished.

Two of the sailors reached into the boat and hauled out a large crate, which clinked faintly as they lugged it further up the shore.

Almost directly below Finch's position, a tall figure emerged from what must have been an alcove or cave at the bottom of the ridge.

"About time you showed up." Norris's voice was loud.

"For 'eaven's sake, be silent," one of the sailors muttered, waving his hands. Norris ignored him and bent down to open one of the crates. The sailor slapped his hand away. "Money first. Wine later."

"What money?" Norris demanded in a belligerent whine. "I let you land here. I expect payment."

"We promised you one crate of brandy. You owe us for the other five you insisted we bring."

"One crate for the risk I've taken?" Norris's hollow laugh rang across the shore. "*One* crate? Are you mad? The profits from that will barely cover my household expenses for the month."

"It is your choice. We can always leave." Even from atop the ridge, Finch could see the sailor's Gallic shrug as he turned his back on Norris.

Fast as lightning, Norris's fist shot out and clipped the Frenchman on the ear. The sailor bellowed and wheeled on Norris, his own fists doubled. He'd just managed to land a glancing blow on the taller man's arm when another voice shouted, "*Qu'est-ce q'y se passe?*"

"*Rien.*" The sailor's voice was surly as he turned to face a man who had just climbed out of the boat. At this distance, Finch couldn't be certain, but the man who had shouted resembled the Frenchman he'd seen Norris consorting with in Portsmouth. Similar build, similar way of moving. Not surprising that St. Amour would be here.

"Nothing is happening? Good," St. Amour said as he came closer. "I would hate to see a flaw in the plan at this late stage."

"This scoundrel says you want blunt for this brandy." Norris's whine grated on Finch's ears like fingernails on a slate. Someone really should tell the man the basic arts of persuasion.

"Was that not our arrangement?" St. Amour, on the other hand, had the silky voice of a diplomat. Perhaps he had been one, before the war had made diplomacy a rather pointless profession.

"So you say. But I say differently, and I can make things very difficult—"

St. Amour held up a hand. "Stop, Norris. You can 'ave your wine. But this is the *last* wine we will bring you."

"But—"

"Would you prefer I tell some of your fine friends in London about our arrangement?"

Norris snorted. "Who do you think is buying the wine? This bloody brandy is the only reason I *have* fine friends in London, as you call them."

Finch permitted himself a moment of silent congratulation that he had correctly divined the market for Norris's ill-gotten gain.

"And you'd hardly be able to expose me without exposing yourself as well," Norris continued.

"Neither can you," the Frenchman replied.

A momentary silence fell between the two men, until

St. Amour waved his hand. "Enough wasted time. The wine is not the point. We must get these men ashore and to their lodgings." He turned toward the water. "*Vite, mes amis. La nuit est courte.*"

The night is short. Finch's stomach tightened as he looked to the east. A very dim glow had begun to illuminate the horizon. If he were fortunate, the spies would be far from the beach before sunlight revealed his position behind the fence.

He cast another glance at the horizon and decided not to rely on Fortune. She had not been particularly kind to him in the past.

As silently as possible, he slithered on his elbows away from the men huddled on the beach, following the line of the fence. Five agonizing minutes later, he had dropped down behind a small hillock. He heard several sets of feet pounding along the path from the beach, out of his sight.

Part of him longed to follow them, but he knew that would be suicidal. Better to use what he knew to trap the conspirators in the act in London.

Who were Norris's customers? Finch wondered as he heard the footsteps receding in the distance. And were they the real movers behind the spy ring? It was evident that Norris didn't have the wit or the stomach to play that role.

Finch sighed. He would need to find a plausible excuse to return to Town. But even in London, it was doubtful Barton would be able to spare any agents to assist him. If Finch was to keep an eye on this growing band of conspirators, he was going to need to convince Charlotte to accompany him. And that, he suspected, would be almost as much of a challenge as catching the spies.

* * *

Charlotte struggled, and failed, to grasp the idea that Lord Finchwood—Finch— had just presented to her. Surely she had heard incorrectly.

"You are going to London?" she asked, as she watched him pace before the fireplace in the Gilhurst Hall drawing room.

He nodded. "Yes. I believe Norris will be making his way there within days, possibly to meet some higher placed associates in the plot. London is my best chance to snare him, and this wedding invitation I received this morning will provide a most fortuitous excuse. Thank goodness for military acquaintances whose fiancées are set on having a ceremony early in the season." He tossed an engraved card onto her desk. "I shall need you to compose a reply, of course."

She nodded, turning her attention to the unthreatening invitation.

"And, as I mentioned, I would be most appreciative if you would come to London with me."

She swallowed as she looked up at him. The expression on his face was an odd combination of hope and stubbornness. She had not been mistaken. He did want her to come, and he knew she would resist.

"Surely you must know that would be improper?" She had agreed to write his correspondence. She had agreed to work with him to entrap Mr. Norris. But she most emphatically had *not* agreed to put her reputation in jeopardy for him. She had risked scandal just by being seen in his company—luckily for her, the village had approved of his public conduct in the months he'd been in Hampshire, and the whirling speculation about his rakish habits had settled down somewhat. But just imagine how Mrs. Kane's tongue would wag if Charlotte were to announce that she was traveling with the viscount to London! By nightfall, it would be common knowledge throughout Gillington that Charlotte Gregory was Lord Finchwood's lightskirt. Given

the difference in their circumstances, no one would assume that he was wooing her.

All that being said, a small, secret part of Charlotte relished the idea of courting her, even as the finer part of
her nature ruthlessly suppressed it.

*What would it be like to feel his arms around her in a dark,
private carriage? To kiss him? Quite delightful, she would imagine. Akin to the guilty thrill she'd experienced when he'd held her
to arrest her progress across the lawn at Cliffholme—without the
fear of detection.*

Stop it, she told herself in a silent voice as firm as any
she used on misbehaving students. That is not what he is
suggesting, no matter how it may look to outsiders. Letting your imagination run riot will do no one the least
bit of good.

"There will be nothing improper about it, I assure
you." He finally stopped pacing and settled into the
Queen Anne chair. "I should have been clearer about my
idea. Lady Gilhurst will accompany us. She is eager to
visit London for at least part of the season, but she does
not wish to spend an extended period alone in the family's London home. For various reasons, most of her
close friends do not plan to be in Town. Since my father
has no interest in Town amusements, she had given up
hope of visiting the capital this year. When I proposed
that you and she stay there together, she was overjoyed.
So you see, you would be doing her a great kindness."

Charlotte stared at the viscount, but his face was as ex-
pressionless as a sleeping cat's. She had to give him
credit. He knew she would feel guilty about denying the
kind marchioness a stay in Town. But there were other
elements in her life to make her feel guiltier.

"What about the school?" she asked. She knew she
sounded belligerent, but she had to find some way to de-
flect him from this mad plan. "I have a responsibility to
my students."

"School is due to break for the summer at the end of next week, is it not? Surely Miss Carter can keep things functioning in your absence. Or are you uncertain that she is qualified?" An almost undetectable smile flitted across his face.

He knew she had utter confidence in her assistant. Jane was more than able to run the school until the end of term.

"My father will expect me to help after service on Sunday," she protested, her excuse sounding weak even in her own ears.

"Your father raised you to be reliable and responsible, did he not?"

"Yes." Charlotte sensed that the battle was nearing its end.

"And he knows that you have agreed to be my secretary, correct?"

She nodded.

"So he would be more disappointed to see you shirk your duty than he would to lose your assistance for a week or two, I should think."

She was silent. He had deftly parried her every concern. Now the only excuse she had left was her strongest reason for resistance. Charlotte didn't want to go to London with the viscount because she knew that every minute she spent in Lord Finchwood's presence would only deepen her infatuation with him.

Of course, she could hardly tell him that.

"Well?" He grinned with the assuredness of one who knows he has won the war. "Have you not always wanted to see London?"

She had not, in fact. Unlike many people in Gillington, she had never suffered from a vague uneasiness that theirs was perhaps too limited a life. While she sometimes longed for new experiences outside her daily lot, travel to the wider world was not one of the activities she craved. She had always been content here, surrounded by places she knew and people she loved. What little she had heard of London had led her to believe it was a vast, dirty, unkind place. It was only the opportunity to see it in the viscount's company that had made the prospect at all appealing.

And it was appealing.

Charlotte brushed her hands down the front of her dress, as though she could flick the annoying idea away from her. "Very well. You have battered down all my defenses. There is no reason I could plausibly give to refuse your request. So I suppose we are going to London." She picked up the invitation and moved to the escritoire, where she unscrewed the cap from the inkwell.

"Try to contain your excitement." The viscount's wry smile showed that he was not a man used to having his plans met with anything less than enthusiasm. "That scowl will look most out of place at Lucas Darnwell's wedding."

She put down the cap and inhaled slowly before replying. "I have not been invited to the wedding, and I can hardly go without an invitation." She picked up the cream-colored card and held it aloft.

Lord Finchwood waved away her protest with a gesture that would have looked impossibly arrogant had anyone else made it. "When you reply, let Luke know that I shall be bringing a guest."

"To what purpose?" Charlotte knew her voice was shrill, but she could not help it. Was he setting out deliberately to embarrass her?

"In case you've forgotten, we are going to London to learn more about the French agents and their plans. Norris may well know Luke; they are of an age, and I believe they both attended Harrow. In any case, it is clear that persons with both money and breeding—the 'fine friends' St. Amour mentioned—are involved to some degree in this scheme. Darnwell's fiancée is the Duke of Saltington's daughter. Most of the *ton* will likely be in attendance, and no one will want to create a scene. Those facts make the wedding a perfect ground for a little investigation, but the size of the ceremony means surveillance will be complicated. I need your help if I'm to have any hope of eavesdropping on even one-tenth of the guests." He leaned forward and picked up his teacup. He sipped, then made a face. She'd poured it for him a good fifteen minutes ago; it must be cold by now.

"Besides, you got a better look at that mysterious Frenchwoman at Norris's party than I did," he said as he replenished his cup. "If she makes an appearance, we'll be able to focus on her, reducing the amount of wasted effort we expend."

Charlotte felt beads of perspiration prickling her brow. She was almost weak with embarrassment. How could she even have dreamed that Finch had asked her to accompany him to the wedding with anything more than business on his mind? She was his assistant. Of course he would wish her to participate in many affairs in Town.

"Charlotte?" His voice was low, and hearing her Christian name on it was more thrilling than she cared to admit. "Are you well?"

She realized that she had been staring into space like a ninny. When had she become such a bufflehead?

She knew exactly when: the moment she had collided with Finch outside the village pub. The fact that he could destroy her calm, serious demeanor without even trying made it brilliantly clear that going to London with him was a very bad idea.

But she had already agreed. And the last thing she had to cling to at the minute was her integrity. Charlotte Gregory had always kept her word.

"I am perfectly well," she replied to his kind enquiry

with a bit more vinegar in her voice than she had intended. "I was simply working out in my mind how best to arrange my affairs before we depart."

He stirred a lump of sugar into his tea and grinned. "I knew I could bring you around to my point of view."

How could she possibly find a man so smug, so engaging?

ELEVEN

Charlotte felt as confused as a small child visiting a huge, exotic shop. Everywhere she looked she saw something of interest: a man wearing a huge sign hanging from his shoulders urging passersby to visit a pastry shop, a house with beautiful blue shutters, a magnificent pair of matched chestnuts pulling a phaeton so high that she was astonished the occupants did not tumble out into Oxford Street.

At least, she thought their carriage was still in Oxford Street. The jumble of street names and neighborhood appellations had long ceased to make much sense to her. London appeared to be one vast, senseless sea of carriages, mounted riders, pedestrians, and people pushing wagons.

"Are we almost at Burnham House?" she asked, and then immediately wished she could have sewn her lips shut. By asking when they would arrive at the Gilhurst townhouse, she had sounded for all the world like one of the youngest students at the academy, petulantly demanding when dinner would be served.

Neither Finch nor Lady Gilhurst appeared perturbed. "Almost," her hostess replied with a smile. "I am most fatigued, and I suspect you will also be glad to finally leave this confined space." She shot a shrewd glance at her stepson. "And if we are longing to stretch, I suspect Finch is as well."

As if the very suggestion had made him realize how cramped he was, Finch arched his back against the tufted squabs of the carriage and stretched his long legs as far as the small space would allow. Charlotte instinctively shifted away to give him more room. Again, he gave her a knowing look.

Bother! He was perfectly aware of the effect he had on her, and he was playing it for all it was worth. Then again, Charlotte suspected there were few women who did not respond to him. When that stray lock of hair tumbled onto his forehead, as it did just now, he looked like an irrepressible boy trapped in a rake's body.

The thought brought her up short. Of course he was used to playing on his looks to seduce women. He was a rake, after all. She sometimes forgot, when they were sitting together working on his correspondence or discussing ideas for trapping Norris, that he was not an honorable gentleman in the eyes of the *ton*. She supposed that, now they had arrived in Town, she would witness more of the behavior that had earned him a prime place in London's scandal sheets.

"I will be glad to see the end of this trip, that is certain," he replied in response to Lady Gilhurst's statement.

"We're now in Mayfair," the marchioness informed Charlotte as she turned her attention once more to the passing scene. "My goodness, Lord Alcon has painted his front door a most lurid shade of red! He has long been known for his leadership in matters of design, so I don't doubt that red will soon be all the go for every house in Mayfair." She sighed happily. "It is lovely to be back in London. I wish I understood your father's hostility to the place, Finch."

A frown creased the space between the viscount's

brows. "I am the last person you should ask for insight on understanding my father."

Lady Gilhurst exchanged a speaking look with Charlotte. "I do so wish that you and your father would make amends. It is unfortunate to see William and his only child still at odds."

Finch straightened his shoulders. "I am sorry that the poor relationship between my father and me causes you worry. But I was not the one who did not correspond for five years. And I am not the one who refused to receive his *only child* unless said child appeared on his doorstep and threatened scandal." He scowled. "I have tried—you have witnessed it, Amelia. Just last night, I tried to suggest that he join us for dinner. But my father repulses my every move to make amends. I will not grovel." Every word was delivered in sharp, cold tones.

Charlotte suppressed a shiver. For the first time, she sensed what the foreign agents Finch had questioned in Spain must have faced.

No wonder he had been so effective in his work. It would be hard to resist the temptation to placate such steely animosity.

Like Lady Gilhurst, however, Charlotte found it tragic that Finch and his father had spent so many years at odds. She swallowed. Her father had always said that God's work was rarely easy. And surely making amends between parent and child was something of which Providence would approve.

"Do not think of it as groveling," Charlotte heard herself say.

Both passengers in the carriage swiveled their gazes to her. Lady Gilhurst's was hopeful. Lord Finchwood's was stony.

Charlotte cleared her throat. From what little experience she had with men, she knew that their pride was of paramount importance. She would have to tread with care.

"Think, instead, that you are the better man," she began. Lady Gilhurst, likely hoping to defend her husband, leaned forward and took in a deep breath, but Charlotte shook her head and gave the marchioness what she hoped was a pleading look. The blonde woman subsided against the velvet cushions.

"Your father is older and more set in his ways," Charlotte continued. "It is up to you, as the younger, more flexible man, to turn the other cheek."

"I am sure such sentiments are well received from your father's pulpit, Charlotte," he said. "But in the army, he who turns the other cheek—or hand—is likely to find it slashed and bleeding within moments."

The reference to his injury made her flinch, but she plowed ahead. "Would you rather you had never joined the army at all then?" she countered. "You could have lived a life of safety in Hampshire or London. But you took the risk, and you took the sword. And in so doing, you may have saved hundreds of soldiers' lives in that ambush you told me about. Are you sorry?"

Finch was silent for so long that Charlotte assumed he would not answer. "No," he said in a tone of voice that sounded almost surprised. "No, I am not sorry. I regret losing the use of my hand, but I have learned to adapt. And if I were to make my decisions over again, knowing that I would be injured at Badajoz, I would not change anything."

Charlotte sensed she had made some headway, and years of teaching children had taught her that one had to immediately reinforce a lesson if the pupil was to retain it. "So wouldn't it be worth taking a risk to restore your relationship with your father?" she pressed. "You may sustain injury, but the greater good might be worth it."

The viscount folded his arms across his solid chest and

stared at her. The spark of comprehension had faded from his eyes, and his face was as immobile as marble. "Perhaps," he said, in a tone that put the lie to his word. "But at least in Spain, the enemy was willing to come to the battlefield. If my father ever gives any indication that he wishes to speak to me, I will not turn him away."

"But—"

The viscount held up a hand. "Don't press this issue, Charlotte." He shot a warning look at his stepmother. "And that request applies to you as well, Amelia." He sighed. "I would like nothing more than to make amends with my father. But I will do it in my own way, in my own time."

"Just remember, Finch, that your father is aging," Amelia said in a faint voice. "Sometimes we think that time is infinite."

Finch nodded but did not speak, turning his attention once more to the scene outside the window. Lady Gilhurst, eager as always to smooth over any tension, resumed her lively commentary on the doings of Mayfair's wealthy residents. Charlotte responded in kind, and soon the knot of tension between her shoulder blades dissolved somewhat.

Within minutes, the carriage had drawn up to the curb before a tall, rather austere townhouse fronting on Grosvenor Square. No sooner had it stopped than two liveried footmen materialized to throw open the carriage door and fold down the steps. Charlotte stepped out after the viscount and the marchioness, feeling suddenly cowed. She had known the butler at Gilhurst Hall since childhood, as he was a parishioner of her father's church. And even though he had always been perfectly polite to her on her visits, there had been none of this overweening formality. Charlotte stifled an urge to tell the young men in their velvet jackets that she was just as much a servant as they were.

"Come along, Charlotte," Lady Gilhurst admonished her. With a nod to the footmen, the marchioness swept up the stairs and through the open front door.

"I know this must all seem a bit overwhelming." Finch's voice was close to her ear.

Charlotte shrugged. "It is no grander than Gilhurst Hall. Smaller, in fact."

"But London—the noise, the people—"

"When you've spent all week in a school with thirty girls, you become used to chaos. I seem to recall that even you seemed taken aback by it." Silently, Charlotte congratulated herself on her ability to present a façade of *savoir faire*, despite a roiling stomach and trembling hands.

"Believe me, even that roomful of minxes is nothing compared to the *ton* in high season." Finch stood back to allow her to enter first.

Charlotte had been prepared for opulence. After all, the Marquis of Gilhurst was well known to be plump in the pocket, and Gilhurst Hall was maintained and furnished in the latest stare of style. But Burnham House was entirely different.

The foyer was a riot of delicate plasterwork in soft shades of green and peach. Cherubs, griffins, garlands and medallions marched in classical precision around the walls. A small pier glass and table, obviously designed specifically to match the décor, nestled beneath a grand staircase. Despite the fact that she knew it would make her look like a green country girl, Charlotte threw back her head to get a good look at the elaborate ceiling. Accomplished paintings of mythological scenes were encircled in yet more plaster garlands.

Charlotte thought about her small, plain room at the academy, and the similar room she had shared with Eliza growing up in the vicarage. She felt like a barn kitten mysteriously elevated to the status of lady's lapdog. She didn't belong here. The only problem was that neither Lady Gilhurst nor Finch seemed to realize it.

"Charlotte, Maisie will show you to your room," the marchioness announced, indicating a slight young girl who curtsied prettily.

"No need to curtsey to me," Charlotte murmured. "I'm no one important."

"Don't say such things!" Lady Gilhurst exclaimed. "You are here doing important correspondence work for Lord Finchwood, and while you are my guest you are as important as anyone in this house."

"Yes," the viscount added from the doorway, his expression odd and unreadable. "Do not denigrate yourself on account of a few pounds of plaster and paint."

Charlotte felt a wave of weariness course through her veins, as though she had just returned from a long, exhausting walk. She longed for her simple bed at the academy and a roast joint at her father's dinner table.

Her presence here in London was about bigger things, however. She had to keep reminding herself that she might play a role in keeping a ring of spies from infiltrating Britain's defenses. In a small way, she might help ensure that no more men returned home maimed and broken, like Finch. She put away her foolish concerns.

"Thank you, Lady Gilhurst, Fin—Lord Finchwood." She looked toward the enticing staircase. "You are very kind. I believe I shall take your advice and repair to my rooms to rest for a short while."

But even as she followed the young housemaid up the stairs, she realized she had one small task she wanted to perform before allowing herself the luxury of sleep. "Would you be so kind, Maisie, as to bring me some stationery?" she asked, as a plan took root in her mind.

* * *

Charlotte's first few days at Burnham House went by in a blur of calls, social engagements and long, elegant dinners. The news that the marchioness was in residence had traveled through the *ton* like Queen Anne's lace through a garden, and within a day of their arrival a stream of friends, relatives and acquaintances had left their cards with the increasingly beleaguered butler. By the second day, they had begun paying calls, which Lady Gilhurst received with delight.

She had insisted that Charlotte join her in this enterprise. When Charlotte had demurred, on the basis of her status as Lord Finchwood's secretary, the marchioness had waved off her concern.

"La," she'd said, giving Charlotte a quick hug. "I shall simply introduce you as my friend—which, indeed, I consider you—and no one will think to ask questions. Even if they do, my dear, being a vicar's daughter and a correspondence secretary is no source of shame. The *ton* is a more accepting place than you might imagine."

Charlotte suspected that the marchioness's charitable view of *ton* attitudes was shaped to a great extent by the lofty titles borne by her husband and father—after all, what would a marchioness know of aristocratic snobbery? But it suited Charlotte's purposes admirably to meet as many members of society as possible, just in case anyone should let slip a morsel of news that might be useful to the investigation. So she acquiesced to the marchioness's invitation and tried to settle into her role as an almost equal member of the household. It transpired that membership in society was a rather exhausting affair.

"It is wonderful to be back in Town," Lady Gilhurst confided to Charlotte on the morning of their sixth day in residence. They had been receiving callers for the better part of an hour in the sunny salon, whose large windows overlooked the square. "It is not that I mind Hampshire, and I do miss the marquis dreadfully, but there is just nothing to compare to London during the season."

On that point, Charlotte could agree with her hostess. She had never seen anything remotely akin to the frenzied gaiety that appeared to grip the *ton*. Calls were loud but brief, full of exclamations about new dresses and hairstyles, discussions of the latest plays, and *on-dits* about countless strangers Charlotte didn't have a hope of keeping straight.

The *on-dits* appeared to be the most valuable currency of all. No matter how she tried, Charlotte could not become accustomed to the casual way Lady Gilhurst and her friends traded the most shocking information.

After a guest named Mrs. Southmore had departed, having regaled them with a long tale about an elderly married duke who had begun a liaison with a pretty young actress, Charlotte tentatively asked whether everyone in the *ton* was so eager to spread bad news.

Lady Gilhurst's eyes widened. "Oh, Charlotte, you mustn't think these people are evil. It is simply that they wish to be *au courant*. No one is harmed."

Charlotte was loath to criticize the marchioness, whom she suspected didn't have a cruel bone in her body. "But what if the gossip gets back to the people discussed? What if their reputations are damaged?"

"Sadly, that is just part and parcel of living in Town. It is unfortunate, but trying to rein in gossip would be akin to trying to prevent the sun from shining. Besides, sometimes you learn things it is important to know—which young men have a reputation for compromising innocent girls, for example. Those sorts of things rarely make it into the newspapers. In Gillington, such information would likely be common knowledge. Everyone would know the man in question and be able to form judgments based on personal experience. But London's society is so varied that one must rely on this sort of news just to keep one's head above water."

Charlotte conceded that this could be true, although she still did not approve of the gleeful way people shared tragic stories. But she realized that she would have to restrain any qualms she had about such things, if she were to hope to learn anything of use to Finch. So she simply nodded and said, "Of course. I did not mean to criticize."

Lady Gilhurst leaned across a small table laden with cakes and other sweets, and patted her hand. "I know. You are just a better person than I, and I respect your high morals."

"I'm not sure my morals are particularly high," Charlotte said with a smile, thinking of the fitful hour she had spent the previous night, trying to drive inappropriate thoughts of Finch from her mind. He was staying at his townhouse a few streets away, and she had seen little of him since their arrival, which was perhaps the reason she found her thoughts turning to him even more often than usual as she tried to fall asleep. "It is just that when one is raised a vicar's daughter, certain ways of looking at the world become entrenched."

Before she could say anything else, however, the butler scratched at the door and entered the room. "Mr. Seabrook is downstairs, my lady. Are you at home?"

Lady Gilhurst twisted her hands in her lap. "Yes, Johnson. Please just give me a moment or two to compose myself."

When the butler had bowed and departed, Lady Gilhurst sighed. "I am most curious to meet the man who has been the cause of such tension between my husband and stepson. Finch bears him no ill will, but William cannot say a good word for him. In fact, they were debating his character the night before we left Hampshire. I suspect that the marquis would not approve of my decision to receive Mr. Seabrook, but I feel that the dictates of good breeding require me to do so. He has done no wrong, and he is a distant relation."

Charlotte nodded, excited for her own reasons to meet the viscount's cousin. Would she be able to find any evidence to support her theory that he was in league with Mr. Norris?

"I must confess that I am also curious," Charlotte said. "He is a harmless dandy, according to Finch." She tested the viscount's nickname on her tongue for the first time. It felt illicit, even though he had given her permission to use it.

A few moments later, the door opened again and the butler announced Mr. Seabrook. Charlotte and Lady Gilhurst both smiled as he entered.

He was indeed as dandified as Finch had said. His bright blue jacket and richly embroidered waistcoat would have been enough, alone, to bring him to prominence in any gathering, but they were just the first of his sartorial splendors. From the depths of his stiff cravat winked an enormous emerald pin, and a jeweled quizzing glass dangled from his buttonhole. His shirt points were so high they almost brushed the tips of his blonde sidecurls. His hair was fashionably curly, although Charlotte suspected those curls might owe some debt to the ministrations of a skilled valet armed with a crimping iron.

"Lady Gilhurst!" he exclaimed in a warm voice as he crossed the room. "What a pleasure to meet you at last!"

She held out her hands to him, and he raised one to his lips.

"The pleasure is all mine," she assured him. "May I introduce you to my friend, Miss Charlotte Gregory?"

The extravagant dandy turned his attention to Charlotte. His smile broadened into a grin as he bowed to her. She felt a small *frisson* as he kissed her hand. Such gestures were not unknown in Hampshire, but they were certainly uncommon among the informal society there.

"Delighted, Miss Gregory," he said, straightening and looking straight into her eyes. She noticed a scar near his left eye that had been partially hidden by his tousled hair. That eye, she noticed, drooped in an unnatural manner.

Realizing that she might be staring rudely, she shifted her gaze to his other eye.

"Do not be embarrassed, Miss Gregory," he said, his words nothing but kind. "My eye isn't the most attractive thing in the world, and I fully understand why it shocks people. I was injured on the Peninsula. Usually, I wear a patch, but the weather was so fine today I thought I would go without."

"So you have served in the army?" Lady Gilhurst asked. "I did not realize that."

"It was a very brief career," he said as he settled into the small Sheraton chair the marchioness had indicated. "Not like your stepson's."

Lady Gilhurst smiled. "It is tragic that you were both injured in the service of your country, but I admire you for stepping to our defense."

He smiled. "You are very kind, my lady, but I went for the adventure more than any high-minded ideals of service. I found more adventure than I anticipated, and I am heartily glad to be back in London, wearing clean clothes and eating warm food." He leaned back in his chair and eyed the platter of sweets on the table in front of him.

"Mr. Seabrook, excuse my poor manners. May I offer you some tea and cakes?" Lady Gilhurst asked.

"Your manners are perfect, and yes, I would love some refreshment. I've spent most of the morning paying calls, and I am parched." He favored them with a lop-sided grin.

"I believe we have an acquaintance in common, Mr. Seabrook," Charlotte interjected. She might never have a better opportunity to probe the young man's possible connections to the espionage plot. "I know your niece, Miss Emily Templeton."

"Oh, Emily!" he said, clapping his hands. "What a delightful young woman! I am greatly looking forward to her debut later this month. Her mother—my sister—has almost run herself into exhaustion with the preparations. I've told her that she will do Emily no good if she collapses in a heap, but Anne simply will not listen to me. That is nothing new, of course. To her I shall always be a feckless baby brother."

Charlotte searched for evidence of dissembling on Mr. Seabrook's face as he discussed the party, but she could see none. It appeared that Finch was correct after all—that the wine his cousin was contributing to Emily's party was legitimate and not linked to Mr. Norris's smuggling ring.

She felt the muscles in her neck and back tense as she prepared to ask her next question. It might be a bit too obvious, but he would have no reason to suspect her of any connection to the Foreign Office investigation.

"Emily tells me that you were most helpful to her mother in planning the party. I believe she mentioned a fortuitous discovery of a cache of French wine in your basement. How delightful that you were able to save the day!"

"Yes," he murmured, flicking his eyes down to the slice of butter cake on his plate. Was he interested in the food, or trying to hide something? "Every so often, it is amusing to play Uncle Bountiful. Is this your first visit to London, Miss Gregory?"

He had switched the topic very quickly, but perhaps he was just being polite. As the visit continued, he revealed himself to be a witty conversationalist, and

Charlotte slowly allowed herself to relax. She had asked as many pointed questions as she dared.

Mr. Seabrook and Lady Gilhurst exchanged much gossip about mutual acquaintances, and Charlotte did her best to listen with an open mind. Most of his news was funny rather than cruel, and none of it seemed at all suspicious.

Charlotte repressed a sigh of frustration. Lord Finchwood had advised her to keep an eye out for "anything suspicious," without elaborating in any detail what exactly that might mean. She doubted that anyone associated with the spy ring would suddenly begin to wax eloquent on England's shortcomings and the glories of France, or even offer her a good price on some contraband cognac. Her news that Mr. Seabrook had provided French wines for Emily's come-out had been the closest she had come to discovering something of interest—aside from the Frenchwoman she had encountered at Mr. Norris's house—and she suspected now, after just a few minutes' conversation with Mr. Seabrook, that Finch had been correct in dismissing the idea of his cousin as a traitor.

If only she could forget that moment when he couldn't meet her eyes. Was there something else he could be hiding related to his niece's party? If there was, Charlotte couldn't guess what it might be. She would raise the matter with Finch when next they discussed the investigation.

Mr. Seabrook had been engaged for several minutes in retelling the story of a minor *contretemps* that had erupted when the Duchess of Felstone and a woman named Mrs. King had arrived at an open house three nights previously wearing the same dress. Each had accused the other of bribing their shared dressmaker for access to the design, and one woman had broken down in hysterics. His frequent laughter and gestures revealed his relish in recounting the scene. In fact, since the moment he had walked in, he had not mentioned one topic of anything more than lightweight interest.

He had just concluded his tale of the gown scandal when Lord Finchwood sauntered into the room.

"I didn't think it necessary for Johnson to announce me," he said as Seabrook rose. "Good day, Amelia, Miss Gregory, Seabrook." He bowed to the ladies, then shook his cousin's hand.

From her position behind Mr. Seabrook, Charlotte watched the two men exchange pleasantries. To her surprise, she saw that his left hand—which remained behind his back as he shook Finch's—was clenched.

Did he have other war injuries that made shaking hands painful? He had not mentioned them. And if anyone should find the exercise uncomfortable, it would be Finch, but he had told her that a lingering ache when it rained was the only pain his injured hand ever gave him.

Could it be that Mr. Seabrook harbored some grudge against Finch? Perhaps he resented the viscount for standing as heir to such a prosperous estate, when it would otherwise all fall to him? That was something she might mention to Finch later, although she suspected he would find her lingering suspicion amusing. She listened to the gentlemen's conversation, but could detect no note of enmity from either man.

She dug her fingers into the arms of her chair. She was useless at observing people. Perhaps she should suggest to Finch that she return to her role as secretary, and leave the espionage to him.

Just as the idea took hold in her mind, she dismissed it. She had promised Finch she would help him, and she would uphold that promise. But if she was to be of any use, she had to insist that he give her more direction— preferably, before his friend's wedding the day after tomorrow.

With that issue resolved, she settled back in her exceedingly comfortable wing chair to enjoy the conversation.

"Have you had a chance to enjoy many of London's sights since your arrival, Miss Gregory?" Mr. Seabrook asked.

"Not as yet," she replied with a smile. "I have been greatly entertained just meeting Lady Gilhurst's acquaintances here at Burnham House."

"If she can spare you for an hour tomorrow afternoon, would you care to accompany me on a drive in Hyde Park?" Mr. Seabrook grinned. He had a cheerful, easy manner. It would be a welcome diversion to spend some time in his company, Charlotte thought.

She flicked a glance at Finch and was surprised to see him frowning. She wondered whether it was improper for her to accompany Mr. Seabrook.

"I can certainly relinquish Charlotte for the afternoon," Lady Gilhurst piped up with a laugh. "It would be good for her to see some more of the city than these four walls."

If it was not improper, then why on earth was the viscount so displeased by the proposal? Perhaps he had hoped to meet with her tomorrow to discuss the investigation. Well, that meeting would just have to wait. It would be difficult to decline Mr. Seabrook's invitation without a logical reason. And she might acquire just as much news in Hyde Park as she would here in Lady Gilhurst's salon. She had heard that the afternoon circuit through the park drew the cream of Town society. In addition, if Mr. Seabrook *was* involved in the plot— which a very small part of her still suspected—she might be able to learn something incriminating.

"I would be delighted, Mr. Seabrook, thank you," she said, gratified to see the blond man's eyes light up at her response.

The conversation moved into other channels and continued for several minutes before Mr. Seabrook took his leave. As Lady Gilhurst returned from accompanying him to the door of the salon, she glanced at a small clock on a side table.

"Good heavens, is it that time already?" she exclaimed. "I promised Cook I would speak with her about the menu for tonight's dinner. I doubt we shall receive any more callers today, so would you think me terribly rude if I took my leave?"

Lord Finchwood shook his head as he stood. "Of course not. I must be on my way shortly myself, although I need to speak to Charlotte about some correspondence matters first."

Lady Gilhurst smiled and hurried out. A few moments after she had left the room, Finch spoke to the footman stationed next to the door.

"Please attend us outside," he said. Charlotte devoutly hoped that news of this irregular arrangement would not reach the wagging tongues of London society, although she suspected that the marquis's Town servants were as discreet as his Hampshire ones and so she had little to fear.

The footman bowed, left the room and closed the door softly behind him. Charlotte reflected that she was becoming almost accustomed to these clandestine meetings. When she finally returned to Gillington, it would be difficult to become used to the idea of a chaperon once more. It would also be difficult to acclimate to life in Hampshire without Finch, but she would come around to both situations in time.

"So you are off for a ride about the park with my cousin?" Lord Finchwood asked, his face unreadable.

"Evidently. It should be amusing and I may learn something."

"That it will be amusing, I have no doubt. Seabrook is

well known as a witty raconteur. Whether you will learn anything of substance is debatable."

Charlotte hesitated. Should she inform Finch of his cousin's strange reaction to their handshake, or should she just dismiss it, as she was sure he would? It would do no harm even if he did laugh it off, she decided.

"Mr. Seabrook seemed oddly tense when you came into the room."

"Did he?" Finch's voice evinced little interest as he stretched one arm along the back of a small settee. "I would have thought Seabrook didn't know the meaning of the word *tense*."

"He had his fist clenched behind his back."

Finch raised an eyebrow. "That is odd. Perhaps he is in financial straits again. His income is rather smaller than he would like, and Seabrook occasionally comes to me for a loan. He may have been debating the propriety of approaching me in front of you and Amelia, and decided against it."

Charlotte nodded. That would explain much. It was not enmity that lay behind the clenched fist; it was embarrassment. And yet, that explanation seemed too simple. If he was hoping for money from the viscount, would he not have approached him the moment he heard Finch had returned to Town?

Perhaps not. What did she know of *ton* etiquette?

"I will keep this odd tension in mind, however," Finch continued. "As I've told you, it never does to dismiss any possibilities—even one as unlikely as Seabrook being a master spy. I say it is unlikely because the man has always been as transparent as glass. It's one reason I am fond of playing cards with him." He stretched his legs out in front of him with a grateful groan. "Forgive me as I work the stiffness out of my body. I've been holed up in a room at the Foreign Office for half the morning, and the chairs there are deuced uncomfortable."

Charlotte wondered whether some careful pressure applied to the back of his neck would help him relax. As soon as she had the thought, she dismissed it. His physical comfort was none of her business. "Does Lord Barton have anything new to report?" she asked quickly.

He rotated his shoulders, probably trying to assuage more of the stiffness caused by Whitehall furniture. Charlotte tried to ignore the way the motion stretched the fabric of his blue superfine jacket across his torso. "Not really. I appear to be one of the only people assigned to investigate Norris and his colleagues. Intelligence officers are rather thin on the ground these days, as most men in that line of work are on the Continent." He stopped circling his shoulders. "Have you gleaned any useful information?"

"Not particularly, unless you want to know which countess is in debt to her *modiste* for more than one thousand pounds, or which younger brother of a baron became so inebriated at a dinner party that he pitched face forward into the soup?"

Finch chuckled. "For someone as loath to gossip as you, it must seem as though you have landed in purgatory."

Charlotte smiled. "It is my cross to bear in order to serve my country."

"I suspect we will have better luck at the wedding. I did find out through friends that Norris plans to attend."

Before she could stop it, a tiny sigh escaped her. She prayed the viscount wouldn't notice.

"Are you feeling anxious about attending the ceremony?" he asked. Charlotte should have known that not only would he notice her expression of unease, but that he would also divine its cause.

She considered denying her anxiety, but there would be no point. "Somewhat. Everyone has been most pleasant to me so far and has fully accepted the explanation that I am Lady Gilhurst's friend—"

"Which is true."

Charlotte smiled. "I am honored she considers me a friend, as I do her. But the fact remains that I am no one to these people, and they may find my presence at their gathering unseemly."

"There is nothing unseemly about it. I informed Luke that you would be there."

"Not unseemly in terms of etiquette, but—"

Finch cut her off. "Not all members of the *ton* are as idiotic as Lawrence Binks."

Charlotte felt her skin turn to ice. No one had uttered that name in her hearing for five years. When she regained her voice, she asked carefully, "What do you know of Lawrence Binks?"

"I know he is a blind fool," he said, resting his elbows on his knees and leaning toward her.

How on earth was she to answer that? "Is Mr. Binks an acquaintance of yours?"

Finch shook his head, and then looked directly into her eyes. "I've never met the man."

"Then how . . . why—" She knew she sounded like the worst kind of bufflehead, but she couldn't help herself. What had he heard about her erstwhile fiancé?

He continued to hold her gaze. "I am in the business of learning about people. When I asked people in Gillington what they knew of your character, the subject of your broken betrothal came up."

Of course it would. It had been the talk of the village at the time. Charlotte had simply fooled herself into thinking that everyone had forgotten.

"No one thought the worse of you," he continued. "The general consensus was that you were well shot of the man."

Charlotte heartily agreed, despite the fact that she felt most uncomfortable discussing the affair with Finch.

"Even though I was not the one to break the engagement?"

"*Particularly* because you were not the one to do so. Mrs. Kane held forth at some length on the fact that any man who would do such a thing to someone as sweet as 'that dear gel' must be a scoundrel of the first order."

So no one in the village thought less of her? Charlotte thought the viscount might be gilding the lily, at least a little. But she decided not to question him on that aspect of his story, because another question struck her as far more pressing. "So you have known of this aspect of my history for all these months, and never once raised it with me?"

He shrugged. "It did not bear upon our relationship in any way, so I thought it best to permit you your privacy."

Charlotte blinked. "So why bring it up now?"

"Because I suspect that it is at the root of your reluctance to attend *ton* functions, even to receive visitors with Amelia. Preposterous as it sounds, I believe you consider yourself unworthy. But believe me, Charlotte," he said as he leaned forward even further, "you are worth twenty high-born *ton* misses put together."

Charlotte closed her eyes, partly to distract herself from that magnetic stare, partly to absorb the confused emotions swirling through her brain.

The embarrassment of those first few weeks after Mr. Binks had cried off washed over her, but it was mixed with a small, sweet flame of elation. Finch found her worthy of respect.

She felt his fingers, warm and tentative, on her forearm. Her upbringing screamed at her to snatch her arm away, but she could not bring herself to do so.

"Do you wish to tell me about the affair?" Finch asked, his voice gentler than she had ever heard it. "I am happy to listen, just as you listened to the story of my injury. But if you do not wish to discuss it, I will respect your privacy."

She opened her eyes to see him still gazing at her, his eyes soft with concern. Charlotte had never seen him this unguarded. She realized, with surprise, that she *did* want to tell him about Lawrence Binks.

"We were engaged on just a few weeks' acquaintance," she heard herself begin. "Mr. Binks was looking to marry quickly, but only later would I learn the cause. His father is the Earl of Miston. Lawrence, as you likely know, was the youngest of five sons. The Earl has a very large family."

Finch nodded.

"Lawrence had a wild reputation, so wild that there were few families in his own neighborhood who would even consider him suitable, despite his lofty origins," she went on, wondering just how much Finch had learned of her former *beau*'s drunken exploits and scandalous liaisons. Enough, she decided, that she did not need to elaborate.

"Lord Miston was urging Lawrence to marry and settle down, and had threatened to write him out of his will if he did not do so with all haste. Lawrence was willing to marry but had no intention of settling down. What he wanted was a docile wife who would raise his children and say little. I don't think I quite suited the picture he had in mind." She smiled. Years ago, she had learned to laugh at small bits of the unpleasant tale.

"*Docile* is not a word I would associate with you myself," said the viscount. His voice was kind. She looked away from him, for fear she would become weepy under the force of his sympathy.

"Mr. Binks was as well behaved as a curate during our courtship. I had no cause to doubt his sincerity."

"It angers me to see an unprincipled man take advantage of trusting people," the viscount ground out. "How did you happen to meet?"

"I was working as an assistant at the school, while Miss Moore still owned it. Mr. Binks's younger sister had just enrolled at the academy, and he conveyed her to school for her first term. We met, and he apparently decided that I would do as well as any other female, particularly since I knew nothing about him." Charlotte failed to keep bitterness from seeping into her words.

"I have seen men paper over all manner of sins when they have sufficient incentive." Finch's fingers still lay on her forearm. He squeezed, and pure longing jolted through her veins. What would it be like to always be able to rely on such caring, when life's problems were wearing on one?

"When did the situation go awry?" Finch asked.

Charlotte shrugged. "A few weeks after we became betrothed. It was a quick courtship, which should have been my first clue that all was not right. He offered for me two weeks after we met."

"Did you love him?" The viscount's voice was suddenly harsh, and Charlotte started.

"Forgive me," he added hastily. "That question was out of bounds."

Charlotte shook her head. She was reluctant to speak of the events of that time—not because she still harbored any feelings save anger for Mr. Binks, but rather because she felt so foolish. "Not at all. In truth, it is rather a relief to tell you about it." She shrugged. "I suppose I thought I was in love. He certainly courted me with enthusiasm—taking me on long drives, squiring me to local dances, and paying me the most extravagant compliments. I suppose I was flattered."

"As any young woman would be."

This new, empathetic Finch was almost too enticing for Charlotte to bear. She slipped her arm out from under his hand and leaned back in her chair.

"Perhaps you're right, that any woman would have had her head turned," Charlotte continued. "We had a number of enjoyable conversations about everything from politics to literature, and I relished the opportunity to debate with him. He is a fairly intelligent man, whatever his other faults. However, as time went on, he increasingly refused to concede any argument, even when he did not have the correct facts. I remember one discussion we had about the revolution in France. He argued that Charlotte Corday did not murder Jean Paul Marat."

"Obviously, he is the only man in England who has not seen David's painting, with Corday's name boldly written on the letter in the dying Marat's hand."

"Anyone can make a mistake, and I dismissed it thusly. Even when our disagreements became more frequent, I put it down to the fact that he was simply feeling more comfortable speaking his mind in my presence. I thought that was a good thing."

"It can be, when done with respect."

"He was usually very respectful, until I accepted his offer. But once we were betrothed, his manner toward me changed markedly. It was as though he had been wearing a costume and had suddenly changed into his habitual clothes." Charlotte tried to soften her words with a small laugh, but it stuck in her throat.

"Everything began to unravel one night at the vicarage. My mother was still alive then, and she had invited Mr. Binks to dinner. He arrived two hours late. We were terrified that he had met with some sort of misfortune on the road between his inn in Wenfield and Gillington. He had met with misfortune, but not of the sort we thought."

Finch nodded, a small scowl playing about his face.

"He had encountered a friend from Cambridge, and they decided to spend the afternoon in the public house near the inn," Charlotte continued. "By the time he arrived at the vicarage, he was so inebriated he practically fell off his horse."

She smiled ruefully. "I was more than prepared to

overlook that. Every man deserves to enjoy time with his friends, and I do not agree with the more radical religions that say all consumption of alcohol is evil. So I helped him in and got him seated at the table. It was what happened next that proved insurmountable."

She paused, lost in unpleasant memories she had not recalled in years. The tight-lipped displeasure on her mother's face. Her father urging her sister Eliza to go upstairs. The horror that had twisted her own stomach when she realized just what sort of man she had agreed to marry.

"The alcohol had loosened his tongue, and he began to explain what a great favor he was doing our family by marrying me. Then he told us his opinion of our 'small, tedious world.'" Charlotte bristled—that memory among all the others still had the ability to provoke her to anger.

"He thought the academy laughable and my father's career equivalent to tilting at windmills. He mocked the vicarage, saying it would not be considered fit quarters for stable hands on his father's estate. And he regaled us, in quite lurid detail, with his plans to continue his association with his mistress after he and I had wed."

"Lucky mistress," Finch remarked dryly. She appreciated his attempt to make her laugh, but she was too consumed by mortification to respond.

"My father and I both tried to speak, but Mr. Binks spoke first. He said he had done his best to fulfill his father's wishes, but he did not think he could bear a life under the same roof as an opinionated bluestocking who did not have the sense to recognize her station." She winced. "That last part is an exact quote."

"Scoundrel." Finch's mouth was set in a thin, hard line.

Charlotte didn't trust herself to respond to his sympathetic anger without unleashing other emotions she did not care to explore. So she kept talking.

"Before I could tell him that I had no wish to live under the same roof as a man with such an overweening opinion of himself and his class, he cried off. He even had the audacity to slam our door on the way out."

She shrugged. "That is the complete tale. It isn't a terribly original story; I am certainly not the first woman in England to have her head turned by flattery, nor the last to find herself the subject of a jilt when the man in question could no longer maintain the charade."

Finch did not reply for a long moment. Then, in a low voice, he said, "It was not your fault, Charlotte."

"You are too kind. I should have been a better judge of character. And I should have—"

"Shhh." He laid a crooked finger across her lips. "You are entirely too self-critical. I can tell you from experience that such an approach to life leads only to melancholy."

A riposte leaped to Charlotte's brain, but she found herself unable to reply, so distracted was she by the sensation of Finch's finger. She felt her breath becoming fast and shallow. Against her better judgment, she looked directly into her employer's eyes.

What she saw there wiped all thoughts from her mind.

Take your hand away, Finch urged himself. *Don't begin something that you have no intention of finishing.*

He twitched his finger. But instead of removing it, he used it to very gently trace the outline of Charlotte's lips. So soft. So warm. He watched as she closed her eyes.

Her story had made him so angry that it had been a struggle to keep his voice encouraging. What right had scoundrels like Binks to run around England affiancing themselves to innocent women, then destroying their fiancées' confidence with a few ill-chosen words?

Even as the thought crossed his mind, he rejected it. Binks may have soured Charlotte's opinion of her fitness to mix with the *ton*, but, thank God, the idiot had not completely shredded her self-possession. Finch recalled her demeanor in front of her roomful of students: poised, authoritative, in control. He remembered the way she had moved through the Gillington assembly rooms, clearly comfortable with everyone in the room.

No, Binks had not destroyed her. But that small mercy was due solely to the fact that Charlotte was a stronger woman than any other female Finch had ever met.

He realized he was still idly stroking her mouth with his fingertip. But he wanted more. Within seconds, he had stood, then dropped to his knees, his face level with hers.

"If you wish me to move back to my chair, I shall," he said, silently willing her to reject this last detour from the course they were hurtling along. He could hear his blood roaring in his ears like a waterfall.

She hesitated for only a fraction of a second before shaking her head. As she did so, a small curl escaped her simple coiffeur and slid down the side of her neck. "No," she whispered. "Please stay."

At her words, his heart slammed into his chest with the force of a boxer's right hook. He caught the errant curl and wound it gently around his finger. It was soft and sleek. Without thinking, he reached up and extracted a long hairpin. Several other russet curls fell past her shoulders. He ran his fingers through the rippling mass, and refused to dwell on the implications of his actions.

"Do you have any idea how beautiful you are?" he asked her. All the thoughts he had harbored late at night, long after she had left Gilhurst Hall to return to the academy, threatened to tumble from his tongue.

She smiled. "I could ask the same thing of you, except that 'beautiful' is not the right word for a man and I cannot seem to think clearly enough to recall the correct one." She reached forward and pushed a lock of hair from his forehead. "Although I think it unwise for a man who cannot seem to keep his own hair out of his eyes to be attempting to dress mine."

Her smile was so warm that he could resist temptation no longer. With a groan, he gathered her into his arms and lowered his lips to hers.

Rockets of sensation exploded in his body as he tasted Charlotte for the first time. She was redolent of cinnamon and honey, and something far more earthy and wondrous. He longed to deepen the kiss, but he didn't want to frighten her.

Instead, he squeezed her and slowly began to stand, raising her as well. She moved smoothly to her feet and leaned against him, her hands on his shoulders and her body snuggled against his chest. And then, to his astonishment, she slid her hands beneath the collar of his jacket.

He stood back from her, took a sorely needed deep breath, and looked down into her flushed face.

"I thought your shoulders were tense," she murmured. She shifted her gaze around the room, but to her credit refused to dissolve into missishness and returned her focus to his face. "Earlier, you were flexing them. I wanted to help, but your jacket is too thick."

"That is a problem easily solved," he replied. Grinning as he flicked open the buttons of his Weston coat, he shrugged out of the garment and flung it onto the chair behind him. He should not have done so, he knew. But the improprieties were accumulating so quickly now that he thought it would be hypocritical for him to even worry about them. He grasped her hands, which had fallen to her side, and replaced them on his shoulders.

"I would be most grateful if you would help me relieve the tension."

Her eyes were dubious. "I have only tried this action on myself. But I find it very soothing." She placed her hands at the base of his neck and began to knead it with firm, deft strokes. He closed his eyes and leaned his head back. Demme, but that felt wonderful. Ripples of pure pleasure radiated down his back and arms.

She moved her hands to his shoulders, still massaging his tired muscles with surety and skill. Her ministrations felt wonderful, but the relief they brought to his stiff joints was only a minor aspect of his delight in her movements.

He could feel her fingertips through the light muslin of his shirt, soft as tiny pillows. But suddenly, she stopped. He opened his eyes just as she stood on the tips of her toes and buried her fingers in the hair at the base of his neck, lowering his head to hers.

The knowledge that she was eager to kiss him again sent him hurtling over the edge of propriety. He seized her, and this kiss was not as gentle as the first. Crushing his lips against hers, he kissed her as he had never kissed any woman before. As though he could know her, claim her, possess her through her lips alone. She responded in kind, digging her fingers into his shoulders and arching her back.

Dimly, he became aware that only the thin muslin of his shirt and the even thinner muslin of her fashionable gown lay between them. Innocent that she was, she probably had no idea how the sensation of her breasts crushed against his chest inflamed him. Breaking the kiss, he moved his right hand to her ear and traced a slow, meandering path to her throat and then to the low neckline of her gown. Her eyes were fixed on his face as his hand lightly skimmed her smooth, warm skin. He hesitated. The urge to continue his exploration was almost overwhelming. But an irritating voice in the far back of his mind reminded him that such an action would be folly. He couldn't remember why, but he knew it to be true.

The small voice grew louder, even as he tried to smother it. *Charlotte is your assistant, your friend, your colleague. She will never leave Hampshire, and you will never stay. You are as caddish as Binks if you do not stop right now.*

He stepped back, letting his arms fall to his sides. "Charlotte, I should not have done that."

The dazed expression on her face faded as she stepped back, to be replaced by one so sad he longed to take her in his arms again just to erase it. "I am not at all sorry you did. That we did," she said in a low, strained voice. "But you are right. We must stop."

A silence descended on the small room. As it grew, the walls seemed to close in on him.

What on earth had he been thinking? Had five years in the army taught him nothing about denial and self-control? Evidently not, if Charlotte's disheveled hair and flushed face were any indication.

"Let me at least re-pin your hair," he said, knowing that she could not possibly leave the salon and return to her room in such a state without attracting such attention that even his father's well-trained servants would be hard pressed not to talk among themselves and their acquaintances in other Mayfair houses.

She shook her head as she dropped to her knees. "I can do it," she said, as she retrieved several lost hairpins from the carpet. "It has been lovely to have the skills of a lady's maid at my disposal here at Burnham House, but I am well used to arranging my own hair." Her voice was subdued and distant as she stood and moved toward the gilt-framed mirror above the fireplace.

Dash it, he had ruined everything. "Charlotte, please let me apologize."

She turned from the mantel. "Truly, there is no need. I was just as willing a participant as you were." An odd expression crossed her face that might have been a strangled smile. "But I think it would be wise if you left now, and if we did not speak of this again. We have work to do, and we cannot afford to let ourselves become distracted by . . . other considerations."

Work. Yes, of course. The wedding, Norris, the investigation. Any career he might hope to have with the Foreign Office rested on his success in this endeavor. And to succeed, he needed to focus all his efforts on the task, and not on the taste of honey and cinnamon that still lingered on his lips.

"You are right," he said in a stiff, unnatural voice. Her detachment unnerved him. How could she seem so calm, when everything he thought he knew about himself—and about her—had been torn from its moorings?

"I shall come and collect you at half-past ten Thursday morning," he said as he turned toward the door.

"Thursday morning?"

He twisted his head back at the note of confusion in her voice. "For the wedding. Lucas Darnwell's wedding."

"Oh, yes. Yes, of course." She looked away. "I shall be ready."

He said no more as he opened the door and left. But it was oddly comforting to know that Charlotte Gregory was not nearly as undisturbed by their encounter as he had thought.

TWELVE

Charlotte tried to focus on the familiar words of the marriage ceremony, but they washed over her with all the comprehensibility of birdsong, so distracting was the presence of the man seated next to her.

She glanced at him out of the corner of her eye. Finch was dressed in the latest stare of fashion, and as usual his clothes were exquisitely tailored. The black wool jacket sat on his shoulders as though it had been molded in clay.

Just the thought of his jacket caused a fount of mortification to well up inside her. Had she really slipped her hands beneath his coat the other day? Had she really felt the taut, sinewy muscles of his shoulders beneath her hands?

She shifted uncomfortably in her seat. Such questions, and their inarguable answers, had been swirling through her head for two days. They had bedeviled her as she attempted to converse with several friends of Lady Gilhurst's at a small supper party two evenings ago. They had arisen with alarming frequency during her ride in Hyde Park with Mr. Seabrook, when she found herself making ceaseless comparisons between the perfectly nice gentleman and his distant cousin, and finding Mr. Seabrook wanting.

And the thoughts had kept her awake for most of the last two nights, with the result that she felt drained.

Drained, and yet oddly aware, as a tight cord of excitement twitched throughout her body during her long waking hours.

She stole another quick look at Finch. If the dark circles under his eyes were any indication, their kiss the other day was causing him sleepless nights as well. It was not surprising. He was as cognizant of the impossibility of any romance between them as she was.

Desperate to refocus her attention, she glanced around the elegant church. Even though Finch had told her that St. George's in Hanover Square was considered one of London's plainer churches, Charlotte found it much more imposing than the tiny church in Gillington.

An elaborate, two-level reading desk stood to the left of the altar, while an elaborate canopy covered the pulpit to the right. The nave seemed immense, the arched ceiling soaring far above their heads. She leaned against the back of their box pew, as much for support as to distance her body from Finch. He seemed to be radiating heat like a roaring fireplace this morning.

Her gaze traveled over the assembled congregation, several hundred people from England's grandest families. As if he were indicating the local butcher, baker and candlestick maker, Finch had pointed out the impossibly young Duke of Devonshire, the magnetic Lord Byron and the famed Almack's patroness Lady Jersey, among many others. Finally, Charlotte spied the one person she'd been looking for. Anthony Norris was seated toward the back of the church. She swiveled her head away from him, eager that she shouldn't appear to stare, and immediately spotted Henry Seabrook. That did not surprise her, as he had mentioned during their ride in Hyde Park yesterday that he planned to attend the wedding.

In fact, he had regaled her at length with amusing yet not cruel stories of the bride and groom. She had enjoyed herself, even as she had become more convinced that Finch was right—his cousin was a charming light-weight and nothing more. She felt abashed that she had even suspected him of wrongdoing.

A murmur sweeping through the crowd drew her attention to the front of the church. She realized that the rector had ceased speaking and was about to present the newly married couple to the congregation. The bride and groom turned and began to make their way back down the nave to the accompaniment of a crashing Handel fanfare.

As they passed Charlotte's row, she glimpsed the bride's radiant face. With a sharp pang, Charlotte realized that the only man likely to engender such an expression on her own face was sitting next to her on the long polished bench. And she knew that marriage to him was impossible, for reasons almost too numerous to list.

Despite his assurances, she knew that their differences in station could cause comment among the *ton*. He cared little for society's opinion now, but it might rankle as the years went on.

A much more serious concern was the difference in their approaches to life. After little more than a week in London, Charlotte was exhausted. The noise and dirt, the lack of privacy and greenery, had her longing for the quiet lanes of Gillington and her room at the academy, where she woke each morning to the sounds of cows in the fields rather than the shouts of costermongers in the street. She could not wait to return home.

Finch, however, was in his element in Town. Despite the uncomfortable furniture, he had clearly been elated to be back at Whitehall. Since their arrival in the city, he had become even more alert—more alive—than he had been at Gilhurst Hall. If forced to rusticate in the country, he would slowly wither. She was certain of it.

"Miss Gregory?" His voice, formal and correct, cut

across her gloomy thoughts. Of course, she thought, he would be unlikely to address her by her Christian name in a public gathering. "Shall we make our way outdoors?"

Slowly bringing her attention back to the church, she realized that many guests had already taken their leave. She unlatched the door to the box pew and bolted into the aisle. "Of course, Lord Finchwood," she answered as she scurried in front of him. She felt tension ebbing from her arms and legs as she increased the physical distance between them. Without a backward glance, she moved swiftly toward the porch and out into the morning sunshine of Hanover Square.

A knot of well-wishers surrounded the newlyweds. Charlotte twisted her way through the chattering throng, keeping her eyes open for Mr. Norris. The crowd had spilled from the shelter of the church portico to the steps and onto the cobbled street. A good number of people had even washed up on the opposite pavement, where they leaned against an iron fence surrounding a small green park.

Charlotte's gaze swept along the fence until she spotted a familiar face. Mr. Seabrook was chatting with a dark-haired woman in an elegant but subdued blue gown. A small poke bonnet partially concealed her profile, but something about her stance struck a chord with Charlotte. On a hunch, Charlotte moved behind a pillar of the church portico and continued to observe the pair.

"What has caught your interest?" Finch's lips were so close to her ear she could feel his breath on her neck.

She scuttled to the left and turned to face him. "Mr. Seabrook is speaking to a lady across the square. I feel I should know her."

Finch turned his gaze in the direction she indicated. "Yes, she seems oddly familiar to me, too." He squinted just as Mr. Seabrook handed the lady a small, nondescript bag, which she slipped into her reticule.

"Most unusual," the viscount muttered as the lady nodded to Mr. Seabrook and turned away. As she wheeled to leave the square, her face was briefly visible from the church steps.

Charlotte gasped. "Finch!" she breathed, in her excitement forgetting that she should be calling him by his title. "She's the Frenchwoman we followed at Cliffholme—the one you chased to the water's edge!"

As she turned to look at him, he muttered, "She's more than that. She's Betty Lincoln."

"The singer?" Charlotte felt her jaw drop open as the implications of that information sank in. "Mr. Norris's . . . ladybird? But I'm fairly certain that the woman I saw was French."

"She may well be. Most actresses and singers take stage names."

They both watched closely as Mr. Seabrook melted into the crowd in the street in front of the church. Then Finch murmured, "I owe you an apology, Charlotte. If Seabrook is in the habit of giving mysterious packages to Mr. Norris's mistress, who in turn is in the habit of jumping into rowboats on the Hampshire shoreline in the dark of night, your initial intuition very well may have been right." He lowered his voice even more. "But of all the men in England I would have suspected of treason, Henry Seabrook would have been the last."

"Why were you so reluctant to investigate him?"

Finch shrugged. "I believed I understood him. We've known each other since childhood, and he has never given me the least cause to suspect him of anything duplicitous. He served in the army, for heaven's sake. He was even instrumental in helping me secure my commission."

"How?"

"A friend of his father's was a high-ranking officer in

the regiment I wished to join. Seabrook placed a few well-chosen words in a few ears."

Charlotte shook her head. "But his actions do look incriminating."

"They do, indeed. I believe I may pay a call this afternoon to Sue Brightman."

Finch's former *paramour*? Charlotte could feel her features contracting into a frown, despite her best attempts. What did she care? His liaisons were none of her affair.

Even as she tried to tell herself this fiction, she knew why she cared. Because she had fallen deeply, irretrievably in love with Francis Burnham, Viscount Finchwood.

What a disaster.

"To find out more about Betty Lincoln, of course," he added in a sharp tone that showed he had registered her dismayed expression.

Charlotte winced. "Of course."

"If you don't mind, I believe I will forgo the wedding breakfast. In a crowd like this, I shall barely be missed. And if I leave now, there is a good chance I will find Sue at home and . . . alone."

Charlotte felt a blush staining her cheeks. "Of course," she said again, desperate to avoid any further discussion of Mrs. Brightman's social life.

"Jenks can drive you home. I'll take a hackney to Chelsea, and rejoin you at Burnham House after I've spoken to Sue."

"Is there anything I can do in the interim?"

Finch shook his head. "Your sharp eyes and unclouded judgment have already been immensely helpful. And I'll need you this evening. I suspect we may be paying a visit to the theatre."

Without another word, he strode down the steps and across the cobblestones, heading in the direction of Oxford Street. For some reason, she suddenly remembered the small pistol he'd showed her as they stood in the rain

outside Cliffholme, and his comment that the people
they were pursuing were likely carrying firearms as well.
Despite the sunshine beating down on Hanover Square,
a chill rippled along her skin.

"She's definitely French. I would have mentioned it in
my letter, had I known it was important," Sue said. She
picked up a cup of coffee, which she far preferred to tea,
and sipped before continuing. "She said she took Betty
Lincoln as a stage name because no one would be able
to pronounce her French name. And not many people
outside the theatre even know that she's French, since
she usually sings in a chorus, where you can't distinguish
one voice from another."

"It's no matter," Finch replied. The last thing he
wanted to do was to arouse Sue's suspicions by display-
ing unusual curiosity.

"So are you seeking a new ladybird?" she asked with a
grin, stretching along the blue chaise like a sleepy cat.
Finch remembered, with a tinge of shame, how often he
had settled into that chaise with her. He realized, now,
just how sterile those afternoons had been. Sue was fun,
and they'd both enjoyed their encounters, but there had
been no more substance to their relationship than there
was to morning mist. He didn't have the slightest desire
to renew it.

Unlike his encounter the other day with Charlotte
Gregory, which seemed to have worked its way deep into
his skin. Into his brain. Into his dreams.

How could he have ever settled for simple physical
pleasure when there was so much more a man and
woman could share? Laughter, tears, challenging conversation, a common purpose, dreams and fears . . .
some of them things he'd almost forgotten existed.

He cut his thoughts short. He and Charlotte had a

deep connection, without doubt. But such a connection was not enough to build a life on. The fact remained that she would be miserable in London, and he would be tortured in Hampshire, living always under the shadow of his father's scorn, with nothing useful to occupy his days.

"Considering Mrs. Lincoln as my new ladybird?" he repeated Sue's question. "Perhaps." It was as logical a story as any.

"You and the rest of the world," Sue answered with her musical laugh. "Perhaps it's that French mystique, but Betty has them lined up outside the door. If she's not careful, she's going to spark a duel one of these days."

"So who am I in competition with for her favors?" he asked with studied casualness.

"Lud, I don't even know half the gents' names, but they certainly run the gamut. There's a retired colonel, and a gangly youth with terrible skin. Don't know why she puts up with him—he's obviously one step away from the workhouse. Then there's a tall man named Andrew or Anthony or something who shows up occasionally. I think he lives outside London."

That would be Norris. The colonel might be involved in the plot, too. The spies had to be getting their military information from some source. As for the boy, Sue was right. Popular singers and actresses usually had better things to do than tolerate the attentions of poor, unattractive men.

"Do they all come to meet her at the theatre?"

"Usually. Some skulk around the green room, but the smart ones loiter about the door leading into the alley. She's usually very quick to leave of an evening. Always seems to have somewhere to go."

That was intriguing. "Is she ever late for a performance?" he asked.

"Late? You don't know the half of it. If she wasn't just

a chorus girl—and so popular with the male patrons—
Cannings would have given her the sack months ago.
Some nights she never shows up at all. Disappears for
days at a time."

Those absences could easily coincide with the times
Finch had spotted Betty in Portsmouth and at Cliffholme.
"So there are other men nipping at her heels, other than
the gentlemen you mentioned?"

"Oh, scores. There's a man who never comes back-
stage, but I've seen her with him several times in
out-of-the-way places. Frightful dandy, he is. Shirt points
like arrowheads sticking in his ears."

Seabrook.

He didn't dare press his questions further. "Sounds
too competitive for my liking," he said, rising to leave.

"Hardly," Sue replied. "You could give any of her *beaus*
a run for their money. They're nothing special, except
for the blond dandy—and he's far too effeminate for my
taste."

Finch smiled and dropped a light kiss on Sue's cheek.
"Thanks for the advice and support, Sue. I am glad to
see that all is well with you."

"As well as ever," she said, rising to walk with him to
the door. "Any interest in who my new protector is?"

"It is none of my business," he said as he collected his
hat and gloves from a small table.

"That's what I always admired about you, Finch," she
said, as she held the door open for him. "You're one of
the only people in London who believes in privacy."

If you think I'm discreet, you should meet my friend Charlotte,
he almost said. He walked through the open door and
smiled. "I trust that if I mind my business, others will
mind theirs."

Sue grinned. "If that's a subtle hint to keep our conversation today private, consider it done."

"Thanks, Sue." He turned, walked down the pathway of

her little cottage and hoped he could find a hackney quickly. One of the only men in London who valued privacy planned to spend the evening shadowing the movements of the city's most popular singer. The irony was not lost on Finch as he made his way toward King's Road.

Forty minutes later, he leaped out of a hackney and took the front steps of Burnham House two at a time. He could not wait to tell Charlotte what he had learned from Sue. If he could catch Betty Lincoln with anything incriminating, he might well have enough evidence to bring in the whole ring: Norris, Seabrook, St. Amour, the mysterious retired colonel, the lot.

Johnson opened the door almost as soon as Finch dropped the knocker. "Good afternoon, Lord Finchwood," he said. "Everyone is upstairs in the salon."

Finch suppressed a sigh as he handed Johnson his gloves and hat. He had been hoping that his stepmother would be out, giving him the opportunity to discuss the latest news with Charlotte in privacy. But it would not kill him to make small talk with Amelia for a few minutes before squiring Charlotte away on the pretext of attending to some correspondence.

"Shall I announce you?" asked the butler as Finch hastened up the staircase.

"No need, Johnson, thank you. I know my way."

"By the way, your—" The end of the butler's sentence was muffled by a burst of feminine laughter from within the salon. Finch opened the salon door.

As he walked in, three pairs of eyes swiveled to meet his. Charlotte's. Amelia's. And his father's.

Finch stopped short. What in blazes was the marquis doing here? Finch would have thought his father was only too glad to be shot of him. And his parent detested London.

Finch bowed. "Father. What brings you to Town?" He

straightened and raised his eyes, fully expecting his father to stalk from the room now that Finch had appeared. To his surprise, the marquis stood, bowed and managed a small smile.

"A most unusual letter I received several days ago," his father said, with a quick glance at Charlotte.

A letter? What the deuce was he talking about?

Finch looked at Charlotte as well. She appeared somewhat pale, and she was nibbling on her lower lip.

"Miss Gregory took the time to write me a note that explained a few matters that had puzzled me," the marquis added as he dropped back into his chair, his knees cracking in protest.

Finch felt his eyebrows shoot up in alarm. Surely Charlotte had not revealed the nature of his work in Hampshire—and, even worse, sent that news through the public post? That did not make sense. Throughout their association, she had proven herself capable of absolute discretion.

"You are speaking in riddles," Finch said to his father as he eased onto a small settee. "What matters puzzled you?"

"Well, for one thing, the reason you joined the army."

"Joined the army . . ." Finch was struck dumb. The questions were flooding his brain faster than he could address them. What the devil was Charlotte doing writing to his father in the first place? And about the army? And what had she said that had prompted the marquis to get in his carriage and come to London? He rubbed his temples.

"Yes," Charlotte piped up. "I told him how you are just as devoted to England as he is—just in a different way. How you went to the Continent to protect the rest of us, not just for adventure."

He recognized bits of his speech to the girls at the academy coming back to haunt him.

"And she explained that your, well, notoriety in London was due to lack of purpose rather than a true inclination toward darker pursuits," Amelia chimed in.

It sounded as though the letter had been somewhat longer than a short note. "I see," Finch said noncommittally, still trying to absorb this turn of events. So Charlotte thought she understood him, and thought she had the right to interfere in his relationship with his father? Had he not specifically said he would resolve that issue in his own time, in his own way?

"She mentioned that you would be interested in taking up responsibilities on the estate, should I be in need of assistance." His father's voice was subdued, as well it might be.

"I told you the same thing more than a year ago, in the letter I sent from Badajoz," Finch said, keeping his voice level with difficulty. "Was I unclear? Or did Miss Gregory simply express it in more flowery language?"

Such blatant disrespect was bound to drive the marquis from his chair. Finch rather hoped it would. This conversation was most uncomfortable, particularly since it was being conducted in full view of an avid audience.

Despite Finch's hopes, his father remained seated. "There is no need to be sharp. You did tell me. The problem was, I was too angry to listen."

"You were still angry that I'd joined the army, after five years? Isn't that rather a long time to hold a grudge?" Finch was struggling, but failing, to sympathize with his father. With a fierceness that surprised him, he longed for the civil conversations they had had when he had been an undergraduate at Oxford. Before he started butting heads with his father at every opportunity.

"Part of me was still angry. That's why I didn't answer any of your letters from the Continent, at first. It was childish, I admit." His smile was rueful. "My anger over the manner of your departure eventually ebbed, but as I read the papers and your letters—"

"You actually read my letters?"

"Every one. Many of them so often that they fell apart in my fingers."

"It's true, Finch," Amelia said.

This conversation was becoming more perplexing by the second. "But if you cared enough to read them, why didn't you answer them?"

His father sighed. "It was clear from your missives and from the newspaper reports that Spain was a very dangerous place."

"Of course it was. Wars are rarely safe."

A nod from the marquis. "I understand that, of course. In the abstract. But the idea of you, my only son, in the line of fire—possibly captured, maimed or tortured—well, every time I thought of it, I would become so incensed at what I saw as a needless pursuit of glory that I would become angry all over again."

"It wasn't, as you call it, a needless pursuit of glory."

The marquis sighed. "I see that now. But for years, I was blinded by the idea that you had thrown away all the opportunities I so wanted for myself, in pursuit of something I couldn't understand."

"This all goes back to my refusal to remain at Oxford, doesn't it?"

"I suppose. I had so wanted to pursue a higher degree." The marquis's expression was distant for a moment. "When you threw the opportunity to do so back in my face, I suppose I resented it."

Finch raised his hands, then let them drop to his lap. "But surely you realized that I don't have an academic bone in my body."

"Miss Gregory tells me you have quite a facility with languages."

He longed to shoot her a speaking look—longed, actually, to sequester her in a room and shout himself hoarse until she apologized for meddling—but her interference was a separate issue. He focused on the matter at hand. "But languages were more a hobby than anything else. I nearly went mad in the years I spent at Oxford as it was. Sitting in a room with a book is not my idea of life. I was desperate to see the world."

"I know." His father's voice was sad. "And I suppose that was another reason I was reluctant to let you assume your rightful place at Gilhurst Hall when you returned from Spain. Part of me wondered whether you would become bored and leave again. That would do the estate no good."

Finch blinked. "Of course I would not leave. I have always known that Gilhurst was my birthright. Believe me, five years in Spain have cured me of any desire to spend my life wandering the globe."

"But would you be happy living the life of a rural landowner?" his father persisted. "Attending to prosaic things like leaky cottage roofs and new agricultural techniques and the complaints of the local magistrate?"

Finch hesitated. His father raised an excellent point. Finch had been so focused on bullying his father into accepting him back into the family fold that he had not stopped to think whether he would find such a life constraining.

"I'm not sure," he answered slowly, wishing for his sake and his father's that his answer were more positive.

From the corner of his eye, he thought he saw Charlotte's shoulders slump. She obviously sensed the failure of her tidy plan to bring harmony to the House of Gilhurst.

The marquis nodded. "Give it some time. Think about it." He took a deep breath. "But no matter what you decide, I want to—" He stopped and looked away.

"Just say it, William," Amelia urged.

His father looked back at him. "Dash it, I want to apologize. I've acted like a righteous boor all these years. And while I don't think I'll ever quite forgive you for haring off to the Peninsula, I understand much better why you put yourself at risk." He glanced at Finch's ungloved right hand. "I think that's what made me angriest of all," he added in a soft voice. "The thought that you would never ride again. You were such a skilled rider. Remember? Took all the prizes at the Gillington fairs."

The marquis subsided into silence, and Finch found himself incapable of reply. His father had apologized. In all of his wildest fantasies, he would never have believed it would come to this.

What a stupidly proud family they were.

"You didn't speak to me because you were sorry I was injured?" Finch finally managed.

His father nodded. "Not very manly of me, I admit."

Finch felt his throat tighten as it hadn't since he had sat by his batman's bedside the night the young lad had died. And even that feeling was not as overwhelming as this.

"It is I who should apologize," he said, astonished even as the words fell from his lips. "You have been right, and I wrong, about many things." He was thinking of his father's implacable hostility to Seabrook, but of course he could not, yet, tell the marquis he had been correct about that.

"I should have been more willing to talk, and less willing to argue. I should have come to Hampshire as soon as I returned to England. And," Finch murmured, as though he were once again the small boy who had been caught in the neighbor's apple tree, "I should not have brought shame on the family by . . . carousing in London. I know it has pained you."

His father shrugged. "We have both hurt each other. Perhaps it is time to stop keeping score. I am an old man, and I find that I'm less interested in saving face than I once was."

"As am I." Finch instinctively held out his right hand to his father. "Shall we bury the hatchet?"

Instead of shaking his hand, the marquis flipped it over and looked at the calloused scar. "It looks like you already have." His voice was raw. Finch suspected his throat was as constricted as Finch's own.

Finch chuckled, surprised yet again that he could laugh about an injury that had caused him so much anguish, both mental and physical. "It could have been worse."

"That's very true." The marquis's voice was solemn. "It could have, indeed."

With those words, a silence drifted down on the foursome. It was a largely contented and companionable silence, although Finch detected some tension from Charlotte. He wasn't surprised. Now that the initial elation of his reconciliation with his father was past, he found that another, much less pleasant emotion was nibbling at the edges of his consciousness: annoyance. He knew he should be grateful to Charlotte for engineering this *rapprochement*, and he was. But her blithe disregard of his express wishes left a sour taste in his mouth. She had properly taken him to task for trying to interfere with her school. She should have known better than to do the same thing to him.

Presently, the marquis stood and yawned. "It was a long journey from Hampshire, and I was up early this morning. If you'll excuse me, I believe I'll go upstairs to rest."

"I'll join you," Amelia said, scrambling to her feet as well.

Within moments, Finch was alone with Charlotte. Without being asked, the footman moved to the door and closed it behind him.

"Well," Finch said.

"I'm so pleased to see that you and your father have begun to repair your relationship," Charlotte burbled in a bright, unnatural voice.

"As am I. I am less than pleased, however, about the manner in which that reconciliation was brought about." His words fell into the quiet room like nails on marble.

"Yes. Well." Charlotte looked him straight in the eye. "I know I was out of line, but it was obvious that you would dally forever before you swallowed your pride enough to make a move."

"Pride? You, Charlotte, are a fine one to speak of pride."

She winced. "I know. But just because I suffer from the same vice does not mean it enhances either of us."

He drummed the fingers of his uninjured hand on the arm of the chair. "It also does not give you *carte blanche* to ignore justifiable pride in others. Did you ever plan to tell me of this letter?"

She shook her head. "If it did not work, I did not want to raise your hopes. I also did not want to incur your wrath for no reason."

He appreciated her candor. "When did you write it? And why?"

"The day we arrived in London, because you seemed so sad in the carriage as we discussed your feud with your father. I could not bear to see you unhappy."

"And you had no ulterior motive in trying to mend fences between my father and me?"

She frowned. "Ulterior motive?"

He stood and wandered over to the far side of the room, picked up a china figurine from the mantel, examined it and put it down before replying. "If I made peace with the marquis, it would increase the chances that I would return to Hampshire permanently."

Charlotte's eyebrows flew up into her hairline. "Do

not flatter yourself. I did not go to the trouble solely to avail myself of your esteemed company."

"Oh, don't turn missish on me, Charlotte. You cannot deny that you have been attracted to me for some time now." His words sounded arrogant, even in his own ears. "As I have to you," he added in a somewhat softer tone.

Her face was flushed. "Both facts were more than apparent the other day. But I assure you, my feelings for you were not my primary motivation in writing your father. Indeed, you just told him that you may not return to Hampshire, despite your reconciliation."

"That's true. Then why did you write the letter?" He leaned against the mantelpiece and crossed his arms on his chest.

Charlotte sighed. "It's something that is difficult to explain. It is just that my own family is very dear to me. The thought that you and your father would let years go by without trying to recapture some of that richness for yourselves seemed sad. I saw a way to try to help, so I did." She shrugged. "That's it. I am sorry that I overstepped the mark, but I'm not sorry that I tried to help."

A smile tugged at the corners of his mouth, even as the vestiges of irritation clung to his thoughts. "At least you are honest."

"It's one of my few virtues."

He could think of a few others, but none of them were fit for discussion in polite company. And he did not want to continue berating her for her interference when there were much more serious matters to address. "Let us put this discussion behind us. I have interesting news to report about Betty Lincoln." He summarized what he had learned from Sue. At the end of his synopsis, Charlotte nodded.

"So now all we need to do is witness someone in the ring trading something tangible that can be used as evidence?" she said.

"You make it sound so simple. It could take months."

"But you don't think it will." It was a statement, not a question.

"No." He retook his seat. "There are some military matters afoot that I'm not authorized to tell you about. I learned of them at Whitehall the other day. If these plans are scuttled, it will deal a serious blow to Britain's efforts in both Spain and France. I suspect that Norris and Seabrook have arrived in London with much bigger matters on their mind than Lucas Darnwell's wedding. And tonight, I'm going to test that hunch."

"May I come along?"

Finch had been debating that point all the way back to Mayfair in the hackney. If she were a male agent, he would say yes without question. But because she was female, and because she was Charlotte, he hesitated.

"You hired me to do a job. You brought me to London to finish it. I want to help."

"It may be dangerous, Charlotte."

A shadow passed over her face. "All the more reason to bring assistance."

"I will do my best to protect you, but if the situation moves in unpredictable directions—"

She reached out and covered his hand with her own. "You cannot control the whole world, Finch. Let me help."

It would be immensely useful to have two sets of eyes and ears this evening. London wasn't Spain, or France, or Portugal, he reminded himself. There would be no snipers hiding behind walls, no shrapnel raining down, no dysentery lurking in unexpected quarters. He should be able to keep her safe.

He nodded. "But this time, you *must* listen to me. Not the way you listened to me in the matter of my father. I must insist on your obedience."

She nodded. "Of course. You are the expert in these

situations. I disregarded you the last time only because, in matters of the heart, I think I outrank you."

He felt a grin split his face. "Well then, now that we are agreed on these matters, let me explain what we're going to do this evening."

THIRTEEN

Charlotte craned her neck but could see nothing untoward in the alley behind the theatre. She and Finch had been huddled in Finch's carriage for the better part of an hour, and while many people had passed through the dark lane, the viscount had deemed none of them worth his attention.

She shifted in her seat.

"Bored?" Finch whispered.

"Somewhat. But not unbearably."

"Good. At least we're not perched at the top of a tree in the rain."

"Small mercies, indeed."

He glanced out the rear window of the carriage and exhaled loudly.

"Mr. Barton's men have not arrived, I take it?"

Finch shook his head. "He said he would do his best, but that he could not guarantee us any support. Several investigations are under way in the city, and most agents were already committed elsewhere by the time I informed Barton of my suspicions late this afternoon. If we must proceed alone, we must." He smiled briefly. "It's fortunate that you are no stranger to unilateral action."

Finch obviously still harbored some lingering resentment toward her for the letter she had sent to the marquis. She understood his anger, but she was still not sorry. She would never be Finch's wife, but she could take consolation in the fact that she had been able to help him in one small way.

His resistance to the idea of moving to Hampshire was all the proof she had needed that they would never suit. Despite her protestations, some small part of her had hoped that he would return to Gilhurst Hall, and that, in time, they might be able to overcome the prejudices of society and build some sort of permanent future for themselves. But it was clear that the viscount's heart lay with the Foreign Service, and hers was still firmly lodged in Gillington. Even if she could imagine herself living in London, which she couldn't, she simply couldn't abandon her father and her school.

She became aware that the noise on the street outside had increased. "The theatre appears to be emptying," she said.

On the other side of the carriage, Finch nodded. "At least some of the performers will emerge from that back door any moment now."

And indeed, they did. The first few people to leave were male. Charlotte kept her eyes trained on the door. Then she heard Finch suck in his breath.

"Look who's here," he murmured, nodding toward a man who had slipped into the alley as the actors were departing. "It's my esteemed cousin."

As Charlotte watched, Seabrook strode to the stage door and waited. After a minute or so, he pulled out a pocket watch, examined it in the dim light from a window, and put it back in his pocket. He brushed at the sleeve of his coat as though he had just spotted a speck of dust.

"He looks impatient," Charlotte observed.

"All the better for us. Nervous people make mistakes."

After about five minutes, the stage door opened and

Betty Lincoln hurried out. Charlotte watched with interest to see how Mr. Seabrook would approach her.

His manner erased any suspicion she or Finch might have had that Betty was his mistress. He grabbed her roughly by the arm and half-dragged her along the alley. As they came close to Finch's plain carriage, Charlotte prayed that the almost fully drawn blinds would conceal herself and the viscount from Seabrook's view.

"What could you have been thinking, taking so long?" His voice drifted up to them through the slightly open carriage windows.

"It is not as though I 'ave no admirers," came a female voice. "It was *difficile* to get away."

"You're a chorus singer, and not a very good one at that," Seabrook muttered. "If you didn't have other talents, you'd be hard pressed to surround yourself with male admirers."

"You take that back, 'enry," she cried.

"Be quiet." That was the last thing they heard him utter before the squabbling pair moved out of earshot.

Finch opened the door slightly and called up to Jenks in a stage whisper. "The blond man with the dark-haired woman. They're the ones we need to follow. And remember—be discreet."

"Yes, my lord," came the reply.

"You have very understanding servants," Charlotte commented.

"As I've said before, Jenks makes a perfect coachman. Obedient, tight-lipped and not terribly swift. It would never even occur to him that most peers don't make a practice of trailing chorus girls."

Peering through the gap in the curtains, Charlotte observed Seabrook and Betty climbing into a dusty hackney. She released a pent-up breath. Now that Finch's cousin and his associate were also traveling by carriage, it would be somewhat less obvious that she and Finch were following them.

The streets were crowded and lively. No matter how long she spent in London, Charlotte thought, she would never get used to the numbers of people out and about long after everyone in Gillington would be fast asleep.

She and Finch said little for the next few minutes, both concentrating on keeping the hackney in sight. When the hired carriage took a quick left turn, however, Finch exclaimed, "Good Lord, they're going to Vauxhall."

"Vauxhall? The pleasure gardens?"

Finch nodded.

"How do you know?"

"I'm not certain. But this road leads directly to Westminster Bridge, and Vauxhall is the most popular place on that side of the river at this time of night."

"You seemed displeased."

Finch let the curtain fall back into place. "Vauxhall is large and even more chaotic than the streets around Drury Lane. We shall have to keep our wits firmly about us if we want to keep Seabrook and Mrs. Lincoln in view. They likely chose this venue precisely to avoid detection." He paused. "Thank you for agreeing to accompany me. Your assistance will be most valuable."

Charlotte hoped so, as the carriage rattled across Westminster Bridge. She peeped through the curtain at the vast city stretching out before her on both sides of the glittering Thames. The calls of boatmen mingled with the laughter of merrymakers on their way to the gardens and the clatter of horses' hooves. Charlotte felt very small in the midst of so much activity.

At the end of the bridge, Jenks turned right. Within a few minutes, the carriage slowed, then stopped. "This is it," Finch said, wrenching open the door and signaling Charlotte to precede him.

"They're about fifty feet straight ahead, my lord," said the coachman as Charlotte and Finch awkwardly jumped to the ground. There was no time to fuss with the carriage steps.

Charlotte looked into the distance and spotted Mr. Seabrook's blond head. He and Mrs. Lincoln were making speedy progress through a swirling mass of people.

"Right," Finch said, grabbing Charlotte's hand. Together, they pushed and pummeled their way forward, always keeping Mr. Seabrook in view. Charlotte's forehead was beaded with perspiration. When they reached a gate, Finch hastily shoved some coins into an attendant's hand.

"They're turning left," Charlotte called, no longer worried that their quarry could hear them. She could barely hear herself above the clamor of a thousand excited voices.

Finch nodded and propelled her in that direction. "Are you all right?" he shouted at one point. Charlotte nodded, too winded to reply.

Eventually, the crowd thinned somewhat. From alarming, it improved to merely overwhelming. From a safe distance, they watched as Mr. Seabrook and Mrs. Lincoln headed down a gravel path lined with trees.

"That path leads to the Dark Walk," Finch explained as they followed. Once they reached the walkway, Finch moved to the verge, tugging Charlotte into the gloom. "Due to its dimness, the Dark Walk is rather notorious as a location for secret liaisons." He paused. "Many people feel it is scandalous for an unmarried woman to even be seen in its precincts. If you wish to turn back, now is the time."

Charlotte took a deep breath. The chances that any of her students' parents would see her here was small, and the chances that she could help Finch—and by extension, the war effort—by proceeding were great. She knew Finch would not ask her to take this risk if it were unnecessary.

"I do not wish to turn back," she said in a steady voice.

He nodded. They walked on for perhaps ten minutes, and the crowds finally petered out to just a scattered few souls. About forty feet ahead, Mrs. Lincoln sat down on a bench in the shadows. Mr. Seabrook remained standing, but continued to address his companion. Judging by his stiff stance and her gesticulating hands, they were in the midst of an argument.

"I wonder what they're debating," Charlotte breathed.

"Something I would dearly love to overhear," Finch replied. "But we dare not move closer. I suspect they are here to meet someone."

Mrs. Lincoln looked over her shoulder into a small copse of trees behind the bench. She appeared to call out something. Then a small, dark man emerged from the shadows and kissed Mrs. Lincoln on the cheek.

"For once, Fortune is on my side," Finch muttered.

"Pardon me?"

The viscount nodded toward the little man. "That's Pierre St. Amour."

"One of the men you saw in Portsmouth with Mr. Norris?"

"Yes. And the man both Barton and I suspect of being the ringleader of this little group."

As they observed from the shadows, Mrs. Lincoln stood and appeared to introduce the two men to each other. Then she departed, alone, down the path that stretched away from Finch and Charlotte.

Finch leaned forward, like a cat about to pounce.

Mr. St. Amour reached under the bench and extracted what appeared to be a single sheet of folded paper. Glancing about, he pressed it into Mr. Seabrook's hand. Mr. Seabrook took the paper, folded it again several times, removed his hat, and tucked the sheet into the lining.

"I'll be damned," Finch breathed.

Charlotte raised her eyebrows.

"Sorry."

"Forget the language," Charlotte whispered. "What has you amazed?"

"The information we suspect is being traded tonight will likely be used for sabotage purposes. As such, the recipient of the information is likely the saboteur himself."

Realization dawned. "And you were expecting Mr. Seabrook to give something to Mr. St. Amour?"

Finch nodded. "But if my suspicions are correct, I've continued to underestimate my foppish cousin. Seabrook, not St. Amour, appears to be the mastermind."

"Mr. Seabrook?" Charlotte's voice was rich with disbelief.

"See how difficult it is to picture him as anything but a lightweight dandy?" Finch asked. "But you were right all along, and we've just seen the proof."

"Is what we've just witnessed enough proof to convict him?"

Finch shook his head. "Not likely. That paper he secreted in his hat might suffice, however."

"Shall we approach him?"

"No." Finch's voice was low and intense. "Never provoke a fight when you're outnumbered, unless absolutely necessary. If we can capture Seabrook alone, there's a good chance we can overpower him."

"We?" Charlotte tried, but failed, to recall any training Finch had given her in overcoming tall male spies.

"I shall try to overcome him. You grab his hat."

Mr. St. Amour appeared to be making preparations to leave. He stood, clapped Mr. Seabrook roughly on the back, and turned in the direction Mrs. Lincoln had gone.

"So now we have a fighting chance?" Charlotte murmured.

"Indeed. Just follow me."

He waited a moment until Mr. St. Amour had disappeared around a bend in the path. Then Finch grasped Charlotte's hand, tucked it through his elbow and led her from the shelter of the trees onto the gravel path. They might as well have been promenading in Hyde Park, so unconcerned did Finch appear.

They reached Mr. Seabrook just as he rose from the bench.

"Seabrook!" Finch cried. "What are you doing here? I figured you'd be into your second bottle of claret at White's by this hour of the evening."

"Finch." Seabrook's eyes were vacant as he looked at his cousin. Then, suddenly, they cleared. "Miss Gregory. How unexpected."

"It is a night of surprises," Finch said, as he brought his left fist down with such force on the back of Mr. Seabrook's neck that Charlotte winced. With a sharp cry, the blond man crumpled to the ground. As he did so, his hat fell from his head and rolled into the gravel path. Mr. Seabrook grabbed for it, but Charlotte seized it first. She clutched it to her chest and stepped back. At the same time, Finch placed his boot in the small of his cousin's back.

"Give me my hat, you stupid chit," Mr. Seabrook growled.

Charlotte shook her head, too frightened to reply. There was a look in Mr. Seabrook's eyes that unnerved her. Something wilder and more disturbing than mere anger.

"Give up, Seabrook," Finch muttered.

So quickly that Charlotte couldn't shout a warning, Mr. Seabrook twisted and yanked on the foot Finch had not planted on his back. Finch stumbled and crashed to the gravel.

With amazing speed, the blond man regained his feet. Reaching into his pocket, he extracted a small pistol and pointed it directly at Finch's heart.

Charlotte felt all the blood drain from her face. Why had she not tried to convince Finch to wait for reinforcements? Why had she never asked him to teach her to use a pistol? And why, in heaven's name, had she been too missish to tell him that she loved him?

"Miss Gregory," Mr. Seabrook ground out, his gaze never leaving Finch's face. "Give me my hat."

"Don't do it, Charlotte!" Finch shouted.

"Oh, *Charlotte*, is it?" Mr. Seabrook's voice was low and full of hatred. "Don't tell me you've developed a taste for the moral life all of a sudden, Finch? That you've tired of lightskirts and actresses and decided that it's finally time to be a good blue-blood and settle down?"

As Seabrook spoke, his attention focused solely on Finch, Charlotte tossed the hat behind a shrub and reached into a pocket of her pelisse. Her sister had often teased her for ruining the line of the garment by sewing in pockets, but Charlotte had needed somewhere to hide her mobcap, and she disliked carrying a reticule.

Never had she thought those funny pockets might save a life. Her fingers closed around a cool, smooth object she'd placed there before leaving Burnham House. Sliding it out of her pocket, she twisted the lid open with one hand. Her heart crashed against her rib cage like a terrified bird.

"Make haste, *Charlotte*," Mr. Seabrook said. "Or your *beau* won't be quite so handsome any more."

She moved toward him, her hands behind her back. She prayed that he would think she was concealing the hat. When she was in the line of his peripheral vision, he turned toward her. She brought her hand out from behind her back and tossed the contents of a vial of perfume into his eyes.

"Arrgh!" he screamed, dropping the gun as he clawed at his eyes with both hands. Within seconds, Finch had risen to his feet and kicked the gun across the path. Standing behind Mr. Seabrook, he wrenched one of his cousin's wrists behind his back. With his right arm, he grabbed Mr. Seabrook around the waist and gave a swift jerk to his stomach. Seabrook doubled forward, gasping for breath.

"Your sash," Finch shouted. "Give it to me!"

Charlotte squirmed out of her pelisse and quickly unwound the strip of silk from her gown. But instead of handing it to Finch, she moved toward Seabrook and reached for the arm Seabrook continued to fling about like a madman.

"Charlotte, get back!" Finch roared. She seemed to have no concept of the danger she was in. Of the danger he had put her in.

"You brought me here for a reason," she shouted back. "Two can do this more effectively than one."

She knew. She knew Finch would find it almost impossible to subdue and tie up Seabrook with only one good hand, unless he could shoot the scoundrel or render him unconscious.

She knew, and she didn't care. All she cared about was the job at hand.

From women who had mocked him because he could no longer cut his meat normally, he had progressed to a woman who didn't care that he couldn't save her life single-handedly. If they managed to escape Vauxhall Gardens intact, he would make it up to her. If it took his entire life.

"Finch!" she shouted.

With one swift move, he released his right arm from

Seabrook's gut and smacked his gnarled fist into Seabrook's free arm.

Seabrook howled but stopped flailing.

Charlotte looped one end of the sash around the limb and tied it tight, then held on to the rest of the sash with both hands. Finch grabbed the fabric from her and wound it around Seabrook's other wrist, then looped it back and forth in a figure eight pattern several more times. Charlotte helped him tie it to the loose end that still flapped from Seabrook's right wrist. He yanked the silk to ensure it was tight.

"Blast, Finchwood," his cousin cried. "Demme, haven't you done enough to me already without trying to kill me, as well?"

"Done to you?" Finch spat out. "What in the name of heaven have I ever done to you?"

"Well, for starters, you haven't even offered me a handkerchief to wipe this infernal scent from my eyes."

"Not sure I care to.'"

"You've got me trussed like a Christmas goose. I'm not going anywhere."

That was true. Finch reached for his handkerchief. After he had wiped Seabrook's eyes, Finch looked up to see Charlotte proffering Seabrook's hat. Her eyes were alight with admiration. Finch reached inside the hat to extract the slip of paper. He unfolded it and scanned it briefly.

"You'll find nothing there to incriminate me," Seabrook muttered. "It's just a list of artworks I'm interested in buying."

Finch raised his eyes from the paper. "What sort of fool do you take me for, Seabrook? These are details of the troop movements planned for Portsmouth next week."

"What? You read Italian now?"

"Enough to get the gist of it." Finch permitted a mirthless laugh to escape him. "Were you too green even to use code?"

"I begged them to use code," Seabrook muttered. "Stupid Frenchman couldn't get the hang of it. I had to teach myself rudimentary Italian just to accommodate him."

Finch yanked on the sash binding Seabrook's hands. "So far, astonishingly, we've managed to avoid attracting the attention of the few passersby who've made it this far into the gardens. But we may not be so lucky soon. Would you prefer to air your dirty laundry in the middle of Vauxhall Gardens, or would you prefer to do so in the privacy of my carriage?"

"I won't tell you a thing unless you torture me. And I doubt you'll want to do that in the middle of Vauxhall Gardens."

Finch nodded. "You're right." He prodded Seabrook along the path with a firm hand in the small of his back. "But I can't speak for my friends in the Foreign Office."

He wrapped his left arm around Seabrook's waist like a vise. The maneuver not only concealed Seabrook's bound hands from public view; it also made it almost impossible for him to run off without difficulty.

With his other hand, Finch motioned to Charlotte to join them. He slung his right arm around her shoulders, and felt a pang as she collapsed against him. It had been a long, brutal night for her. For all of them.

The odd little party made its way back through Vauxhall Gardens to Finch's waiting carriage. To an onlooker, it might appear as though Finch was merely supporting two friends who had imbibed more than was wise.

Charlotte raised her face as another burst of fireworks lit the sky. Around her, the crowd sighed in awe.

If anything, Vauxhall was more crowded this evening

than it had been two nights ago when they had captured Mr. Seabrook. Of course, this wasn't just any night. It was a grand *fête* to celebrate the Duke of Wellington's stunning triumph at Vittoria. The Prince of Wales and all his brothers were supposedly here.

Charlotte wasn't here to see the fireworks or the royals. She had asked Finch to bring her here as a farewell treat before she left the next morning to return to Hampshire. Foolish as it was, she wanted her memory of the famous pleasure gardens to be, well, pleasurable.

But no amount of fireworks or sweets or concerts would lift the heavy weight around her heart. For she was leaving tomorrow, and Finch was staying in London. Lord Barton at the Foreign Office had been delighted with his work in catching Mr. Seabrook and his co-conspirators, and had offered him a permanent post at Whitehall.

As she had feared, she and the viscount really did live in two different worlds. She had lain awake for much of last night, pondering the advisability of telling him she'd be willing to move to London. She would do it, much as she would hate living in Town, if she thought it would make any difference.

But Finch had been distant in the two days since they'd captured Mr. Seabrook. She'd barely seen him. It was clear that, now that the spies had been caught, there was no more point in continuing their association. She had no doubt that he felt as strongly about her as she did about him. That was not the issue. The issue was that they both realized those feelings had no future.

Another brilliant rainbow of artificial stars exploded above their heads with a monumental boom.

"So what reason did Mr. Seabrook give in the end for his actions?" Charlotte asked. Even here, where there was no possibility anyone save Finch could hear the words she practically had to shout in his ear, she was reluctant to use the word "treason." When a crime was punishable by death, it was not a term to bandy about in public.

"I'm still not certain," Finch admitted. "He was half raving by the time I got him to Whitehall. The gist of it was that he was more bitter than he let on about losing his eye at Talavera. Thought the entire British Army leadership was incompetent. Along with that, he resented me for standing between him and the Gilhurst inheritance. That's why he worked so hard to help me secure a commission. He was hoping I'd be killed in Spain."

"How dreadful," Charlotte breathed.

"When my father married Amelia, that seemed to send Seabrook plummeting over the edge of sanity. He believed Father hoped to ensure the succession by marrying a young wife who could help him begin another family."

Charlotte smiled. "On that score, your family's luck just may be changing."

Finch looked thunderstruck. "Is Amelia . . . ?"

She nodded. "She believes so. It is too soon to be certain, but the possibility is good that you may soon have a baby brother or sister."

Finch laughed and squeezed her hand. "I am so pleased for Father and Amelia. I know it is something they both want."

"So you have had a chance to speak further with your father?"

Finch nodded. "We met at White's yesterday afternoon to discuss many things we should have talked out years ago. We may not exactly be the best of friends, but the groundwork has been laid." He paused. "I feel I did not thank you graciously, or even properly, for your part in bringing that about. You were right, of course. It might have been years before I swallowed my pride enough to make the first move."

"I'm just glad it's resolved."

"So am I," Finch said, an odd light in his eyes. "It

would be deuced awkward living permanently in the same house and being on poor terms."

Charlotte blinked. "Living in the same house? But aren't you staying in London?"

He smiled as he shook his head.

"What about the position at the Foreign Office? You worked so hard for it—"

"Sometimes, Charlotte, you can spend months, or years, or a lifetime, working for the wrong goal." He sighed. "Ever since I returned from Spain, I thought I wanted a Foreign Office job. But in the last few weeks, what I've realized is that what I needed above all else was a sense of purpose. The Foreign Office would offer me that, of course. But so would taking up my responsibilities at Gilhurst Hall."

Charlotte nodded, but didn't trust herself to speak.

"My father and I have agreed on a number of duties I can take from his shoulders. As you and Amelia both tried to tell me, he is no longer a young man. Many men could fill that position I was offered at the Foreign Office. But only one can be my father's heir. Now that I know he will let me help, I am happy to go back. I hadn't quite realized how much I missed Gilhurst and the village until I returned."

"You won't be bored, rusticating in the country?"

He looked down into her face. "Not in the slightest. Not if I have you by my side."

A wave of happiness engulfed her as the import of his words sank in.

"Charlotte, you've been with me through an ordeal such as many husbands and wives never experience. Through it all, I've never once doubted that I could trust you." He took a deep breath. "You made me believe in myself again, and for that gift alone I can never repay you. And now I'm going to ask you for another gift, because we blue-bloods are all impossibly greedy."

She smiled through the tears that were leaking from her eyes.

"Would you marry me?"

She was so overwhelmed she could not speak.

"I will pay off all the school's debts, if that's what's worrying you. You'd have to let me this time." He grinned. "It says so in the marriage vows. Something about obeying, if I remember."

She nodded, returning his smile.

"But in all seriousness, you must stay just as involved in the school as you like. Or sell it. I don't care—as long as you're happy."

The tears were coursing down her face in earnest now.

"There will be time enough to sort out the school," she said gently, reaching up to touch his face. As she thought how close she'd come to losing him, here in this very park, her heart clenched. She threw her arms around his neck, threw back her head, and laughed.

"Yes, Finch. Nothing would make me happier than to be your wife."

Overhead, a great volley of rockets exploded. At least Charlotte thought the rockets were overhead. As she closed her eyes and surrendered to Finch's kiss, she thought that perhaps they were in her heart.

More Regency Romance
From Zebra